"Hawkins has again crafted a story which makes the reader spellbound, itching for the next installment, wondering what sort of trouble the next MacLean can create, and what it will take to get out of it!"

—Fallen Angel Reviews

TO CATCH
A HIGHLANDER

"Love and laughter, poignancy and emotional intensity, endearing characters, and a charming plot are the ingredients in Hawkins's utterly delightful tale."

—*Romantic Times*

"Karen Hawkins's best book to date! Fast, sensual, and brilliant, it tantalizes and pleases all in the same breath. . . . This is romance at its best!"

—Romance and More

TO SCOTLAND,
WITH LOVE

"Hawkins brings another hardheaded MacLean brother and a sassy miss together in a sensual battle of the sexes. Her humor, intelligent characters, and story are simply delightful."   —*Romantic Times*

"Strong characters, delightful humor, and sizzling sensuality. . . . The hero is deliciously sexy while the heroine is strong and humorous. *To Scotland, With Love* delivers it all and then some! A not-to-be-missed treat!"

—Romance and More

Love a good book? So do we!
Pick up a bestselling
Romance from Pocket Books.

FEEL THE HEAT
A BLACK OPS, INC. NOVEL
Cindy Gerard
A relentless enemy...
A merciless temptation.

UNTRACEABLE
Laura Griffin
Be careful what you look for...
You just might find it.

MAKE HER PAY
Roxanne St. Claire
A BULLET CATCHERS NOVEL
Sometimes it takes a thief to catch a thief...

OUR LITTLE SECRET
Starr Ambrose
Keeping secrets can be deadly
...or delicious.

A DIFFERENT LIGHT
Mariah Stewart
The beloved classic—now revised and
revisited by the bestselling author!

Available wherever books are sold or at
www.simonandschuster.com

HOW TO ABDUCT A HIGHLAND LORD

Also by Karen Hawkins

❧

THE MACLEAN SERIES

How to Abduct a Highland Lord
To Scotland, With Love
To Catch a Highlander
Sleepless in Scotland
The Laird Who Loved Me

CONTEMPORARY ROMANCE

Talk of the Town

Available from Pocket Books

KAREN HAWKINS

Lois Lane Tells All

POCKET STAR BOOKS
NEW YORK LONDON TORONTO SYDNEY

Pocket Star Books
A Division of Simon & Schuster, Inc.
1230 Avenue of the Americas
New York, NY 10020

This book is a work of fiction. Names, characters, places, and incidents either are products of the author's imagination or are used fictitiously. Any resemblance to actual events or locales or persons, living or dead, is entirely coincidental.

First Pocket Star Books paperback edition April 2010

POCKET STAR BOOKS and colophon are registered trademarks of Simon & Schuster, Inc.

For information about special discounts for bulk purchases, please contact Simon & Schuster Special Sales at 1-866-506-1949 or business@simonandschuster.com.

The Simon & Schuster Speakers Bureau can bring authors to your live event. For more information or to book an event contact the Simon & Schuster Speakers Bureau at 1-866-248-3049 or visit our website at www.simonspeakers.com.

Cover design by Min Choi
Cover photos: dog by Juniors Bildarchiv/Photolibrary, woman by Caroline Schiff/Getty Images
Interior design by Julie Schroeder

Manufactured in the United States of America

10 9 8 7 6 5 4 3 2 1

ISBN 978-1-4165-6027-2
ISBN 978-1-4391-7126-4 (ebook)

To my wonderful brother, Roy Smith
(aka Tech Support), for the following
Beyond Mere Brotherly Assistance:

1) keeping backup copies of all of my
manuscripts in your bank vault,
2) being on-call for my emergency
computer needs (Really? Muffin crumbs
will do *that* to a keyboard?), and
3) personally hand selling my books to
every attractive woman who wanders into
your local bookstore.

Thank you!
I owe you a drink (or ten).

ACKNOWLEDGMENTS

I would like to acknowledge the hard work and exquisite tact of my editor, Micki Nuding, who encourages me to challenge myself with every word I write.

Thank you for assisting me in taking my work to the next level and for doing it with such innate grace.

Chapter
1

Dear Bob,

My new boss is impossible to get along with. He acts like I don't know what I'm doing, though I'm the one with the degree and far more experience.

How can I tell this jerk to back off and let me do my job? He is the boss, after all.

Signed,

Angry and Determined

Dear Determined,

Recognize your boss's problem for what it is—an attempt at compensation for having a small "member." Men who boss women in such a fashion usually need a good kick in the ass and a healthy dose of that medicine they sell on late-night TV that promises "instant satisfaction."

If neither of those work, then quit. He'll miss you and come crawling back.

Sincerely,

Bob

The Glory Examiner
June 24, section 2B

⌒

"What is *this?*"

The newspaper landed on Susan Collins's desk with a *thud*, slapped down by a large masculine hand.

Susan leaned back in her chair and faced her pain-in-the-ass and thankfully temporary boss, Mark Treymayne.

Fortunately for the readers of *The Glory Examiner*, their new editor-in-chief wasn't intimidated by men—not even hunky, dark-haired, blue-eyed ones.

She smiled at him. *So the column hit the mark, did it?* Her Ways to Irk the Boss List was growing quickly. "You'll have to be a bit more specific, Treymayne. What is *what?* The font? The layout? Give me some specifics."

She reached out and rubbed the edge of the paper between her thumb and forefinger. "If you mean the stock, I'd call that thirty-pound newsprint with low-rub black ink."

His mouth thinned with displeasure, probably because he had no idea what thirty-pound stock was, let alone low-rub black ink.

"Damn it, I'm talking about the Dear Bob column, and you know it."

"Oh, *that*. Hmm. I probably wrote that two or three weeks ago. Let me see." She tugged the paper from beneath his fist. Then, with a great deal of exaggeration, she read the column as if she couldn't quite remember it.

Finally, she tossed it back onto her desk. "Yup, that's a good one."

He placed his hands flat on her desk and leaned forward. "Don't push me, Collins."

"Why on earth would I do that?" She met him gaze for gaze, mainly because she couldn't look away from his eyes. They were such a vivid, sexy blue, with thick, black lashes framed by rimless glasses. Smoky, sooty eyes that were still unmistakably masculine.

Why, oh why had God put such a damnably *sexy* man in charge of the paper? Things would be so much easier if she didn't have a boss who made her stomach flutter just by glaring at her.

And he did a lot of glaring. You'd think she'd be used to it by now, since they'd been working together off and on for almost ten months, but no. One laser lock from those brilliant blue eyes, and she had to fight to keep her thoughts straight.

Which was a real problem. Here in Glory, North Carolina, where everyone knew everyone else, she'd never met anyone who sparked such outrageous chemistry, and she had no idea how to react to it. She wasn't used to feeling hot and bothered, and in defense, she found herself lashing out in a way that surprised her.

Mark's temper was none too even, either, which kept them at loggerheads. His idea of running the newspaper was a complete anathema to her and she was pretty sure he felt the same about her theories. Their ideas were as different as their personalities; he was precise and neat, she was more general and creative. He was the big city and she was small town. He prized organization, while she prized the freedom to create. He was all about crunching the numbers and nothing *but* the numbers, while she understood the value of the newspaper within the community.

No two people could be more different or have more diverse opinions on how to accomplish the same job—namely, to make *The Glory Examiner* the most profitable, healthiest newspaper possible.

He scowled now, which was nearly as potent as his glare. "You wrote that Dear Bob column about me, didn't you?"

She pretended to be shocked, which was hard to do when a grin was threatening to break through. "Why, Mark! Why on *earth* would you think that?" She leaned forward. "Was it the part about 'compensation' for having a small member? Did that strike too close to home?"

She seriously doubted her annoying new boss had any "compensation" issues; he was a walking billboard for virility—which was utterly annoying at times.

His jaw tightened. "No. It wasn't that. The article uses the word 'jerk,' and you called me that at last Monday's staff meeting, when we were arguing about why we weren't getting a new copier."

"We didn't argue about anything; we *discussed* it."

"I would say 'argued,' seeing as how you threw your notebook onto the table so hard it overturned my coffee cup."

She wrinkled her nose. "I forgot about that. OK, I'll let the word 'argue' stand. *But*, I did *not* write the Dear Bob column about you." *I wrote it about my issues with you.* "Now, if you'll excuse me, I have work to do." She picked up a random folder and pretended to study its contents.

Glancing over the edge, she could see him standing with his arms crossed over his broad chest, feet planted as if ready for a fight. She had to stifle a giggle because he unknowingly stood adjacent to a poster of Superman, who was in the exact same pose, only wearing a cape and blue tights.

Ever since she'd read her first comic book at age six, Susan had developed a thing for Superman, so much so that she'd decided to become Lois Lane, which was why she'd gotten her degree in journalism. It was also why her office was decorated in what she liked to call "Early Krypton." Not only was there the almost-as-big-as-life Superman poster by Mark but also framed rare Superman comics, a hologram of Lois Lane shaking her fist at Lex Luthor while supporting an injured Superman, a vintage Superman lunch box, and other items that had once decorated her bedroom.

She wondered how Mark would look in tights, then decided she'd rather see him *without* tights. Under those khakis, did he wear boxers? Briefs? The man was hot enough for the cover of GQ, though the thought of him *au naturel* was far—

"Prove it."

Susan almost jumped at the sudden demand. "Prove what?"

"Prove you didn't write that damned column about me."

"How?"

"Show me the original letter."

She sniffed. "Sorry, that's privileged information. I never reveal my sources."

His jaw tightened and she could see he was getting more irritated, which was kind of fun. Susan enjoyed seeing Mr. Perfectly-in-Control a bit *out* of control. Every clipped, well-thought-out sentence he uttered begged for a quip of some sort and she'd found she was just the woman to deliver. "I receive letters throughout the week, I select the most promising one, and I answer it." If there weren't any letters, then she made one up. But that was her business and no one else's.

"Collins, the legal definition of a source is—" He began a stiff-lipped speech.

Susan let him lecture as she enjoyed the view. He had great arms, which one wouldn't expect of an accountant. They weren't bulging with muscles like the arms of her next-door neighbor and poker bud, Ethan; even Ethan's muscles had muscles. But she liked a man with a bit of finesse. Someone like Clark Kent here, only with a sunnier disposition. Someone who was muscled but smooth, like Lance Armstrong or—

"You didn't hear a word I said, did you?"

"Sorry, your arms—your *arguments*—distracted me."

Oh God, did I really say that?

"Stop trying to change the subject," he said gruffly. "Show me the letter that spawned this Dear Bob column."

Why couldn't Mark *ask* for things instead of *demand* them? She'd been in charge of her own life since she was twelve, and she wasn't about to allow someone else to tell her what to do now, especially not in such an odiously superior tone of voice. She might not be the most sophisticated woman around, but every inch of her was independent and she liked it that way.

In fact, before she'd accepted the position of editor of *The Glory Examiner*, she'd been the county dispatcher and had worked with the sheriff, Nick Sheppard. They'd gotten along fine, since Nick knew her limits and never stepped on them. Mark, meanwhile, pushed them every chance he got.

She showed her teeth in a not-so-nice smile. "Ask nicely and I'll let you see the letter."

He grimaced out a "please" that had a *damn you* tone to it.

Sheesh. He was so uptight. Which was a pity, as he was so intriguing in a Clark-Kent-nerd sort of way. The trouble was that there wasn't enough common ground between them to strike a match. When Mark's sister, Roxie, had asked Susan to become editor of the newspaper, she'd jumped at the chance. Little did she know then that the job would come with the caveat that Roxie's big brother would oversee the financial side of the paper until it began to operate in the black.

Susan cast a glance at Mark from under her lashes, noting the way his dark hair fell over his forehead and made his eyes seem bluer. While she admired his looks, he remained stubbornly aloof and she knew very little about the actual man. She knew he owned an accounting firm in Raleigh and that he was divorced, but everything else was pure speculation. Rumor had it that Mark's ex had been as wild as she was beautiful and—if rumor was to be believed—he was still pining after her even now, two years after the divorce.

Perhaps he thought all women were unstable, which was why he didn't trust Susan's instincts with the newspaper.

If only he understood that she loved her job and was good at it, everything would go smoother. She was an excellent editor, a good writer, a thorough investigator, and she knew everyone in town. People trusted her because she'd been the calm voice responding to every 911 call to the sheriff's office. Now she was wearing a different hat, but one that still served her town.

She waved her hand at Mark. "I'll find the letter and bring it to the next staff meeting." That would give her time to write one.

"Collins, while I may get on your last nerve, I'll thank you to remember that I'm a licensed accountant."

"So?"

"So I'm not a pushover. Not for the IRS and not for you." He rubbed his chin, his eyes suddenly glinting with sardonic humor. "In fact, I'll wait while you locate the letter from 'Angry and Determined.' "

Now, that could be a problem. To buy some time, she said "Fine!" and opened a random drawer and dug through all the pens, rubber bands, and a variety of Post-its.

He crossed his arms. "You don't have it, do you?"

"Of course I do," she replied in a lofty tone. "I just haven't filed it yet, so I can't lay my hands on it at the drop of a hat."

He glanced around at the piles of papers and books. "You *file*?"

"Once a year, whether my office needs it or not."

He grinned and shook his head. "I couldn't work like this."

"And I couldn't work at your desk, either. It's too sterile."

He stiffened, his smile disappearing. "My office is not sterile."

"There's nothing on your desk. Not even a pencil holder."

"I like it clean."

"You like it *barren*. Deloris Fishbine came in yesterday to talk about the new library reading room and thought your office was a spare. She even asked if we'd donate the space as a call center for the next library fund-raiser."

He pointed to her desk. "Find. The. Letter."

She sighed and opened another drawer, this one filled with coupons and recipes she'd been meaning to take home and transfer to her cookbooks. As she pretended to search the drawer, she looked at Mark from under her lashes.

He was so attractive, his dark hair mussed and his glasses slightly off center. She felt an almost physical pull to lean across the desk, straighten his glasses, and plant a kiss right on his firm lips. Her cheeks warmed at the thought.

She looked up from the drawer. "Wait. I just remembered . . . I think I filed it already."

He lifted a brow. "Just find it."

She pulled a random stack of files forward. "Do you know that Dear Bob is one of the most popular features in the paper?" She was extraordinarily proud of that, since she'd come up with the idea for the column three years ago and had worked hard to convince then-editor Ty Henderson to give her a chance to make it work. And he had, too, until he'd been arrested for kidnapping and extortion and a bunch of other charges.

"I know the Dear Bob section is popular," Mark said. "I've seen the results from the focus group. That doesn't make you less responsible for the content. If anything, it makes you more so."

She opened a drawer and picked out a thick file and slapped it down on top of the newspaper. "I've kept every letter that's been sent to Dear Bob over the past two years." She eyed the folder. It was thick, but not *that* thick. She reached back into the drawer, grabbed another fat folder, and tossed it on top of the first one. "That's all of them."

"Good God, there must be hundreds."

"Thousands." She stood and collected her interview notepad and pencil. "The letter I answered in this week's column is in one of those files . . . somewhere."

"I don't have time to read through all of these." He pushed the files her way. "Find it."

She used her hip to close the drawer. "I would, but I have an interview with the mayor about the budget cuts that may affect the local animal shelter's no-kill policy."

"Right now?"

"Very shortly."

Mark shook his head. "What kind of a filing system do you have?"

"A very private one that only makes sense to a trained journalist." What was in those two folders, anyway? She eyed them for a moment. Ah, yes. One held her office expense invoices, while the other contained . . . she wasn't sure what, but the folder was dusty so it couldn't be anything important. She gave a fake sigh. "Before you go through those files, I should warn you about certain women's issues."

He removed his hand from the top folder, his blue gaze suspicious. "What women's issues?"

"Lots of women write to Bob requesting information on lumps, cysts, periods, menopause—that sort of thing."

He looked at the folders with a mixture of horror and fascination. "No way."

"Yes, way."

He shoved his hands into his pockets. "You know, Collins, I think I'll let you find the letter after all."

Thank you, God. She scooped up the folders, dropped them into a drawer, and slammed it shut. "I always have to cull the letters to find something that might make a good interpersonal sort of story."

His suspicious look returned. "For some reason, I feel like I just got played."

She lifted her chin and said in a cold voice, "Sir, I am not a liar." *I'm a bluffer. And if you weren't such a starched shirt who never played poker, you would recognize the difference.*

"What you *are* is a troublemaker," he stated.

She fluttered her lashes. "Why, sir, ah do believe ah am offended!"

He grinned and Susan's stomach tightened. He looked so approachable when he smiled. So cute. She really wished he wouldn't do that.

She grabbed her purse. "I'd love to stay and chat, but I have to catch the mayor before he follows his secretary home for their daily slap and tickle. After that, I have a source meeting at Micki & Maud's."

"Drinking a latte and gossiping with my sister is not a 'source meeting.' " He tucked the newspaper under his arm. "I'll cede your point on the Dear Bob column this *one* time, only because I don't have time to comb through your mess of an office. But I still have my suspicions. You made the exact same Cialis statement in the hall yesterday."

Good God, he'd heard that? What else had she said? Surely that wasn't the worst. "You shouldn't eavesdrop."

"And you shouldn't complain so loudly outside my office door."

"If *someone* hadn't made a storage room out of the break room—"

"We have a break room."

"That closet?" she scoffed.

"It's bigger than our offices."

"That's another prob—"

He held up a hand. "Collins, don't start."

She scowled, but knew she'd be wasting her breath. Mark had never seen the old newspaper office in its heyday. When he'd arrived the place had been a hot, dusty mess, and before she'd known what he was about, he'd cleaned it all out and erected this appalling cubicle farm. Dilbert would be proud.

"Fine. My meeting's in five. I'm off to City Hall." She tucked her notebook into her purse and moved around her desk. Unfortunately, the size of her cubicle forced her to squeeze past Mark, who just stood there, the amused look on his face letting her know that he was perfectly aware that he had her cornered.

Susan wasn't a timid sort of woman, so she stood where she was, well within his personal space, so close she had to tilt her head back to look up at him.

That was a bit disconcerting. Not only was she even more aware of the intensity of his blue gaze, but she could smell the spicy scent that always seemed to surround him. She didn't know if it came from his shampoo or if he wore cologne, but the scent was tantalizingly faint, making her want to lean closer and take a deeper breath. She was just about to do that when she caught his amused gaze.

Hastily, she straightened. "I will be late for my meeting if you don't move."

Mark glanced at the Superman clock that adorned the far wall. He was certain Susan had plenty of time to make her meeting; the entire town wasn't much bigger than a gnat's ass. But that was Glory's one and only claim to perfection; it was a one-note town from top to bottom. There was one post office, one dentist, one cop, one restaurant, one hair salon, and (thankfully) one newspaper. If monotony was your thing, Glory was the town for you.

Not that he was a small-town snob: he just enjoyed Raleigh too much not to be aware of Glory's obvious shortcomings. It always had been and always would be too small, too tightly knit, a gossip hot zone.

His gaze dropped to Susan's breasts. They were another hot zone, but an infinitely more enjoyable one. The thought surprised him. Since his divorce women had come and gone, but none had engaged him like this one. Fortunately for them both, their attraction was based on the determined desire to best one another, whether between the sheets or in the boardroom. As soon as one of them acknowledged defeat, he was certain their unruly passion would disappear.

Susan frowned up at him, a flicker of uncertainty in her blue gaze. "Are you going to move?"

No. No, he wasn't. He was usually cool and in control, but ten months of being dogged by a pert, sassy, too-knowledgeable-for-her-own-good newspaper editor was really getting on his last nerve.

Worse, he was beginning to savor their alter-
cations and the low simmer that always hummed
between them.

Susan stood just a bit too close to him, wearing
jeans that fit her lean curves like a loving hand.
Her well-worn scoop-necked T-shirt was thin
enough that he could make out her bra beneath
it, and one lacy red bra strap peeked out as if dar-
ing him to imagine what she'd look like without
the shirt. His cock ached at the sight . . . and that
was just from thinking about her clothes. When he
thought about what came *with* those clothes—the
long, long legs; the creamy skin; the dark red hair;
the full, wide mouth and her blue, blue eyes—it
wasn't just his cock that ached, but his entire body.

He'd never had such a fierce case of pure lust in
his life, not even for Arlene. And the memory of
that short, purely physical, and brilliantly wrong
marriage shouted that he should ignore any hottie
who made his libido fire up like a pressure cooker.
So far, the memories were fresh enough that he'd
been able to comply.

But now, looking down into Susan's upturned
face, her hair pulled back in an elegant ponytail,
her full lips moistened by a swipe of pale pink
gloss, her blue eyes fringed by a ridiculous sweep
of thick black lashes, his determination to stay

aloof seemed mighty stupid. And that, more than anything she might ever say or do, irritated him to the bone. "You're a smart one, Collins. You figure out a way to get me to move."

Her eyes blazed at the challenge. "I could stomp your foot."

"And slip past while I was hopping around like a cartoon rabbit?" He rocked back on his heels and smirked. "It won't work. I may howl, but I'd be damned if I'd move."

She crossed her arms, the gesture pressing her breasts against the thin T-shirt and making his heart stutter. "What do you want, Treymayne?"

He leaned forward to place a hand on the top of the cubicle wall by her head. What did he want? He was almost afraid to answer that question himself, so instead he asked her. "What do you *think* I want, Collins?"

Susan's heart thundered. His body was now holding her prisoner. Oh, he wasn't touching her—that would be too heavenly. As irritating as this man could be, he was damned *tasty*. Maybe a good roll in the sack would cure them both of their case of the crankies—but she was sure the suggestion would send Mr. Clean Living into shock. To be honest, it sort of shocked her, too.

It was a pity she wasn't the sort to engage in

a brief, no-holds-barred casual fling. Such an opportunity was rare in a town like Glory, where everyone knew everyone else or, worse, was related. Perhaps the time had come to rethink that particular view. She was healthy, over thirty, and it had been a long, long time since she'd felt this sort of attraction for anyone.

She found herself looking at his mouth, hard and masculine. A wave of lust hit her and she had to bite the inside of her lip to keep her expression neutral. Why *didn't* she throw herself into a lovely flirtation with Clark Kent here? What could it hurt? Heck, it might help ease the endless conflict. And the fact that he'd be leaving soon was a huge plus—there'd be no fallout.

Now that she thought about it, this man was a rare, golden opportunity, and if she didn't snag him, someone else would. Probably one of her closest girlfriends. Connie, who ran Micki & Maud's Diner with her mother, had been casting eyes at Mark since he'd arrived in town. Of course, Connie cast her gaze upon every eligible—and not-eligible—man who came her way, so perhaps she was a poor example.

Still . . . Connie wouldn't hesitate, so why should Susan? Didn't she deserve a little warmth and excitement in her life? Heck, *yes*.

She slipped her arms around Mark's neck, rose up on her toes, and laid a good one on him. His eyes widened, his hand dropped from the wall, and his mouth opened in surprise—which allowed Susan to slip her tongue between his lips and do something she'd been dying to do from day one. As her tongue touched his, instant heat flooded her and hot passion swept over her from head to toe. *Good God, why didn't I do this months ago?*

Susan's searching hands and tongue blew every thought from Mark's head. When her tongue touched his, his hands naturally found her rounded ass as he cupped her to him and molded her even more closely. She moaned against his mouth, her tongue driving him wild. Pure passion roared through his body and he soaked it up. It had been so long since he'd felt such a physical thrill for a woman—any woman. He ran a hand up her back and cupped the back of her neck, her silken ponytail trailing over his fingers.

She tightened her hold around his neck, lifting to him, moaning as he deepened the kiss. For a few glorious moments, he didn't think, didn't measure or weigh the cost of what he was doing, he just *did*.

Susan broke the kiss and nipped at his bottom lip, her even white teeth gently teasing his sensi-

tive skin. Damn, the woman knew how to kiss!
Blazing desire raced through him as he saw that
her eyes were closed, her thick lashes crescents
on her creamy skin, a few pale freckles sprinkled
across the bridge of her delicate nose. She was so
naturally sexy, and didn't even know it. It was
hard to believe that anyone who saw Susan would
think—

*Saw? Oh, God. The shade is up and our windows
are directly opposite City Hall's. If just one person
happens to look outside, they'll see—* He dropped his
hands from her waist and stepped back, straightening his glasses, which had gone askew.

Susan blinked sleepily, as if just waking.

Mark raked a hand through his hair. "Damn
it, we shouldn't—" Then his gaze locked on her
chest, where her nipples clearly showed through
her lace bra and T-shirt. *I need to impose a dress
code.* "While on company property, proper, well-
lined *underwear will be worn at all times.*"

Susan slid her fingers along her bottom lip,
the sensual gesture making his cock harden even
more. "I'm impressed. That was a good kiss."

He straightened his shoulders. "It shouldn't
have happened." He nodded toward the open
blinds.

Her smile seemed to freeze in place. "What's

wrong, Kent? Afraid someone might see you kissing the help?"

"Kent?"

"Clark Kent." She jerked her head toward a framed comic book on the wall over her desk. "That's you to a T. Uptight, follow-the-lines, never-have-fun sort of guy."

Mark didn't like that description one bit. "If I'm Clark Kent, then I suppose you're Lois Lane," he scoffed.

"I could be."

"She was always getting in trouble so that Superman had to rescue her. That's a bit lame, isn't it?"

Susan tsked. "You need to get out of the fifties, Kent. Nowadays Lois is mad, bad, and dangerous to know."

Mark glanced at the framed comic book, a bit surprised. "Really?"

"Yup. Lois is a kick-ass journalist now. Independent and capable of saving her own life—and Superman's sometimes, too."

"I haven't really kept up."

"Obviously. But then, I don't know the tax code. To each his own." She leaned a shoulder against the wall, turning slightly toward him. She should be moving away from him, yet her instincts screamed at her to do the opposite. The kiss had unfuddled her brain, and now she knew what she wanted: more of Mark Treymayne. *Lots* more. She wanted to shock and befuddle him, make him think about her without the irked expression he was wearing now.

Why? The kiss had begun well, and he'd taken it over as soon as his libido had checked in. For a moment, she'd thought he might devour her. She shivered at the memory. *Oh, yes, I want more of that.*

Mark glanced at the clock. "You'd better go. The mayor will be waiting."

She caught sight of the time and grimaced. "Oh, I'm late!" She brushed past him, her entire body still aflame.

"When you're talking to the mayor, ask him if he wants a few more ads for Founders Day."

"I can't do that; it'll seem like bribery. You know, 'Buy some ads from me and I'll make you look favorable in this article.'"

"No one would accuse you of doing such a thing."

"The mayor would. I won't compromise my integrity as a journalist just to sell ads, Mark." She sent him a hard look. "If we would focus on improving the content and making the paper more worthwhile, using good reporting and engaging photography, then we'd have more readers and could charge more per ad."

"It's my job to decide the price points, not yours." He held up a hand when she would have argued. "That's a conversation for another time. You have an interview and I've already made you late as it is. I should regret that, but . . ." His gaze flickered across her.

Oh, Lord! He was right. Heart racing, she hurried to the door. "We'll discuss this later."

His eyes glinted, and to her surprise, a faint smile lifted one corner of his mouth. "Later, Lane."

She grinned back like the biggest idiot in the world, feeling strangely light and airy as she ran down the stairs. That devastating half smile, paired with those steely blue-gray eyes, made her tingle.

She'd clearly been using the wrong tactics on Mark Treymayne, but today's little kiss had given her a new path to follow—and follow it she would. She wasn't the sort of woman who avoided romantic relationships. If the opportunity came, she went for it. The trouble was that the opportunity rarely came. Oh, she'd had offers . . . more than one might expect from such a small town, so the problem wasn't availability. The problem was that she was inordinately picky.

It took a *lot* of—well, everything—before she felt even a flicker of interest. She wanted it all; someone who was intelligent and sexy and funny. A real life super man.

In the last ten years there'd only been one man she'd felt anything for, and though he hadn't met all of her requirements, she'd allowed herself to be charmed into a relationship. He'd turned out to be a complete putz with a liar's tongue and a cheater's heart. That had hurt, but it had also confirmed one thing: picky she was, and picky she'd stay. It just made life easier.

She glanced at her wristwatch as she took the last few steps into the lobby. A hot fling with a Clark Kent look-alike was exactly what the doctor ordered. What could it hurt? By the time things went awry, it would be time for Mr. Too Uptight to return to his offices in Raleigh. The entire scenario was perfect; it was just a pity she'd wasted so many months before realizing it. Well, that little mistake could be rectified by—

"On your way somewhere, Miss Susan?"

She grinned at Ray Dobbins, who put down his ever-present crossword, but didn't rise from the overstuffed lobby couch that he constantly occupied. The old man was a relic of a time gone by when every large building had a doorman. The bright orange 'Security' written on the tag hanging from Ray's blue blazer was a mere courtesy title; everyone in town knew the man was nearly blind and couldn't work up a run to save a life, even his own. Just walking across the lobby to the fountain to get a drink left the man wheezing like a slit tire. Still, he was an institution and she couldn't imagine the building without him.

"Yup," she said. "I'm interviewing the mayor."

"Give 'em hell. Charlie Harkins is a crook."

She pushed open the heavy door and grinned. "So I've heard. Back in a few!"

Ray waved and returned to his crossword as she went outside in the sunshine and hurried toward City Hall. This would be a good article; she could feel it. All she had to do was fight Mark for the proper amount of column space; lately he'd become almost miserly in allocating it, preferring to hold it for ads. Her smile faded. Truly, the man needed a lesson in newspaper management. Perhaps she'd take the time to give him one. After a few more of those hot kisses, of course.

Her smile back in place, she raced up the steps to City Hall, her notebook already opened to a blank page.

Chapter
2

Dear Bob,

My mother is trying to set me up with her new husband's cousin's stepsister, who is a stone-cold fox.

My problem is this—the first time I do something to make this gal mad, she'll tell her sister, who'll repeat it to my stepfather, who'll blab it to my mother, and all hell will break loose.

I'd rather not have to watch my p's and q's quite so close, if you know what I mean.

What should I do?

Signed,
Don't Tell

Dear Don't,

Take my advice and resist your mother's matchmaking or you'll come up the loser.

Tell your mother "no" and, when you find a pair, go get your own girl.

Signed,
Bob

The Glory Examiner
June 26, section B2

Susan climbed out of her '98 Jeep Cherokee and rolled her neck, wincing when it popped a half dozen times. "What a day," she muttered. She'd been on edge and she knew the reason—the hot kiss she'd shared with her boss two days ago had her restless and lusting like an unfulfilled high schooler.

She leaned into the Jeep and collected the bags of groceries that sat on the floorboard and used her hip to close the door.

"Hey, Collins!" came a deep voice behind her. "Need some help?"

Susan looked across the hood to see her neighbor, Ethan Markham, leaning against the picket fence that separated their properties. His house was very similar to hers, a low craftsman style with a wide porch framed with solid pillars and heavy wood trim around the doors and windows. The difference was that Ethan's house was . . . not rundown, exactly, but the paint needed updating, the flagstone walk could use a good pressure washing, and the shrubs were badly in need of a trim.

Of course, Ethan was relatively new to the house. He'd inherited it from his elderly aunt, but the house had sat vacant for years before he'd settled down and moved in. Now he was slowly, carefully updating every part of the house. And from what she'd seen, he was doing an amazing job.

Susan put the groceries on the Jeep hood and sauntered over to the low fence. Ethan's front door was propped open, and two sawhorses had been placed on the front lawn. "Whatcha working on today?"

"The downstairs bathroom. I'm going to completely gut it, put in slate tile, new fixtures, a double vanity, and a steam shower."

"Wow! Fancy, aren't you?"

Ethan flashed her a grin. "Got to keep up with the Joneses. You've raised the bar for the whole neighborhood with the work you've done on your place."

Susan leaned against the fence and eyed her own house, deep satisfaction lifting her spirits. "I've done a few things."

Ethan's blue eyes crinkled as he laughed. "You should be on HGTV."

"I TiVo every show."

"You're good with your power tools, I'll give you that. When you get done with your house, feel free to help me with mine."

"Deal." Grinning, she eyed his house. "It's a

shame you planted pansies up your walk. The boys will give you a hard time about that."

The "boys" were her poker buds. Come rain or shine, work or no, she *always* had poker night. It was her special time, filled with her best friends, most of whom were men.

Until Mark's older sister, Roxie, had come back to town, Susan hadn't really socialized with many of the town's women. Oh, she knew most of them and got along with them. But none of them liked to fish, and she did. Before he took a turn for the worse, she and her dad used to fish a lot. Now she had the biggest, fastest bass boat in town and she loved it.

She also loved football, hot wings, and icy beer, but put her in a mall and she felt like a giraffe at a hat-hanging party: she simply didn't fit in.

Her two nods to her femininity were her shoe collection and her biweekly pedi, and then she got in and out with as little chitchat as possible.

She sometimes wondered if she'd have felt differently if her mother had bothered to stick around after her twelfth birthday, but she'd never know. For now, at least she had her shoes. Those reassured her that no matter how many fish she caught, how many football nights she hosted for the town's bachelor force, or how few dates she'd been on in the last few years, she was, indeed, female.

"Sweetheart," Ethan drawled, breaking into her thoughts, "you should learn your flowers. They're not pansies, they're impatiens."

"The guys will love it that you know the name of those flowers."

"I didn't want to do this, but if you force me . . . I'll maintain my status by mentioning how I got to watch you wash your Jeep in those cutoff jean shorts of yours."

She eyed him suspiciously. "You weren't home when I washed the Jeep."

"I came in just as you finished. Noah Baxter and I enjoyed your final gyrations."

"Noah Baxter is married."

Ethan's grin faded. "He and Tiffany are taking a break."

"No! They've only been married two years, at most."

"It happens."

Susan knew that from her own experience. At twelve, she'd watched her own parents' marriage crumble, her father becoming more and more self-destructive until her mother had stormed out, bags packed. Susan had refused to go with her mom; the thought of leaving Dad alone seemed heartless. Mom had been a strong woman and had continued her life, though she'd continually pressed Susan to join her.

Then, three years after she'd left, Mom had been killed in a car accident. Susan had mourned, but she hadn't been as devastated as she'd expected. Mom had moved on, and so had Susan.

She smiled at Ethan now. "I'd better get those groceries inside. I have ice cream."

"Is that an invitation?"

"If you forget you ever saw me in those jean shorts." He didn't answer right away, so she added softly, "Double Dutch chocolate."

He chuckled. "You win."

She enjoyed having Ethan for a next-door neighbor. He was handy with tools and frequently helped her with some of her more complicated home improvement projects. Better yet, he was a terrific poker player and was amazingly easy on the eyes.

Seriously, the man looked like a twenty-something Hugh Jackman with his black hair and blue, blue eyes. He maintained a sexy scruff, too, a bad-boy look that Susan couldn't imagine Mark ever trying—which was a pity. She was sure it would be devastating on him.

She fought back a sigh at the image. She had

enough trouble keeping her hands off of her boss as it was. It was a good thing he didn't know how to work it, or she'd be really gone.

Meanwhile, easygoing and available Ethan had never caught her interest. He was fun to hang out with, but despite his Greek God physique, she had absolutely no desire to throw her arms around him and kiss him the way she had Mark.

She really needed to work on her taste in men. Maybe she should watch more Lifetime and less HGTV.

She pushed herself from the fence. "I'd better get inside. It's getting late and Dad's probably waiting on dinner."

"Your dad's not home, Suse."

"He *left*?"

"A few hours ago on his bike. I guess it was two o'clock."

"Oh." She forced a smile. "I won't need to fix dinner right away, then. Did he . . . did he say where he was going?"

"I asked, but he just waved and left."

She managed a carefree shrug. "He's that way."

Ethan looked at if he might say something more—something serious and sympathetic—so she flashed a fast smile. "Let me know if you need help setting the tile for the steam shower. I know a few tricks there."

She grabbed her bags and carried them up the flagstone path to her house, turning her attention to her neat and tidy home. It was all hers. She'd scrimped and saved and had worked hours of overtime to come up with the down payment. Now, every day when she came home, her soul grinned as she walked up this path, even when she was worried.

There's nothing to worry about, she told herself. *Dad will be fine. He's always fine.*

They said God took care of children, fools, and drunks. She knew from firsthand experience that at least part of that saying was true.

She paused on the front step, admiring how the flowers she'd planted around the front stoop were blooming in a gorgeous array of crimson, yellow, and purple. The sight warmed her, and some of her trepidation eased.

She climbed onto the wide porch, where several welcoming rocking chairs waited, and walked inside. In the living room, her eyes were drawn to the empty easy chair by the fireplace. Where the couch and love seat were comfy plump, well made, and obviously new, the chair was a product of days gone by. Of a muted yellow-and-brown plaid, the

seat sagged, the arms were threadbare, and the recliner part had long since broken, which was why
an equally ancient ottoman was pulled to the front
of it. Around the chair were scattered papers covered in scrawling drawings, stacks of *Popular Science*, *Scientific American*, and *Discover* magazine.

She set her groceries on the front hall table
and went to the chair to collect a few fallen mag-
azines that littered the space. She stacked them
neatly around the sagging chair and was turning back for her groceries when she noticed the
edge of a beer can sticking out from under the
chair skirt. She sighed and fished it out, then another and another. Soon, she had a stack of eight
beer cans.

She carried them to the kitchen and placed
them in the recycling bin. Not a drop dripped
from any of them. "Sucked them dry, didn't you,
Dad?"

Collecting her groceries, she put them away,
then grabbed an empty laundry basket from the
table by the laundry room door and went up the
broad, wooden stairs to the second floor.

The farthest room from the landing was her
bedroom, the largest one in the house. The oak
floor shone, and a large four-poster king-size bed
dominated one wall. The windows were large,

almost to the floor, and covered with plantation shutters that reduced the sun's glare. The bed was covered in a muslin coverlet trimmed with white scalloped lace, while a pile of lavender, sky blue, and sage striped pillows sat against the high headboard. A puffy chair covered in sky blue muslin sat to one side with a friendly ottoman pulled before it. Against the other wall was an antique dresser that matched the huge bed, and across from it, a lovely vanity and mirror.

The walls were painted a soothing sage green, which set off the cream trim and made the dark oak flooring gleam in contrast. It was a beautiful bedroom, one worthy of any decorating magazine. She paused by the vanity, noting that her assortment of antique bottles that lined the polished surface was crooked and she automatically straightened each of them.

Two of the bottles had belonged to her mother. The attic was full of things that had belonged to Mom, but Susan kept only these two items in sight. Some things were better left in the past. She and Dad had made their own way in life, and there was no sense in wishing things had been otherwise.

Susan turned from the vanity and paused by the picture on the wall leading to the bathroom.

It was an old black-and-white print of Phyllis Coates, the actress who'd played Lois Lane in the original TV series *Adventures of Superman*. Of all the actresses who'd ever played the intrepid Lois Lane, Susan thought Coates was the best.

"I bet your Clark Kent didn't try to prove you wrong every chance he got," Susan murmured. The real Clark Kent had a bigger-than-life crush on Lois Lane and did whatever he could to assist her, even when he shouldn't.

Though I'd probably find it annoying if someone did that for me. She opened her closet door, where her laundry bag hung from a hook against the far wall. Like the house, her closet was organized from top to bottom. All of her jeans and a few slacks for special occasions were neatly hung, arranged by color and length; her shirts, the same way.

But what would have surprised her friends was that the entire left wall was covered from ceiling to floor with shoes. Five pairs were her usual sneakers and boat shoes, but the rest were an assortment of the sexiest, finest, most decadent shoes she could find.

With a smile, she ran a finger across a pair of red open-toe sling-back heels. They were made of gorgeous Italian leather with engraved silver buckles across the toes. Just touching them gave her a feeling of satisfaction.

She took the pair out of the closet, tossed the laundry basket on the bed, kicked off her comfy trail shoes, and slipped her feet into the four-inch heels. Crossing the floor to look in the mirror, she admired how the red pumps made her feet look elegant and sexy. They'd look even better if her toenails were a lovely shade of red to match the leather. Perhaps she'd get that at this weekend's pedi.

She walked around the room for a few moments, pleased at the way the shoes made her hips sway with feminine sensuality. She should wear these to the office one day. She tried to imagine Mark's reaction as she strutted in, her do-me red Italian stilettos tapping across the floor.

She made a last turn about the room, then reluctantly replaced the shoes in her closet. Boy, would her poker buds laugh to see her playing dress up! She smiled wryly trailing her finger over a few favorites before she turned off the closet light. "Get to work, Collins. You've got laundry to do and dinner to fix." She emptied her laundry bag into the basket, then went to her dad's room for his dirty clothes.

Only one of his shirts had made it into the

hamper; the rest littered the floor around it. Susan grabbed them all and headed down to the laundry room off the kitchen, eyeing her new granite countertops with pleasure. She was almost finished redoing the house, meticulously creating an elegant and comfortable space. Next up was her garage, and she had big plans for that. When she was done, she'd have the car-fixing/fly-tying/poker-playing center of her dreams.

After loading the washer, she returned to the kitchen and began fixing dinner, baking pork chops, mashing potatoes, and frying apples in butter and brown sugar. She was just finishing when she heard a bicycle creak to a halt outside.

Wiping her hands on a dish towel, she hurried out to the garage. "Dad!"

Her father climbed off his rattley old bike, staggering a bit. In a trice, she was down the two steps into the garage and had his arm.

He grinned and let the bike drop to the garage floor with a crash. "I'm fine." He patted her hand. "Just lost m'footing on this slick floor's all."

The slurred words and familiar smell of beer made her heart sink. "It's a bit early for the Bigger Jigger, isn't it?" It was a waste of her breath to even say it, but she did it because she wanted him to listen to her, because she couldn't stop hoping that one day he would change. At least a little.

"I jus' stopped by to have a beer or two with m'friends. There was no harm in it at all. Besides, Bob broke his own record for sales at the hardware store. We *had* to celebrate that." He grinned at her, his face flushed, his eyes bloodshot, his hair mussed.

She swallowed the lump in her throat and ruffled his hair. "What are we going to do with you?"

"I'm hoping you're going to feed me."

"The pork chops are almost done."

He brightened instantly. "With fried apples?"

She nodded, gave him a final hug, and hurried into the kitchen.

He came to wash his hands at the sink. "I'll set the table."

"Thanks, that would be nice."

"It's the least I can do, seeing as how you did all the cooking." He collected two plates and the correct silverware and made a show of lining everything up properly. "How was your day? The new boss still giving you fits?"

In more ways than you know. "He's been strangely calm these last two days. We haven't had a single argument." *Just a lot of heated glances.*

Dad poured them both ice water and placed it by their plates before he sat down. "Working on any good stories?"

"The biggest one is on the budget cuts to the local animal shelter. I'm also writing a follow-up piece on the Methodist Church singing contest."

"Those should keep you busy for a while."

"You'd think." She put the last of the food on the table and took a seat beside him, and filled their plates, watching from under her lashes as Dad pretended to eat.

He was beginning to look far older than his years, his skin gray, his nose bright red, his hair a faded version of her own red and shot through with threads of silver.

They talked desultorily over dinner. As soon as it was over, Dad began yawning and suggested he was going to sit in his chair. Susan handed him another glass of ice water and sent him on his way to his chair by the fireplace.

She stayed in the kitchen to clean up. A short time later, as she took the final load of clean laundry to the stairs, she glanced into the living room and saw Dad asleep, a tall boy clutched in one hand. "Darn it, where did he—" She clamped her mouth closed. He was very good at hiding his stashes.

She set the laundry basket on the bottom stair, and came to collect the mound of cans he'd stacked on the far side of his chair, out of sight.

She sighed and picked up the only full can, grimacing when she found it to be warm. "Of course it is," she muttered. "He knows that if he leaves them in the fridge, I'll pour them all out."

She stared down at her sleeping father. He'd had eight beers after dinner, and probably as many or more beforehand. She collected a throw blanket from the couch and laid it across him, then bent and kissed his forehead.

Tomorrow he'd wake up with a sick stomach, a raging headache, and enough guilt for a church full of Baptists. Meanwhile, at the same time, she would rise and go to work, where she would become the crack editor she'd always wanted to be— if she could convince her boss to let her.

Sighing, Susan put away the laundry in neat stacks in the perfectly laid-out drawers. If only all of life were so organized and simple.

Chapter
3

Two shrill female voices from the reception area drifted into Mark's cubicle. He winced and lifted his office supply catalog a bit higher. Since he'd left his cubicle door open, they could see straight into his office.

He lowered the catalog and eyed Tundy Spillers cautiously. Of all the women he knew, Tundy was the scariest. She'd once been his sister's maid in Raleigh. Roxie had hired the red-haired, plump, freckled woman to nurse Mother through her heart troubles. Now that Roxie had decided to stay in Glory, so had Tundy, who'd landed a job as assistant to the activities director at the Pine Hills Assisted Living Center.

Few women had Tundy's combination of unorthodox determination mixed with a shocking lack of style. Mark had to grin when he caught sight of her Pepto-pink velour jogging suit and orange flip-flops, augmented by a flaming red tote bag slung over one shoulder. Every part of the out-fit clashed with her bright red hair, which she'd twisted into an implausible topknot, tight red corkscrew curls cascading down to frame her per-fectly round face.

Tundy leaned one chunky arm on the counter and said to Pat, "I want to know where in the hell my ad's gone."

"What ad?"

"I put a personal ad in the paper, paid for it and everything, and it's not there." Tundy's voice was as loud as a foghorn over smooth water. "I've got rights, you know! I paid good money for that ad!"

"Who told you the ad would be in this edition?"

"Mr. Treymayne tol' me that, and I got witnesses."

Mark could feel both pairs of eyes boring through his catalog. Yeah, she had witnesses. One of them, an old lady by the name of Clara, was close to being deaf, while the other was a vague old gentleman called C.J., who only knew where he was about ten minutes of every day. Both of them were stationed by the elevator, watching Tundy the way one might watch a saint perform a miracle.

Mark wondered if the staff at the assisted-

living center knew Tundy took her "gang," as she
called the residents she drove around town, on
her personal errands. Mark doubted it; the woman
didn't have an Off button and wouldn't know a
boundary if one bit her in the ass.

"Here." Pat slapped a piece of paper and a pen
onto the counter. "If you want to make a complaint, you got to put it in writing." With that, she
turned back to what she'd been working on before
Tundy arrived: a bacon, egg, and cheese sandwich
from the diner.

"I don't want to fill out no more papers! Mr.
Treymayne *promised* me it would run today."

Pat snorted in disdain. "Mr. Treymayne told
you that, did he?" Her voice hinted that his word
wasn't worth the air it took to speak it.

"Yes, he did. And I done took three *days* to
write it up, too, because I wanted it all perfect."

"Huh. Well . . . I guess we can look in the book
and see when you turned it in." Papers rustled as
Pat flipped through the personal ads notebook,
trying to look important. Pat was good at looking important in a belligerent, I'll-cut-you manner. Mark suspected it had gotten her many false
confessions over the years.

"Well?" Tundy demanded.

"I don't see it. When did you bring it by?"

"Yesterday morning."

The book slammed down and Pat huffed, "Why, no wonder it wasn't in the paper! It takes two days from the day you pay to run an ad. Didn't you sign a form when you made your payment? It's written right there."

"I didn't have time to read it. I had my gang with me and they were arguing over who got to ride shotgun on the way back to the assisted-living center, and were about to come to blows."

"Was not!" Clara said from where she sat in her wheelchair.

"Did too!" C.J. chimed in, looking pleased he'd been able to contribute.

Clara turned to him, her eyes hideously magnified by her bottle-thick glasses. "C.J., you're disagreein' with me."

He blinked. "Was I?"

"Yes."

"Oh." He thought about this a minute. "Was I right?"

She sighed and patted his hand. "Never mind."

Pat closed the book. "Miss Spillers, your ad will be in tomorrow's paper."

"But that's too late! It's singles karaoke night at the Bigger Jigger, and I need me a date."

"Then you're going to have to wait until next

week. They have singles karaoke every Thursday, so you won't be out much."

"I can't wait until next week. I want me a date *this* week. The ad I wrote was perfect, too." She dug a crumpled note from her huge beach bag. "Here it is. It says, 'Looking for love. Young, sexy, slender Virgo seeks—' Are you laughin'?"

"No, no!" Pat's voice warbled. After a moment, she managed to say in a strangled voice, "Go on."

Mark sank farther in his chair, his catalog shaking with his silent laughter.

"Where was I? Oh, yes . . . 'Young, sexy, slender Virgo seeks hot young man in his twenties, preferably tall, dark, and handsome like Toby Keith, and ready for a good time, if you know what I mean. I am yours for the taking! Call today!' and then I put my new cell phone number on there. Mr. Treymayne *promised* me it would be in this paper."

Knowing she was glaring in his direction, Mark turned a page in the catalog so she wouldn't think he was listening. She was right. He had promised her that, but only if she brought the ad in by Monday. He'd repeated himself twice, but she obviously hadn't listened.

"Mr. Treymayne! Come out here and tell this beanpole to put my damn ad in the paper and to do it now!" Tundy called in irritation.

He turned another page. Pat could handle Tundy.

Tundy harrumphed. "I know you can hear me back there in yo' office, Mr. Treymayne! I can see you!"

"He's not listening," Pat said in a withering tone. "He *never* listens."

Mark was sure Pat was glaring at him. She was a bit intimidating, with her bright blue eyes blazing against her lined, tanned face. Worse, just this past week she'd had her iron gray hair cut in a short, severe style that made him think of Nazi Germany and tools of torture.

Frankly, no woman gave him hives like the militantly angry Pat Meese. At first, he'd thought she was just angry about Roxie promoting Susan to editor over Pat's head, but no. Pat was mad at *him*. In the ten months he'd worked with her, he'd seen her grouse at, to, or about every male who crossed her path. She seemed to think the entire testosterone world owed her an apology.

He'd stopped trying to get along with her after that; he'd be damned if he'd apologize for having a cock. He liked his cock and he rather thought it liked him, too, so that was that.

Besides, he had far more important things to do than worry about Pat. He glanced at a large spreadsheet tacked to the wall beside his door. According to his Master Plan, he would reach his goal to raise the paper's profitability in exactly ninety-three more days, *if* everything went according to plan.

That was a big "if." A really, really big—

The elevator door opened and Susan strode into the reception area, her deep auburn hair tousled in a way that made Mark think of hot morning sex, the kind that made you smile all day long.

She stopped by their two elderly visitors. "Hello, Miz Clara, Mr. C.J. And how is Glory's very own Murder Mystery Club?"

Mark grinned. Though it was hard to believe, Clara and C.J., who both looked frail enough that a good puff of wind might blow them over, were two-thirds of a murder mystery club that had solved a very long-standing mystery. While they'd been totally wrong in their choice of a suspect, they'd stirred up the town enough that the real culprit had felt forced into action, thus revealing himself.

From her wheelchair, Clara held up a coffee tin decorated with pictures of various *CSI* actors, Gil Grissom the most prominent. "We're taking donations."

"Yes, we are," C.J. warbled after her, nodding. "For our own CSI lab."

Clara peered up at Susan through huge, pale pink, eighties'-style glasses. "We're going to order a complete CSI kit off the internets."

"The internets?" Susan's lips quivered, but she managed to say smoothly, "You can order a CSI kit from there?"

"You sure can! Why, we'll have evidence envelopes and crime-scene tape and tweezers and fingerprint dust and—Lord, you wouldn't believe it if you saw it."

"Sounds impressive. I may have to do a story on that when you're through."

C.J. nodded. "We're going to have some real fluorescent lights, too. Just like they do on *CSI: Miami*."

"Wonderful," Susan said. "And where is this magnificent CSI lab going to be?"

"In Rose's bathroom at the assisted-living center," C.J. answered.

"Ah. Is this going to be a surprise for Rose?"

"Hell, no." Clara waved a hand, her vast assortment of Home Shopping Network gemstone rings glittering on her liver-spotted hand. "Rose knows what's what. She's getting her hair done or she'd be with us right now, taking donations. All

we really need is a big case." Clara looked hopeful.
"You don't happen to have an extra one, do you?
A murder, maybe, or extortion?"

"No, I'm afraid not."

"Oh." Clara looked disappointed.

C.J. shook the can at Susan. "Wanna donate?"

"Sure." She slipped her purse from her shoulder
and pulled out a few crumpled dollars and tucked
them into the tin.

Clara brightened immediately. "Woohoo!
Show me the money!"

Susan grinned and sauntered across the lobby
to greet Tundy and Pat. Mark's mouth went dry
just watching that long-legged walk. There was
something about the way Susan moved that just
killed him. It wasn't the self-conscious strut that
Arlene affected, a deliberate roll of her hips that
drew every male eye within eyeball range. Susan
moved in a more natural, subtle way, but one that
was just as sexy for all that.

What was it about her? He'd been trying to
figure it out ever since she'd kissed him, and he'd
decided it was simply that she was just herself—
unapologetically feminine.

He watched her now as she greeted Tundy and
Pat, flashing them a warm, unaffected smile.

Since that kiss, she'd been damned casual

about the whole thing, acting as if nothing had happened.

Was that the norm for her? How many men *did* she kiss in a week? Was the number so high that she didn't bother even counting?

He rubbed his neck, as tense as if he were involved in a high-level audit. He didn't understand her at all. Most women were fairly transparent, but not her. It was as if he'd been given a 120-piece desk to assemble, the instructions all in Chinese, and someone had left out the final "assembled" picture.

He didn't need this kind of aggravation. Since his divorce, he'd thrown himself into his business and had dominated in every aspect. His company was bigger, leaner, and more productive than ever. His personal life . . . not so much. There'd been women and he'd enjoyed himself, but none had kept his interest.

He watched as Susan leaned against the counter and listened to Tundy's complaint. Mark noticed how Susan's thick, dark red hair curled about her graceful neck, how her eyes literally seemed to sparkle when she smiled, how she had the most intriguing dimple in one cheek that only showed up when she gave that deep, throaty laugh, how great her ass looked encased in soft blue jeans—

His groin tightened.

"Miz Susan," Tundy said. "You're the editor now. You can help me."

Pat sniffed and Susan diplomatically said, "Pat's been teaching me everything she knows."

"Well, I got a problem with my personal ad." Tundy leaned toward Susan. "I got to get me a hot date for karaoke tonight and somehow my request got lost."

"It's not lost," Pat said flatly. "She missed the deadline by a day so it's not in the book."

"Ah, I see."

"And now I want my money back," Tundy said, sending Pat a hard look.

"We don't give refunds," Pat said.

"Why not?" demanded Tundy.

Clara pushed her wheelchair over to the counter beside Tundy. "Costco'll give you a refund if you have your receipt. They changed out a ten-pound jar of pickles for me just last week."

"Even the psychic channel gives out refunds," Tundy added.

Pat snorted in disbelief. "You can't believe that silliness."

"It's not silliness. I paid for one of them psychic readings just last week, and the nice voodoo lady said I was gonna be a doctor. She also said I was goin' to get some money and I got paid the next day, so some of it's already come true."

Susan nodded, her eyes sparkling. "I can see where that might seem like validation."

"No, it's not," Pat said flatly.

"Oh, but it is," Tundy said. "How did that lady *know* I was goin' to get paid, huh? She *didn't*. So it was a real prediction and it came true."

"I believe 'em," Clara added. "I wanted to join the psychic network, but they wouldn't take a Medicare voucher."

Pat looked ready to explode, her thin lips folded into a fierce frown. "Psychics are frauds. They either predict broad things—like that you'll get paid—or they keep a dossier from previous calls. I know because my mother got caught up with one, and they took her for a lot of money before she realized what was what."

"A dossier?" Clara's gaze brightened. "I saw a *Rockford Files* once't where they went to the newspaper and there was a file on ever' person in town. You got one of those here?"

"That's called a morgue."

"Like for dead people?"

"Yes. It's where the dead issues go. Sometimes

they'll clip copies—or nowadays just scan 'em—
and you can look for information on all sorts of
people and places."

"Well, I'll be!" Clara shook her head in wonder. "That'd be useful to have."

"Not as useful as a refund," Tundy said in a
stubborn voice.

"Tundy, I am *not* giving you a refund, and that's
that!"

Tundy turned to Susan. "I got to get me a date!
My psychic said I was gonna meet me someone
this coming week when Mars aligns with—or was
it Mercury? I don't remember, but I have until
Thursday. That's tonight!"

"Thursday's paper is already out, so there's
not much I can do for you." Tundy opened her
mouth and Susan held up a hand. "*But* I have a
suggestion."

"What's that?"

"Attend the First Baptist Singles Bowling this
afternoon, so you'll have a date for karaoke *tonight*.
There are a lot of desperate men in the Baptist
church."

"Desperate?"

"*Very* desperate."

Tundy pursed her lips. "You think some of
them might like to sing karaoke?"

"I don't know why not. There's bound to be some choir members there."

Tundy brightened.

"And if they aren't good, then tomorrow, when your ad *does* come out, you'll be able to audition other dates over the weekend to see which one has the best set of pipes."

"Sort of like *American Idol*," Tundy said, awed.

"That's a good plan," Clara said, nodding. "I like *American Idol*."

"I need to pee," C.J. announced.

Tundy patted his hand. "We'll stop by on our way out." She beamed at the others. "Thanks, Miz Susan! That's just the thing. What time does this singles bowling begin?"

"Three. I wrote an article on it last month, and they had four men for every woman present."

"Now those are some odds!" Tundy rubbed her hands together. "Come on, gang! We'll go to my house and you can help me find the right clothes." She pushed Clara's wheelchair to the elevator, C.J. lagging behind.

Susan poured herself some coffee from the machine behind the reception desk, then went to her cubicle.

As she walked past his office, Susan caught Mark's gaze over the top of his catalog.

His neck heated and he offered a sheepish grin. "Thanks for taking care of that."

"You're welcome." She leaned against the door frame. "Hiding?"

"Yes." He dropped the catalog on his desk. "Could you move a few inches to the left? Pat's still giving me the evil eye."

She obligingly shifted her hip to one side, but her expression wasn't as bright as when she'd been talking to Pat and Tundy.

He tried a big smile. "How was your morning?"

"Great. I set up an interview with the new preacher."

"For which church?"

She sipped her coffee. "First Baptist. I also stopped by City Hall to get a copy of the new surveyor's report and overheard the mayor telling that bimbo—"

"Secretary." At Susan's disdainful look, he added, "If you get in the habit of calling Robin Wright a bimbo, you'll slip up and say it when you don't mean to."

"And that's bad how?"

"It's unprofessional and could be interpreted as bias."

"I don't allow my personal feelings to interfere with my work, but that doesn't mean I don't *have* any personal feelings. It just means I don't use them in my articles."

"Still, I'd like us to maintain some dignity in the community. People expect and want that."

Susan looked unconvinced. "How's this? 'The mayor was talking to his evil, will-sleep-with-anything secretary.' "

Mark wondered if anyone else's eyes were the exact same blue as Susan's. They were a gray-blue lit with gold and brown flecks, like . . . well, he couldn't think of anything to compare them to. They were just amazing.

"By the way," she continued, "are we still having a staff meeting Monday at ten?"

"Every Monday."

"I might miss it. Old Pastor MacMillan is holding a Meet the New Preacher Breakfast. I should be there."

He shrugged. "We'll move the meeting back for you."

"Oh." Her nose wrinkled.

"You really hate meetings, don't you?"

"You should see me at the City Council meetings. Boring doesn't begin to describe them. I once fell asleep and they finished the meeting and locked up the place."

He chuckled. "They didn't wake you?"

"Nope. I woke up in the dark in a strange room. Scared me half to death, but it taught me a lesson."

"Don't sleep in council meetings?"

She laughed. "No. Take a pillow and always carry a flashlight. I almost fell over two chairs on my way out."

He chuckled with her, and for one delicious minute, they were in complete accord. Then he noticed her shirt was slightly pulled up on one side and he could see a sliver of pale skin at the low-slung waistband of her jeans.

The sight of that skin made his mouth water, his heart race. He wanted to touch that skin, to trace it with his lips. The image was startling and graphic and suddenly he wasn't grinning anymore.

Neither was she. She cleared her throat nervously and said in a hurried voice, "By the way, the mayor is talking reelection. Looks like he may not have the funds to run, though he said it could be a battle if someone else in town decides to run against him."

Focus on her words, not her hips. "How did the secretary take that?"

"She was hopping mad. Told him that if he lost his office, he lost her, too."

"That could be interesting," Mark said. "Especially if you catch them arguing in public."

"Or at one of the council meetings."

"They argue there? While it's in session?"

"They argue everywhere, all of the time."

"Hmm. Might find out something useful from that."

She gave him a secret smile that turned his libido upside down. "Oh, I have." She turned on her heel and entered her own office.

He stood, determined to find out what she meant by that, but became aware of Pat's interested gaze from the reception area. Crossing his office, he made a great show of selecting a book before he returned to his desk and pretended to read.

Damn it, what was he thinking? If Pat thought there was something between him and Susan, she wouldn't hesitate a second in broadcasting it.

He closed the book and tossed it onto the desk, where it landed on the month's profit margins with a satisfying *thunk*, aware that Pat was still staring. He ignored her and began to go through the spreadsheets. The newspaper office was a fish-bowl, as was the entire town—one of the many reasons why he had no interest in staying in Glory a second longer than he had to. There was nothing for him here. No, that wasn't quite true. There was *one* thing—a potential flirtation with a very hot redhead with a sassy mouth and a penchant for arguing.

Stop it, Treymayne. You're going to get yourself in trouble with that one. Just focus on the paper. The sooner you get it in the black, the sooner you can get the hell out of Glory.

The phone in the reception area rang and Pat had to turn to answer it.

Mark immediately swiveled in his chair so he could see directly into Susan's office, where she was turning on her computer and shuffling files on her desk.

He'd been raised in Glory, and had been taught to believe in beauty as defined by his Southern heritage—demure, sweet, steady, augmented by large hair and larger breasts.

Susan was slender, small chested, eschewed makeup, and always wore jeans, yet she managed to look more feminine than any woman he'd ever met. Perhaps it was her thick, dark red hair that she was even now confining to a ponytail at the nape of her neck with a band she'd pulled from a desk drawer. Or perhaps it was the way she moved with an almost dancerlike grace, even in worn hiking boots, her usual shoe of choice.

Her cellphone rang and she fished in her purse for it. "Hello, this is Susan." She listened intently. "Yes. Yes. I know. So I told him. Well, he'd better not and—are you OK, then? Sheesh. You have to be more careful!"

Who in the hell was that? Mark was almost certain she was talking to a man.

Susan stifled what sounded very much like a giggle.

Mark was on his feet before he knew it. He grabbed the first folder he could lay his hands on and walked to the door of Susan's office. Leaning in, he could detect that her caller was indeed a male and had a very deep voice. Who did she know in town who had a deep voice?

She sent him a startled look and then said into the phone, "Can you hang on just a moment? My boss just walked in." Susan cupped a hand over her phone. "Yes? You want something?"

He wanted to know who the hell could make her giggle like that.

He eyed the phone in her hand with rancor. He should leave; he knew that. A professional, libido-in-the-right-place boss wouldn't even be here. But somehow—

He walked into her office and plopped in the chair across from her desk. "I'll wait until you're done." He waved a hand. "Go ahead."

She frowned. "I can—"

"I couldn't possibly interrupt you," he said, certain his voice was clearly audible to the man on the other end of the phone line. "Go ahead and finish your conversation." He opened the folder and settled into the chair as if already absorbed. "I'll just read my notes while you're talking."

There was a lengthy silence as she looked at him with a flat stare. Finally, she removed her hand from the phone. "Sorry, Jeff. You were saying?"

The deep voice continued, discussing (of all things) barbecue. From where he sat, Mark could make out the faintest hint of a Northern accent. He couldn't think of a single person in town recently arrived from up North.

Mark tried to picture the guy. He'd be short and stocky, have black hair, and wear a lot of gold chains. Yeah. Gold chains and polyester shirts open to his hairy chest. The guy probably had the IQ of a dead horse, and a potbelly.

Mark was feeling better when Susan said, "Jeff,

I almost forgot to mention it, but Deloris at the library says your book is doing well. I—What? You're *kidding* me!" Susan looked at Mark, her eyes sparkling, a genuine grin lighting her face. "The *New York Times* list *again*? That's *amazing*! You have to let me write a story for the paper about you."

Mark's image exploded. How could they have a *New York Times* best-selling author in little Glory, North Carolina? And why was he talking to Susan?

Susan had to struggle to pay attention to Jeff, one of her poker buds. She wasn't sure why Mark was sitting in her office and listening in, but she knew for a fact he was. Every time she said something to Jeff, Mark's expression changed.

She wished he would leave. It was hard enough not to stare at him when he was in his office directly across the hall from her, looking kissable and annoying. How did one man manage to have both deliciously lickable-looking muscles and adorably nerdy glasses? It was more than the glasses that made Mark nerdy—he just had that *look*. And she found it so sexy. She wanted to un-nerd him—to muss his hair, run her hands over him, and shock the living daylights out of him.

When she'd foolishly stopped by his office this

morning, she'd discovered it was difficult talking to a man while having fantasies of climbing over his desk, ripping off his glasses, and throwing herself into his lap, all while wrangling a kiss from his firm mouth.

Having him sitting here, his broad shoulders echoing the Superman in the poster directly over his head, was even more difficult. It was taking all of her effort to talk to Jeff.

"Suze?"

Susan realized that she hadn't heard a word for at least a minute. Cheeks burning, she muttered, "Sorry, Jeff. What was that?"

"I was just asking if you minded if I came by this evening and checked your grill, to make sure you have enough gas to do an entire rack of ribs for the guys at the poker game. Thought I might surprise them."

"Sure. I'll be home at six."

"I have to fly at five, taking Doc Wilson to Raleigh. How about I just stop by in an hour or so? The grill's on the back porch and I can check it—"

"No." She said the word too quickly, because Mark's brows lowered and Jeff went silent. "My dad, ah, he might be taking a nap. But it's no problem. I bought a brand-new tank of gas just last week." She'd stop by the hardware store on the way home and make that lie the truth.

"OK, then." Jeff's voice sounded relaxed again. "Talk to you later. And Suze?"

"Yeah?"

"Don't let that ass of a boss ruin your day."

Mark's expression darkened and she knew he'd heard every word. It served him right for listening in.

Susan fought a sudden grin, feeling as if she were back in control of the situation. "Thanks, Jeff." She hung up the phone.

Mark's blue eyes fairly burned through his glasses. "Jeff?"

"Brockaw. He runs the FBO at the airport."

"FBO?"

"Fixed Base Operation. He provides gas, showers, and beds in case the weather socks in a pilot. You wouldn't believe how gorgeous the facilities are—marble countertops in the restrooms, high-speed internet computers set up in the lounge area, leather couches, and a full kitchen. It's luxurious."

"And people use it here in Glory?"

"You'd be surprised. Doc Wilson flies out once

or twice a week to visit his patients in Raleigh. Mayor Harkins rents a plane every time he has to go to the capitol. Others in town use the airport, too, plus Jeff's a certified flight instructor and gives lessons."

"All that and a *New York Times* best seller, living right here in Glory."

There was nothing rude about Mark's tone, but she couldn't help but feel that he was sneering. "Jeff writes mysteries. You may have heard of him; he writes under the name Thomas Shoreham."

"*Shoreham?* The Leonard Chronicles series? Those have been made into movies!"

She grinned. "I know."

"Have you written about him for the paper?"

"No. He's sort of incognito."

"Not if Deloris Fishbine knows his identity."

"He doesn't mind people in town knowing about it, but he doesn't want the bigger media outlets to pick up on it."

"Hmm. How long have you known this guy?"

"A few years. He plays poker at my house every Wednesday."

Mark's gaze narrowed. "You have a weekly poker game?"

She nodded. An awkward silence grew. *Good*

God, does he expect me to invite him to the game? It's hard enough to have to see him at work, especially after that stupid kiss. She twiddled her thumbs, the silence growing.

Finally, her Southern manners got the best of her. "You, ah . . . do you play poker?"

"No."

"Oh, good."

He lifted his brows and her face grew hot. "I mean, I'd hate to owe you money. I daresay you're very good at bluffing. You don't show a lot of emotion and—" She winced at her own words. "I mean, I just think you—"

"Don't worry about it," he said shortly. "I appreciate the invite, but I have things to do on Wednesdays."

"Right. I'm sure you do." She cleared her throat. "You came in to ask me something, I believe?"

"Yes, I did but—" Mark frowned. "If you decide to do a story on this Jeff guy, be careful to check his story."

"You sound as if you don't believe it."

Mark adjusted his glasses. "I didn't say that."

"Good," she said, bristling, "because he's a friend of mine. He's the real thing and I'll vouch for him."

Mark's lips thinned. "You can vouch for him

all you want, Collins, but if you do a story on him, I want more research than your opinion."

Her jaw tightened. "I would never write an article without checking the facts thoroughly, and I don't appreciate the suggestion that I would. Now, if there's nothing else, I have work to do. I'm actually verifying some of the facts I got from the new preacher this morning." She lifted the phone and angrily punched in a number.

Mark sighed. "Susan, I'm sorry. I just—"

"Hello! Johnson Bible College!" came a cheery voice on the phone.

"Hello," Susan said smoothly. "This is Susan Collins, a reporter for *The Glory Examiner*. I need to verify the graduation dates for a previous student."

Mark sighed and left.

Susan watched from under her lashes as he crossed the hall and made his way to his own office. He sat, staring down at the folder in his hand for a long time. Then, with a sigh of frustration, he threw it down, got up, and walked out. She heard the creaky swoosh of the elevator doors and then nothing.

Susan waited as long as she could before she stood, moving the phone with her as she separated the slats in the blinds and stared down into the parking lot. For a nerdy guy, his clothes fit astoundingly well, his khaki trousers hugging his ass and muscular legs, his polo-style golf shirt stretched across his broad shoulders and neatly tucked in, a belt defining his narrow waist.

Nerd clothing on a hot bod. The fascinating contrast drove her wild. Just watching him cross the parking lot was getting her all hot and bothered. It was a pity all that male sexiness was controlled by a brain so coolly calculating that he was Borg-like: part human—the part that had kissed her—and part adding machine—the part that had *stopped* kissing her and was now causing him to avoid her like the plague.

Barely listening to the automated voice on the other end of the phone, she took her seat behind the desk again. Why, oh why had she kissed him? Now she wanted to do it again, and again, and again, on his desk, in his chair, on the floor. She couldn't remember wanting a guy this bad since high school, including Mark himself. She'd known him then, of course, though not well. Besides, she'd been into the handsome football hero sort, which hadn't been Mark at all. In fact, she barely remembered him, except that he hadn't looked anything like the way he did now. It was amazing what sixteen short years could do for a man.

The cheery voice on the phone broke into her thoughts and, with a sigh, she found a pen and began to take notes. He was a tough egg to crack. For this one, she was going to need help. Fortunately, she knew right where to get it. Wednesday's poker game couldn't get here fast enough.

Chapter
4

Dear Bob,

I've never been the sort of girl that boys ask out. Instead they offer to take me fishing or to see a race—that sort of thing.

My mom is worried that there's something wrong with me and that I should try to look more feminine. She wants me to get a perm and wear dresses and stuff.

I think it would be wrong to dress and act in a way that's not me. What do you think?

Signed,
Tomboy at Heart

Dear Tomboy at Heart,

You have to be true to who you are or you'll never be happy. Tell your mother that you love her, but that you need to decide who you are, and a perm won't do that.

Enjoy who you are and you'll eventually find the right guy: one who will appreciate you for being you.

Sincerely,
Bob

The Glory Examiner
June 31, section B2

Pat limped into the meeting room, dropped into her seat, and said in a querulous tone, "What do you want, Treymayne? I have a hot lead and I don't have time to meet every ten minutes."

"We only have one meeting a week, Pat."

"Yeah, well, you keep having them right when I get my leads." Pat leaned back in her chair and plopped her feet on the table. "Get to it, Treymayne. I've got interviews to do, leads to—"

"Follow. I know. So what are these leads, anyway?"

"A reporter *never* reveals her secrets."

"I think the phrase you're looking for is, 'A reporter never reveals her *sources*.' "

"Same thing." She snorted in disgust. "That's why they should never let a *bean counter* run a paper. You don't know the first damn thing about the news, do you?"

"No. Fortunately, it doesn't take Lois Lane to realize the facts, which are—"

"Did someone mention Lois Lane?" came a sprightly voice. Susan came in, her hands overflowing with cups of coffee and a bakery box. She was dressed in jeans and a white stretch T-shirt that made her look about eighteen.

Pat thumped her feet back on the floor. "You've been to Micki & Maud's!"

"Yup, and Connie's up to her usual magic. She made cinnamon buns that are out of this world. I had two extra but Ray conned me out of one of them."

Pat eagerly tore into the box. "Good God, they're huge!"

Susan placed a coffee in front of Pat and one in front of an empty chair, scooting the third toward Mark. "Thank goodness Ray was there to catch the elevator for me. It was all I could do to carry all of this."

"Excuse me," Mark said politely as Susan and Pat dug into their treats. "As soon as you two are ready, we'll start the meeting."

Susan shot him a look from beneath her lashes and blinked but didn't comment.

It made him crazy when she looked at him like that. No woman blinked with as much effect as Susan Collins. He didn't know if it was the ridiculous length of her lashes, or the way her eyes had a bit of an uptilt, probably a throwback to some Slavic ancestor.

Susan put down her sticky bun. "Before you begin, I have an item I'd like placed on our agenda."

Wow. Participation. He could get used to that. "Sure. What is it?"

"Monday morning meetings."

"Why do you want those on the agenda?"

"Because only a moron would schedule a meeting first thing Monday morning."

Pat banged her sticky-fingered fist on the table. "Hear, hear!"

"What's wrong with Monday mornings?" he asked, indignant.

Susan reached into her large brown leather satchel and pulled out a folder. She flipped it open and removed a dozen phone messages. "These all came in over the weekend."

"What are they?"

She flipped through the messages. "Suggestions from community members about stories."

He eyed the small stack. "Wouldn't we need a meeting to assign them?"

"Pat and I have our distribution method already worked out." Susan tossed the slips of paper onto the table. "Pat, you first."

Pat stirred through the pile, then made an expression of distaste. "Guess I'll do one about the rule changes in the Glory High School Homecoming Parade because of the fire that started on the DECA float last year."

Susan rifled through the papers, finally settling on two small pink squares. "Doc Wilson called to say that his niece just finished her residency and is coming to Glory to join his practice. Someone could do an 'all-in-the-family' sort of piece."

"I know Doc pretty well," Pat offered.

"Okay, you take it. I'll cover the Baptist Bake-Off. There's something wonky going on with it. I need to do some digging."

Pat perked up. "What's wonky?"

"There are rumors that money went missing after the last one."

"How much?"

"A lot. This time they're bringing in an out of towner to manage things, which they've never done, and—oh, a whole mess of things. It wouldn't surprise me if this became a lead story."

"*That?*" Mark asked incredulously. "You have to be kidding."

"People take the Bake-Off very seriously around here," Susan said.

"Seems like a piece for the Living Section, not the front page." Mark ruffled through the remaining pieces of paper on the table. "Most of these stories could be covered with a few phone calls. They're pretty thin."

"That depends on how you write them." Susan

selected one of the notes. "Like this one, for example."

He leaned forward to take it from her, instantly aware of the light, sweet scent of her perfume. He took a deep breath. It was floral and reminded him of a spring rain.

Arlene had worn Chanel No. 5, which was heavier and reminded him of a hothouse flower, which described Arlene exactly—a redneck hothouse flower.

Susan plucked the paper from his fingers and read aloud, "Little PeeWee Rangers Campout."

"So?"

Pat snorted. "Good God, man! Don't tell me you don't know the value of photos of cute little gap-toothed boys and girls?"

"Photos, sure."

"*And* a story," Susan said. "We could include a short history of the PeeWees, get some quotes from adults in town who used to be in the program, and open and close the article with quotes from current-day PeeWees and how the program is changing their lives."

Mark winced. "Sounds like a lot of column inches."

The enthusiasm in Susan's eyes suddenly dimmed and he felt a twinge of guilt. He hated being the one to constantly bring up costs, but someone had to do it. He *had* to get this paper on its feet for Roxie's sake. Few people understood all that his sister had faced in the last year. She'd gone through a difficult divorce that had hurt her badly and had shaken her belief in herself. While she was doing well now, especially since she'd met Nick Sheppard, Mark remembered how haunted she'd once looked. It was a look he never wanted to see again, so he'd decided to personally oversee her investment in the newspaper until it was solidly in the black and could provide her with some security.

It was not going to be an easy task; the paper was in far worse shape than anyone knew. But with careful management, and increased revenue, there was a chance he could turn the paper around. It wouldn't be easy, but he was ready to make the tough decisions. After all, that was what he did for a living: he helped people make the most of their financial decisions, and he was good at it. *Very* good.

Still, there were times when he hated being the voice of reason, a responsibility he'd carried for most of his life. As early as he could remember, Mother had charged from one personal mess to another, offending half of the town for this, accusing the other half of the town of insulting her over that, and generally overemoting her way through life. From an early age, Mark had removed himself from such shenanigans, but he still got caught in the backlash at times, which had made him all the more resentful of emotional decision making. He liked things neat, contained, and organized.

Susan finished off her cinnamon bun and wiped her fingers. "Mark, why do we even have these staff meetings? We never had them before you came."

"Yeah," Pat said. "And the paper did just fine, too."

Mark put down his cup. "No, the paper didn't do 'just fine.' I've been running the numbers and they're bad."

Susan paused in taking a sip of her coffee, her gaze locked on his. "What do you mean by 'bad'?"

"Here, let me show you." He opened his folder and pulled out a large paper, unfolding it until it covered almost half of the table. "This represents the paper's total expenses and income."

Susan leaned forward, the tip of her ponytail brushing the chart.

Mark immediately imagined that ponytail brushing far more intimate things, and his speech evaporated into thin air.

"Wow. It's even in color." Pat's tone conveyed all the respect one might give a fellow classmate who'd not only completed their assignment to draw the solar system, but had brought in a 3-D model as well. "What's all of that red?"

"Expenses," he said briefly.

Pat pointed a bony finger. "What's that little sliver of green?"

"Income."

Susan whistled silently. "That does look bad."

"I'll say," Pat agreed. "Treymayne, you should change the colors. Blue would look better than all that red."

"Pat, this chart doesn't make the paper *look* anything. It tells the way the paper really *is*. The simple fact is this: we're going broke."

Her face reddened. "Times are tough all over and—"

"Not this tough. If we're going to keep the doors open, then things have to change, and all of us—*all* of us—have to work together."

Pat slammed her cup onto the table, coffee sloshing out and staining the chart. "I don't need to stay here and listen to garbage like this." She grabbed her things, her movements jerky. "The paper did just fine before you Treymaynes came along, and it will do just fine once you're both gone!" She stomped to the door, pausing to look at Susan. "You coming?"

Susan frowned. "Pat, I want to hear how the paper's doing. You should, too. Mark isn't trying to—"

"Fine. Stay here, then. I'll be in my office doing the *real* work—reporting the news." With that, she slammed the door behind her.

Susan winced. "Sorry about that."

"You didn't do anything."

"No, but . . . Pat's not usually so difficult. She's just mad because Roxie made me the new editor and not her."

"You have a degree in journalism and are a hard worker. Pat never went to college, and her writing shows it. Furthermore, she may have more direct experience with the paper, but it was marred by her uncooperative attitude. She's been trouble to every one of her bosses, including Ty and his father before him."

"She can be difficult." Susan took a napkin and blotted the coffee from the chart, then threw the wet napkin into the trash can. "I had no idea things were this bad."

"Neither did I, or I would have warned my sister when she decided to buy it." Mark noted the worry in Susan's eyes and quickly added, "I'm doing what I can to save your jobs. If I have to cut personnel, I won't start in the newspaper office."

"If you're cutting personnel and it's not me or Pat, then who—" Her eyes widened. "Ray Dobbins?"

"We don't need a security guard. He's really a courtesy employee, and he's so out of shape that if anything really did happen, he'd be next to useless."

"Mark, he's worked here for over forty years. You *can't* fire Ray."

"I wouldn't fire him; I would just lay him off. He would get unemployment—"

"For a few weeks and that's it. But it's more than that!" Somehow, they were both standing now, Susan's hands fisted at her sides, her face flushed. "Mark, Ray *lives* for this job! You can't do this to him! You can't—"

"I don't want to do it to anyone!" Mark burst out. He caught her amazed look and realized that it had been years—literally *years*—since he'd lost his temper.

What was it about this woman that made him lose control at the slightest provocation?

He pulled off his glasses and rubbed his face, then carefully replaced them. "Susan, why do you think I've been working so hard since I arrived?

I've been trying to save the paper and all of your butts, too. I'll do everything I can to save Ray's job. You should know that."

Susan pressed her fingers to her temples. "You're right. I just—" She dropped her hands and offered a shaky smile. "I'm sorry. You were just explaining things and I got mad—not at you, but at the circumstances. I had no idea things were so grim and it caught me off guard."

"I felt the same way when I first found out. I should have told you but I didn't want you to quit."

She nodded and placed her hands palm down on the table before her, her fingers spread. "Let's start over, shall we? Tell me everything. I promise not to snap at you or quit."

He had to admit, he liked her style. When she was wrong, she admitted it and attempted to do better. He wished more of his vice presidents were so reasonable in their behavior. "What do you want first, the good news or the bad?"

"I'd like some good news, please."

"There are some solid assets on the balance sheets—the building and the land represent some of the most valuable commercial real estate in Glory. That's why I moved the newspaper offices to this floor. If we can rent the bottom floor as office space, it'll take the cost for upkeep of the entire building off the paper's shoulders."

"So if we get some tenants for the downstairs offices, then everything will be—"

"Better, but not fixed. We'll need more than that, though it would be a good start."

"OK, so we need to rent the bottom offices." She pulled a small reporter's notebook from her pocket, flipped it open, and scribbled a line. "What else?"

"The other good news is that while newspapers across the country have experienced dwindling readership, *The Glory Examiner* hasn't."

"We have a loyal base."

"Apparently so. The subscription rate is remarkably steady."

"That's good."

"That's excellent. Also on the plus side is that both you and Pat know and understand this community and are well liked and respected."

To his surprise, she blushed. "Thank you."

He shrugged, oddly touched by her reaction. It was obvious that she cared deeply about her job.

"Is there any more good news?"

He consulted his notes. "No, that's about it."

"Then next up is the bad news." She fixed her steady blue gaze on his. "Go ahead."

"The roof and HVAC on this building haven't been touched in years. It's only a matter of time before one or both die."

She drew a line down the page and began a new list. "I never thought of that." Her pen traveled over the paper. "There's the elevator, too. It's ancient, slower than molasses, and sometimes hangs between floors.

"What would it cost if we had to repair both the roof and HVAC?"

Mark liked that Susan didn't flinch when it came to facing facts. "It could be around $150,000 for a simple repair. For a complete replacement—" He shook his head. "You don't want to know."

"Ouch." She glanced over at the chart. "I see that you've figured in repair of our printing equipment."

"I didn't have enough information to figure out exact repair costs, so I estimated based on past costs." It was a relief to share the bad news, especially with someone able to see the entire picture. He met Susan's gaze evenly. "If the printing press goes out then we're cooked."

"That's Ty's fault," Susan said, referring to the former owner of the paper. "That ass took every penny he could out of the *Examiner* and none of it went back in."

At Ty Henderson's name, Mark's jaw tightened and Susan hurried to say, "Sorry. I shouldn't have mentioned him."

For years, Ty Henderson had used a connection to one of the town's more colorful citizens to perpetrate an elaborate blackmail hoax. When he'd been exposed, he'd taken a hostage—Mark's sister. Fortunately, Nick had been able to save Roxie and Ty had gone to prison. The entire episode still left a horrible taste in Mark's mouth.

Susan leaned forward and placed her hand over his, her fingers warm. "Mark, don't get upset. It happened months ago and Roxie's safe now."

"That asshole—"

"Is in jail and your sister is fine." Susan released his hand. "Back to the *Examiner*. You're right about the equipment; it's so old, we can never find parts. The last few parts had to be custom made, which cost a fortune, and it took weeks."

Susan tapped a finger on her bottom lip. "You know, we *could* outsource our printing to the Asheville paper. They have brand-new equipment and can do it in a tenth of the time it takes us."

"Do they do that sort of thing?"

"Yes, most local papers use them. In fact—" She pulled her notepad close and scribbled across it. "I'll call them today and get a quote so we'll have an idea of the costs."

"Thank you. Would outsourcing make production more difficult?"

"Nope," Susan said. "The layout and content could be sent via the net, then we'd send someone to pick up the finished newspapers."

Mark nodded slowly. "That's an excellent idea."

"Thank you. Any other bad news?"

"That about covers it."

"It's enough." Susan set her pen down and stared at her list. "Mark, I wish you'd told me all of this before now. I thought you were just changing things to be in charge."

"I'm not a capricious sort of person."

No, he wasn't; everything he did and said confirmed that. She should have known better, but she'd been too infuriated by his bossy manner. "I don't know what sort of person you are. You moved away as soon as you graduated, and in high school you didn't even know I was alive."

He chuckled. "Oh, I knew you were alive. I just wasn't about to hit on one of my sister's best friends."

Susan's face warmed. "Roxie and I were never that close. You just never noticed me; admit it."

"I am not going to admit any such thing, Collins." His lips quirked as if he fought a smile.

Susan didn't think he'd ever looked sexier than he did at this exact moment. "You didn't pay any attention to me in high school and—I'll be honest—I didn't pay much attention to you, either."

"If I remember right, you were all eyes for Brian Parker."

"Until he got engaged to Roxie." Susan made a face. "I can't believe he cheated on her like that. At her wedding, I remember thinking how perfect they looked. I was so envious."

"He fooled everyone, including Roxie."

"Sometimes appearances are just that—appearances." She knew something about that from her brief, outstandingly wrong relationship.

"Susan, I need to apologize. I've been very focused on getting the paper back on track and I missed the most important resource the paper has—the employees."

At least he now knew why he'd faced so much hostility with Susan. He'd written it down to Susan's and Pat's lack of acceptance of the new order, when the truth was, he'd apparently been as heavy-handed as hell. "In Raleigh I'm the boss;

I created that firm and when I decide to do something, I just do it. I suppose I've gotten a little spoiled over the years."

Her gaze warmed and she grinned. "You've definitely gotten used to getting your own way."

"Are you saying I'm bossy?"

"Arrogant, high-handed, bossy—" She burst into laughter, her eyes crinkling. "If you could see your face!"

"It's probably a good thing I can't."

She chuckled. "So what's next, Treymayne? You're the bean counter, so tell me about the beans. How many more do we need to save Ray's job?"

"Including benefits? About fifty thousand dollars' worth."

Susan bit her lip, mesmerizing him as her even white teeth sank into her plump lower lip. What was it about her mouth that drew his attention so? Was it the way her bottom lip was fuller and rounder than the shorter top one, giving her a slightly pouty look? Or was it—

"Fifty thousand smackers." Susan sighed. "That's a lot of moola."

"We could do it if we increased our ad sales by a good percent."

"I suppose we could add a sales flyer and—"

"No. If we add pages, it will just increase costs and negate the ad sales. We'll have to reduce the content."

"*No.*" Susan shook her head vehemently. "You can't reduce our reporting space. Why do you think our readers are so loyal? It's because we consistently deliver a quality product. If you really want to see a significant increase in revenue, then add two more pages of content and expand our coverage area to some of the smaller towns nearby. That will increase the paper's value as well as increase our potential readership, which should mean an increase in circulation. *Then* we can raise ad prices to meet our revenue goal."

"Collins, there's no way people would pay more to advertise than they do now. You're at price saturation as it is." Frankly, he was surprised at how much people were willing to pay to put an ad in the paper as it was. "Susan, the simple truth is this: we need more income, which means more ad sales. I'm going to ask you and Pat to start being more aggressive about that."

"Pat and I already cover the entire country's events, *and* write all of the content, *and*—because of you—now we also take turns working the front desk *and* answering the phones. When, exactly, are we supposed to sell more ads?"

She had a point. Again. He pulled off his glasses and tossed them onto the chart. "We'll have to figure out some way to make it happen."

"We'll see." She gathered her notepad and coffee cup. "Meanwhile I'll call the *Asheville Citizen-Times* and get their rates for outsourcing our printing." Susan sent him a fast smile and left.

Mark watched her go. What that woman did for a pair of jeans was almost criminal.

He went to the conference room doorway to watch her walk toward her office, each confident stride long and sexy. When he worked in Raleigh he was surrounded by attractive women—lawyers and accountants, legal assistants, ad execs, and marketing personnel—but none had intrigued him like this blue-jeaned, pony-tailed, sensually charged Lois Lane wanna-be.

He had to admit: they sure knew how to grow 'em in Glory, North Carolina.

Chapter
5

Dear Bob,

I'm a young, sexy, slender Virgo looking for a hot young man in his 20s, preferably tall, dark, and handsome like Toby Keith, and ready for a good time, if you know what I mean.

Where can I find me a man like that? I've done checked out the Baptist Singles Group, but none of them could sing "Lay You Down" by that Twitty fellow without giggling like a fourth grader. I need me a no-nonsense man with a good set of lungs.

Where do I look now?

Signed,

Likes 'Em Younger

Dear Likes 'Em,

Tundy Spillers, is that you?

Boys, here's a hot one for you! If you like to dance and look even vaguely like Toby Keith or a member of his band, call *The Examiner* office today and leave a message.

Tundy'll call you right back!

Sincerely,

Bob

The Glory Examiner
July 9, section B2

Susan put down her beer with a *thunk.* "Bull! Women are *easy* to understand."

Six pairs of masculine eyes stared at her in disbelief.

Poker night was Susan's favorite night of the week. Every Wednesday at seven sharp, she opened her garage to six of the town's bachelors, and over the years she'd grown very fond of them.

Nick Sheppard, the town sheriff and Susan's boss when she'd been the county dispatcher, tossed a chip into the center of the table. "Susan, I don't know what you're drinking, but you should probably get yourself some water or coffee."

René Gaspard, the town's fire chief and re-nowned womanizer, grinned. "Or maybe a nice calming glass of milk?" His faint Cajun accent left most of Glory's bachelorettes panting.

Susan snorted. "You all know I've only had one beer. Admit that it's men who say one thing and do another."

Ethan lowered his cards, his brows high. "And women don't?"

"Not as much as men."

"Susan, *ma chère,*" Rene drawled. "Men are

easy to understand. We want pizza, beer, and nakedness."

Susan would have to pass that on to Connie, who drooled every time René, with his mocha skin and pale green eyes, walked past.

Jeff grinned. "I know some women who're into those things, too."

Susan nodded. "That's true. Personally, I couldn't think of a better way to spend the night." She'd been surprised when Jeff had arrived tonight, since he was supposed to be doing cross-country flight training with a student pilot, but at seven he'd strolled in, saying they'd gotten rained out.

He slid a chip into the center pile. "The real secret isn't beer, pizza, and nakedness. It's in getting them all at the same time."

"That," René declared, flashing a grin that made a dimple flicker across his cheek, "would make me downright mellow."

Steven Van Doren nodded. A fireman, he worked with René and idolized the slightly older man. "Docile, even," he agreed.

"Like a lamb," chimed in Jeff.

Doc Wilson tilted back his head so he could see the cards through the bottom part of his glasses. "I'd be comatose."

Susan sighed. "You guys are never serious, are you?"

René looked offended. "We are being perfectly serious!"

Nick nodded. "I'd do a lot of things if Roxie'd bring me pizza and icy beer in the nude."

"You or her?" René asked, trying to look innocent.

Nick returned the favor. "Does it matter?"

They all chuckled and Susan had to laugh with them. "I thought you all would be a big help, but I can tell I was hoping for too much."

Ethan put his cards facedown on the table and pulled a cigar from his pocket. "Anyone want one?"

"I'll take one." Jeff took one with relish.

"Me, too," Susan said, holding out her hand. She sniffed it and smiled. "Mmm, that's smooth." She placed the cigar on the table and used the edge of a beer cap to slice the end.

"That's a neat trick." Jeff held his out and she cut the end for him. "Thanks, Suze." He lit his cigar and puffed a few times. "So . . . what sort of help do you need?"

Susan took the lighter and lit her cigar. "Advice. You guys have always been there for me."

Doc Wilson lifted his beer. "You know it."

Nick nodded. "Anything you need, just say the word."

"This is about Mark."

"We'd guessed that," René said dryly.

She blinked. "How?"

Nick shrugged. "Because you and he seem inseparable lately."

Though no one looked directly at her, she felt their attention as strongly as if a spotlight lit her. "We're trying to stabilize the paper's finances," she said in a cool voice, flipping a chip into the center pile. "It's all work."

René shrugged. "Working with someone and trying to date him can be tough. In New Orleans, there was a woman I once worked with . . ." He sighed happily. "I don't know what was hotter, the fires we fought at work, or the fires we lit afterward."

"Sounds interesting." Jeff threw two cards facedown on the table. "Two."

Nick dealt the pilot two cards. "René, why haven't you mentioned this firewoman before?"

René sniffed. "Why bring up old news?"

Steve threw three cards onto the table. "He never mentions her here because he's been too busy telling us about her at the fire station. According to

René, she's a long-legged blonde bombshell and a real wildcat in bed."

"Excuse me," Susan said. "I believe we were talking about *me*."

"Oh, right." Steve waved a hand. "Continue."

"Well, I used to love to go to work and write articles about the community and represent Glory—you know, try to show who we really are."

René appeared confused. "Are you talking about *The Glory Examiner*?"

Susan stiffened. "Of course I am! It's an important part of our community. Without it, we'd just be a small section in the Asheville paper. Glory deserves more than that."

Ethan removed his cigar and looked at Nick. "She really loves her job, doesn't she?"

Nick nodded. "I thought she just wrote the Dear Bob column."

Jeff looked up from his cards. "Susan writes 'Dear Bob'? I didn't know that."

"She's written it for years—" Nick began.

"*Guys*, I need some help, damn it!"

They all blinked at her, then Jeff put his cards down and gestured around the table. "You guys, too. She's serious."

They all put down their cards. "OK," Nick said. "Lay it on the table, Collins."

Finally! She put her own cards down. "Mark's in charge of the paper until it begins to turn a profit. He and I have different views on a few things, and, well . . . I have an idea about how to turn the paper around, but I think he might disagree."

"So?" Jeff said, looking baffled.

"So I want him to listen to my proposal as if I were on an equal footing."

"You're not on an equal footing now? You're the editor-in-training and he's just a temp accountant."

"It's not him," she said, exasperated. "I just don't want to appear fatuous when I'm trying to—when I want to— You know how you want to make an impression, and you worry that . . ." She could see by the six pairs of eyes fastened on her that not one of them had the faintest idea.

Maybe she should have asked advice from Roxie or Connie. But Roxie was Mark's sister, and Connie had the hots for him—as well as every other bachelor in town. So neither of them would be unbiased sources for some good old-fashioned advice.

Besides, she'd thought she would get the best advice from other men, who understood the male psyche. The trouble was, none of her poker partners seemed to have spared much thought for how their psyches worked and seemed just as mystified as she was.

So now she was once again stuck. She had an idea—a radical, perfectly wonderful idea—but she was fairly certain Mark would reject it out of hand. The idea had been burning a spot in her too-busy brain for the last four days, and she was determined to present it. But what method would work best with Mark? Should she demand that he follow her suggestion? Or ask politely and hope with fingers crossed that he agreed?

There had to be some way she could present her idea that would slant Mark's approval in her favor. But what?

She sighed. "Look, guys, it's hard to explain." Even to herself. The last week had been crazy-busy. Mark's revelation about the newspaper's financial status had made them partners in a way they hadn't been before.

And as the days passed, she'd discovered more about his fascinating personality. One, that he was adorably devoted to his sister. And two, he was one of the most opinionated men she'd ever met. If he didn't like an idea or person, it took a *lot* for him to change his mind, which was why she wanted to give her idea every advantage possible.

Nick opened another beer. "Susan, if you want something from Mark, just tell him what it is. If it makes sense to him, he'll do it."

"I can't just *tell* him that this is a great idea. I have to *convince* him of it. So I need him to listen to me with an open mind." She looked around the table.

There was silence.

"That's it?" Ethan finally asked. "You don't think he'll listen to your idea?"

She nodded.

"Whew!" Jeff said. "I was afraid it was something serious."

"Me, too," Nick admitted.

"It *is* serious!" Susan snapped.

Doc Wilson leaned back in his chair. "Men, I think our lovely hostess wants our expertise. We should hear her out."

"Thank you. I just wish Mark would try to see where I'm coming from. I think he's beginning to trust my instincts on the job, but I want more."

Jeff nodded. "Makes sense to me."

"To me, too," Ethan said.

"And me." René reached for his cards.

"Hold it! I'm not done."

Jeff groaned.

Steve sighed.

Nick held up a hand. "C'mon, guys. Susan provides beer and beef jerky and the use of her garage for our poker games. She deserves our undivided attention."

"Sometimes I even order pizza," she added.

René grimaced. "Susan, I'm sorry. Tell Uncle René what you need from us."

"I guess I just want your advice—as guys—as how to present my idea to Mark."

"Mark seems determined to make the paper a success and you know more about it than most people," Nick said. "Not that it's not a good paper now."

"I love 'Dear Bob,'" Doc said. "I also like the sports and the comics."

"And the horoscopes," René added.

Everyone looked at him.

"Don't tell me you don't believe in the power of the moon," he said dramatically. He was promptly rewarded when Ethan tossed a wadded-up cigar paper his way.

Susan sighed. "Just forget it." She collected her cards. "Whose turn is it?"

René folded his expressive face into a serious look. "Forgive me, *ma chère*. Tell us about this man you wish to impress. What is he like? Is he bold or quiet? Fierce or subtle?"

"Why does that matter?"

Jeff said, "Because one type of guy reacts better to this, another to that."

"Oh. Well, he's very quiet, except when he wants something."

Ethan chuckled around his cigar. "You could say that about all men."

"Except you," Doc Wilson said. "You talk more than any man I know."

Nick gave a wicked grin. "Except René."

"I don't consider René a man," Doc said, "him being French and all."

"I am not French!" René protested, though his green eyes were bright with laughter. "I am Cajun. There is a difference."

"Back to Susan," Ethan said sternly. "I haven't met Mark, but Nick has. And since he's about to marry Mark's sister, he probably knows more about this guy than the rest of us."

Nick crossed his arms. "Well . . . let's see. He's an accountant by trade and very methodical and mathematical. He's also very—" Nick frowned. "Controlled, maybe?"

"That about sums him up," Susan agreed. "He's an accountant first, second, and third." *And sexy in the most Clark Kentish way one could imagine.*

The men digested this.

René observed, "You two are very different. You're casual and spontaneous and he's strict and regulated."

"Exactly."

Jeff leaned back in his chair. "And you want him to consider your idea, right? Then meet him on his own terms."

"How can I do that? He's a number cruncher and chart maker."

"He likes charts, then give him so many charts he doesn't know what's coming."

Use charts on Mark? He did seem fond of them.

Doc nodded. "The guy sounds like he enjoys numbers, too. Give the man charts *and* numbers. Lots of 'em."

"I think Doc and Jeff are onto something." Ethan rubbed his chin thoughtfully. "If I want to sell a guy on a valve job for his bike, the first thing I do is figure out what he wants from his machine—speed or power or looks. If you want someone to buy into something, you have to speak to them on their level."

That is an interesting concept. I never thought of becoming more like him. I was too busy wanting him to be more like me. "OK. I'll see how that works."

Ethan blew a cloud of cigar smoke and then flashed a grin. "You should dress right, too."

She looked down at her T-shirt and jeans. "What's wrong with how I dress?"

Nick shrugged. "Nothing, if you're trying to land a landscaping job."

René agreed, his pale green eyes assessing her almost clinically. "You could be delectable, *ma chère*, with a little work. You need a suit with a skirt cut to"—he touched his thigh midway—"there."

Doc nodded. "I like a woman in a skirt."

Nick grinned happily. "Roxie had on a miniskirt the other day—" He whistled silently.

Rene smiled at Susan. "See? Men appreciate the effort. I'd say Mark needs a bigger hint that you are a force to be reckoned with."

Susan nodded thoughtfully. They made sense. Perhaps she should dress to impress. Well, that was easy enough. "Anything else?"

"Yes," Nick said, stacking his chips, "if you want him to hear your side of things, then present it to him the same way he'd present it to you."

"I can do that." PowerPoint was her friend. She grinned and picked up her cards. "Thank you, gentlemen. You've been a big help."

They'd played several more hands, then Doc yawned and threw down his cards. "I'm out."

René blinked. "But you are winning! You cannot just quit."

"Sure I can." Doc stood and pocketed his winnings. "I need me some beauty sleep. I didn't get any last night."

Ethan grinned. "The missus keeping you up at night?"

Doc chuckled. "Nope, just vandals. My trash can got knocked over around three. Made a huge racket."

Nick collected the cards to shuffle. "You should have called that in."

"Naw. I know who it was. I jumped up, raced outside in my skivvies, and found the Murder Mystery Club. Nick, you need to put a leash on your Aunt Clara."

"She's a case," Nick said grimly. "What in the hell were they doing out at that time of night?"

Doc shrugged. "I dunno. They must have been looking into someone's house with those damned binoculars. They do that a lot."

Nick frowned. "No one lives out your road but the Dotsons and Pastor MacMillan. The Dotsons are on vacation for most of the month, since Sissy had her baby, and you wouldn't see much of anything if you looked in the pastor's windows."

"You know the Murder Mystery Club. Those

nuts'll look into any window that doesn't have a curtain," Doc said.

"Yeah," Susan said, "they do it to Ethan's house all of the time."

Ethan's brows had snapped together. "*What?*"

"You need to close your curtains when you take a shower. They park across the street from your house at least twice a week."

Jeff slapped Ethan on the back. "Sounds like you've got yourself a fan club!"

Ethan's face couldn't have been redder. "I don't want a fan club."

"What you *need*," Susan said, "is a curtain."

"I'm remodeling and I haven't replaced the rod yet! Guess I'll do it first thing in the morning."

"Crazy club." Doc settled his Braves ball cap on his white hair. "Before I could walk down my drive to ask them what in the hell they were doing, that Tundy woman peeled out, flattened the trash can, and spun off. Took me the better part of thirty minutes to collect all of my trash."

"I'm going to have to have a word with my Aunt Clara." Nick pushed his chair back and stood. "Might as well go by now even though it's late. Apparently that doesn't mean anything to her."

Susan decided to have a talk with Tundy. What

had the mystery club been looking for at that time
of the night?

Doc headed for the door. "See you all next
Wednesday."

Susan waved and everyone else chimed in.
"G'night, Doc!"

As the door closed, Ethan turned to Nick. "I
hope you can rein your aunt in; someone could get
hurt running around late at night."

"I like Tundy and was glad when she became
the assistant activities director out at the home,
but truth to tell, she has no more sense than my
Aunt Clara." Nick stopped by Susan's chair. "I'll
let myself out, but good luck on making your proposal with the numbers guy. When you going to
do it?"

"At Monday's meeting. It'll take me a while to
get everything together. I haven't made a Power-
Point presentation since college."

"Check with Deloris at the library; she's good
with stuff like that." He winked at her and then
headed for the door. "G'night, all."

Everyone else began gathering their things,
then René, Jeff, and Ethan helped move the poker
table to the back of the garage and stacked the
chairs in a corner.

Soon, Susan was back in her own home. Dad

was gone again—who knew to which bar—so she had the place to herself. She put on her pjs and made herself a cup of tea.

So the guys thought Mark would respond to a more structured approach? Well, she could do structured. She would dazzle Mr. Cold and Hard Facts with his own weapons—logic and numbers.

"This had better work, Collins," she told herself as she carried her tea upstairs, flicking off the lights as she went. "Or you're going to feel like every sort of fool."

Deloris Fishbine leaned over Susan's shoulder. "Click on the box with the picture of a chart and— There you go!"

"That was easy." Susan shifted on the hard library chair and stretched her back. "Only four more charts to import and I'm done."

"Mr. Treymayne will be impressed." Sixty-seven years old with dark brown dyed hair that she kept in a careful bouffant, Deloris possessed a sheer gusto for life that always made Susan grin. "You've worked on it for three days and it looks fantastic."

"I hope Mark thinks so. This has to impress him."

"Forget Mr. Treymayne. If you were my employee and turned in such a great concept as this, I'd give you a raise, at least." Deloris slid her glasses down from the top of her head. "Remember to save your work. I'm going to check in with the front desk staff and see if there are more books that need to be shelved."

Susan stretched. "You need to do something about these chairs; my butt's numb."

Deloris glanced at the library's computer sign-in sheet fastened to the clipboard she'd placed on the desk beside Susan. "You've been here two hours, so your time's almost up, anyway."

"I think I'll log out and finish up tomorrow."

Deloris consulted the schedule. "Hmm. We only have one hour open tomorrow and that's at nine."

"*All* of the computers are taken?"

"You'd be surprised how many people use the computers here; some of our patrons come every day."

"I guess that's why you have a two-hour limit on each use." Susan glanced at the clipboard. The first few names were familiar: Mr. Rickers, who used to own the local Safe–Co and now spent his time hanging out on a bench in front of City Hall with his fishing cronies; Joe Bob, owner of the local repair shop; and Lucy Carpenter, the church secretary. Susan gave a silent whistle. "Lucy's in the library almost every day—"

Deloris snatched up the clipboard, twin pink spots on her cheeks. "That is privileged information."

"No way."

"Oh, yes. The American Library Association is very explicit about it. I have a duty to protect the patrons from unnecessary infringement."

Susan exited the computer and slipped her thumb drive into her satchel. "Deloris, you've known me since I was knee-high to a grasshopper. I'm too lazy to unnecessarily infringe anyone; I was simply being a busy-body."

Deloris's lips twitched. "I still have to comply with the ALA and protect the computer usage logs."

"Protect them from whom?"

Deloris looked over her shoulder before she leaned over and whispered, "The *government*."

"Ohhhh. I never knew—" Something rolled across Susan's peripheral vision and she turned just in time to see Clara's wheelchair disappear behind a bookshelf. Seconds later, C.J. stuck his head out from the shelf across the aisle, his white hair disheveled as he looked around. He caught Susan's gaze, gasped, and ducked back behind the aisle.

"That darned club." Deloris's gaze narrowed on the spot where C.J. had disappeared. "That's the third time this week they've—"

"Pssst, C.J.!" Clara's whisper was loud enough to be heard across the entire library. "Get your ass over here!"

C.J. dashed between the aisles, his hands on his waistband as if he feared his pants might fall down, jingling with each rapid step.

Deloris shook her head. "They've been digging through the county archives for days now, photocopying this and that."

"Anything in particular?"

Deloris started to answer, then clamped her mouth closed.

"Oh, right—the ALA. Don't worry about it; I'll ask them myself." Susan swung her satchel to her shoulder and grinned at Deloris. "If you'll excuse me, I think I'm needed in the suspense aisle."

Deloris grinned back. "If you need anything more, I'll be up front."

"Thanks, Deloris." Susan made her way to where C.J. had disappeared. As she turned into the aisle, she caught a glimpse of his bright white tennis shoe disappearing around the corner. She hurried after it and saw C.J. scurrying along, hunched low and pushing Clara's chair while Tundy scampered along in front, bent almost in half, a lime green purse swinging in front of her, her hot orange sweatpants revealing a good inch of plumber's crack.

"Hold it right there!" Susan ordered.

The trio froze, then slowly raised their hands in the air.

"What are you all doing skulking around the library?"

"Can we put our hands down?" Clara asked. "My fingers go to sleep when I hold them up like this."

"No one told you to put your hands up."

Clara looked over her shoulder. "Whew! She ain't packin'. Y'all can put your hands down, too."

"Of course I'm not packing," Susan said, trying not to laugh. "Why would you think I was?"

Tundy shrugged. "I'm packin'." She reached into her large green purse and pulled out a huge handgun.

Susan took a step back. "Tundy! Put that away! Do you even know how to use that thing?"

"Not this one." Tundy reluctantly stuffed the gun back into her purse. "It's a .357 Colt Python and a lot bigger than my old .45, but Rose is going to teach me how to shoot it."

Susan looked around. "Where is Rose?"

"She's back there." With a liver-spotted hand sparkling with some of QVC's biggest gemstone rings, Clara waved in a vague direction toward the back of the library. "In the morgue."

Susan blinked.

Tundy let out an explosive sigh. "Miz Clara, I done tol' you that non-cop personnel don't get all those words."

"Oh, wait," Susan said. "You mean the morgue like we used to have at the newspaper—the old clippings and such?"

Clara nodded. "Yup. Now it's all on computer and micron fish."

"You mean microfiche."

"That's what I said," Clara replied. "Now we got to go and help Rose with the photocopier."

"I have quarters." C.J. jangled his pockets and Susan could see that they were weighing down his pants.

No wonder he was holding his waistband. His pants really are about to fall down. "By the way, Tundy, Doc Wilson told me you guys were on his road in the middle of the night and—"

"Got to go!" Tundy grabbed Clara's chair and

started rolling her down the aisle. "Bye for now, Miz Susan!"

"But wait! What are you all photocopying—" But they had already disappeared around the corner.

Susan shook her head and left the library. Whatever they were into, it wasn't as important as her presentation Monday. *That* would be the beginning of a new relationship with Mr. Clark Kent–Treymayne.

Chapter
6

Monday's meeting got off to a rough start. Susan was late coming to work, Pat showed up dressed in coveralls reminiscent of a serial killer movie Mark had seen in college at the dollar theaters, and the elevator was once again acting wonky, stopping between floors as if too tired to continue.

Pat dropped into her seat. "Can we get this show on the road? I put a taco in the microwave and it'll be ready soon."

Mark surpressed a scowl. "We can't begin until Susan arrives."

Pat looked around as if just noticing her one coworker was gone. "Where is she?"

"She called and said she'd be a little late." But she hadn't said why, even when he'd asked, which irritated him. Over the last week they'd settled into an uneasy truce, punctuated on her side by a faint mistrust and on his with an abundance of lust.

Though she'd been out of her office most of every morning, she'd return at lunch and inundate him with questions, obviously trying to understand the paper's true situation. He'd found himself looking forward to finding her in his doorway, a sheaf of papers in her hand, a perplexed look on her face as she asked yet another question. She was a fast learner, too; he wished some of the employees of his accounting firm were so quick to grasp the intricacies of corporate finance. None of them looked as unconsciously sexy as Susan did while pondering spreadsheets, either, her jeans lovingly hugging the world's most perfect ass.

It took all of his self-control to maintain a proper distance, which had left plenty of awkward silences. *Better to seem awkward than to make a fool of yourself.*

It fascinated him that she was passionate about so many things, and wished circumstances were different so that *he* could be one of those things— at least for a little while. A pity it couldn't be so.

He heard the elevator doors creak open, followed by the click of heels coming through the reception area. Susan came around the corner. Mark's heart stopped, stuttered, and began pounding furiously. Gone were her jeans, T-shirt, and hiking boots. In their place was a trim, short-skirted gray suit. Her hair was piled on her head, small pearl earrings dangled from her ears, and a pearl necklace rested against her throat. But what really stole his breath were her legs, which went on and on.

A man could get lost between a pair of legs like that.

Susan cleared her throat, and he jerked his gaze to her face, his neck prickling with heat at her frown.

Pat snorted. "What's up with you? Got a job interview in Asheville?"

"No. I came to present an alternative solution to Mark's ad sales plan."

He fought to get his fuzzy mind in gear. Her lashes had always looked long, but now they were positively luxurious, sweeping her cheeks when she blinked and framing her amazing blue eyes. Was she wearing mascara?

"I brought a PowerPoint presentation," she announced.

Pat gave a silent whistle.

Mark struggled to follow Susan's words. "What?"

"A PowerPoint—"

"Did you hear the microwave?" Pat jumped up.

"That'd be my taco. Susan, just send me a copy of your PowerPoint."

She was gone before Mark could say a word, leaving him and Susan alone.

For a moment, they just looked at one another.

Susan shifted from one foot to the other and cleared her throat. "Shall I make my presentation?"

"Sure, sure! I don't suppose Pat has to be here." When Susan hesitated, he hurried to add, "Unless you *want* her here, of course."

"No, I don't suppose she has to be here. I mainly did this for you. Well, not *for* you but *because* of you. I thought you might understand this format better." She bit her lip, looking as if she might bolt from the room.

Mark couldn't look away from her plump, glistening bottom lip where her even white teeth were pressed. He imagined biting that lip himself, ever so gently before he—

"Mark?"

Heat flooded his face, which was a good thing as it moved the heat from elsewhere. "Sorry. I was just thinking— Of course, give your presentation. I'm all ears." He was far more than ears, but he refused to name body parts that were not cooperating with his desire to remain in control.

She pulled a thumb drive from her briefcase. "Can I stick this in your USB slot?"

If only she would.

Mute, he pushed his laptop across the table.

She inserted the thumb drive, clicked a few keys, then turned the laptop toward him. The first screen said, "Facts About *The Glory Examiner*."

Susan took a breath before pasting a smile on her face. "We share a goal here at the paper, and that's to see it succeed." She clicked the remote and the slide changed to add "Succeed" to the screen. "However, we have differing philosophies on a few key issues."

She clicked the remote again and "Higher ad costs = ?" appeared.

"We already know we can't increase ad sales, because of the current downturn in the economy and given the nature of the area we live in."

A bold graph appeared, showing numerous lines. Mark knew he should pay attention, but he was too fascinated with Susan. Had her legs always been so long, or did her short skirt just make them seem that way?

She clicked the remote and a new slide appeared. "So increasing ad sales would ultimately result in a loss of revenue." Her gaze met Mark's. "Would you agree?"

He nodded. She was wearing lip gloss, too, and he wanted to taste it—and her. His groin tightened as he thought of all the ways to kiss off her lip gloss.

She turned, and her crisp white shirt gaped at the neck and he caught a hint of a white lace bra. *White lace bra, a white lace thong, and those heels . . . if she'd worn just those, he'd be—*

"That leaves us with only two other options."

He didn't know what her options were, but his were to tear off her clothes and assuage his burning lust right there on the conference table.

She caught his gaze. "You want to increase the number of ads without adding pages. The problem with that is that the purchasing value of the paper is reduced." She clicked the remote and a pie chart appeared. She began to expound on a cost analysis of ad space in relation to content.

Mark tried to listen; he really did. She was speaking his language, and she was doing it wearing his familiar armor, a business suit. But on Susan, that suit looked damnably sexy.

She clicked the remote, her face flushed, her eyes sparkling. She was warming to her presentation, enjoying the logic of it, the way she was making point after point. To be honest, he was, too. He loved the way her primly pinned-up hair was already falling in wisps about her face, and how she was glowing with enthusiasm.

He wiped a hand over his eyes and forced himself to listen.

"So we need to increase the readership. Then, we can charge more for the ads we *do* sell."

That caught his attention, and he looked at the chart on the computer screen. "You really want to raise ad prices? Will the market bear it?"

"Most of our advertisers already pay higher prices to place ads in the Asheville paper. If we can prove our readership is strong and growing stronger, I think we can adjust our prices as we go, little by little."

He leaned forward. It was a thought. Actually, it was a good thought . . . *if* they could pull it off. His mind began to kick around the numbers and he opened his folder and flipped through some papers, finally pulling one out. "The subscription numbers." He looked through them. "They haven't dropped the way many of the nation's larger publications have."

"That's because there's no coverage of this area in any other paper."

He began jotting down numbers, locating his

pocket calculator and running the figures. Finally, he put down his pen.

"Well?" Susan sat on the edge of her chair, her gaze fixed on him.

"We can do it if—"

"I knew it!" Susan's face was pink, her eyes shining.

"*If* we increase subscriptions by twelve percent. That's not realistic."

"Yes, it is." Susan clicked through two screens on her PowerPoint. "These are our subscription rates. See the increase here?"

"Fourteen percent in just one month? But then it went back down."

"Yes, but not all the way. We retained eleven percent of those subscribers."

"What caused that leap?"

"That was the month Clara's Murder Mystery Club solved their first case."

Mark looked grim. "And Ty Henderson kidnapped my sister."

Susan hurried to add, "But she wasn't injured and Ty was apprehended and he confessed."

"He'll be in jail for a long, long time."

"With no chance for parole." Susan sent a glance at Mark from beneath her lashes, relieved to see the storm cloud had disappeared. "This highlights the fact that people in Glory appreciate their news. Especially when there's excitement or controversy of any kind."

Mark nodded. "But you can't count on that."

"No, usually we go out there and find something but sometimes, if we're lucky, the news finds us." She tucked a stray strand of hair behind her ear, and he realized she'd also gotten a manicure. Her fingers were pink tipped.

How he'd love to see those fingers trailing along his—

"Which brings us to part two of my proposal."

"Excuse me?" She was talking, but he couldn't quite hear her through the loud panting of his libido.

He caught a flash of irritation on her face before she repeated in a slower voice, "Part two of my proposal."

I have got to control this. Mark put one of his heels on the big toe of his other foot and pressed hard. The pain that shot through him cleared his mind in a jiffy. "Right. The second part."

"We move Ray Dobbins here, to the newspaper office, to answer the phone and to sell ads."

A new chart appeared and Mark tried to wrap

his mind around the information. "This says that if he sells only four percent more ads than we're selling now, he'll pay his own salary."

She leaned forward, earnest and flushed, overwhelming Mark with a wave of fresh lust. "And he'll sell much more if we give him a cut of anything above that. He's well known in town and everyone likes him. He's a natural salesman."

She put down the remote and turned to him. "Well? What do you think?"

He thought he might burst into flames if he didn't touch her soon, drag her onto the conference table, slide her skirt even farther up her slender thighs, and—

"Mark?"

He forced air into his lungs. "I agree."

She blinked, a slow, disbelieving blink. "With *all* of it?" She looked shocked.

He'd better have her leave her thumb drive with him. When she was gone, and he was able to think about something other than how incredible her legs looked in that skirt and how it followed the curve of her ass so well, he might be able to focus long enough to understand what she'd just said.

Her gaze narrowed in suspicion. "You agree with every single thing I just said?"

"Much of it." He hoped.

"Even," she continued, "that you should increase the quality of the content until the value of the paper is driven up? And that at that point you increase ad prices—not by much, but enough to add a double page to the center—which gives you additional ad space and thus revenue?"

He didn't remember a word about adding a double page, but it didn't matter. If her ideas worked the way she thought they would—the way the numbers indicated that they might—he'd be a fool not to give it a shot. She looked so hopeful, so earnest—and suddenly he *had* to listen to what she had to say. Not because of her presentation and damnably sexy clothing, but because she *wanted* him to understand. Because he could see how very, very important this was to her.

He thought through the parts of the presentation he'd managed to absorb through a red haze of lust. "I am beginning to accept that perhaps I don't know as much about things as I thought I did." *Like the effects of a severely tailored jacket on the male psyche.*

"It's a slower process, but studies have shown how—" She dropped the remote and bent to pick it up, continuing to talk as she did so.

Holding his breath, Mark leaned forward, his gaze glued to her ass as she reached way under the table and—

"Finished my taco." Pat came in and grabbed a chair, smelling slightly of onions and hot sauce. "What did I miss?"

Susan straightened up, the remote in her hand, looking flushed and radiant and far too much like a woman who'd just been thoroughly loved.

She grinned at Pat. "Mark's agreed to increase the paper content!"

Pat blinked. "No way!"

Susan nodded, smiling. "Didn't you, Mark?"

Had he? He didn't really know. But right now the last thing he wanted was to remove that smile from her face. "Yes. We'll try it your way for a month and see what happens."

Her smile dimmed slightly. "A month won't be long enough. We'll need at least two months."

If she'd asked him for the moon right now, he'd have started building a rocket. "Two months then, but no more."

"Perfect. *And* he's agreed that we should ramp up our efforts to be more controversial in our reporting, to stir public interest."

Good God, had he agreed to that?

But perhaps it was for the best. If they tried it

and it failed, he'd have the staff's unequivocal co-operation. "If circulation doesn't improve in that time, then we go back to my way. Agreed?"

"Agreed," Susan said immediately. She looked at Pat, who was gazing intently at the chart. "Agreed?"

"What?" Pat blinked. "Oh. Yes. I was just thinking . . . the newspaper does sell well when there's a commotion, doesn't it."

"Much better."

"Hmm. Wish we had one right now." Pat pushed her chair from the table. "Guess I'd better get on the stick and see what controversy I can find."

"Good idea," Susan agreed. "There's more, though. Mark is going to move Ray Dobbins into the reception area so we can spend more time focusing on doing in-depth investigative reporting."

"I like that, but who'll do security?" Pat looked at Mark as if she expected him to jump in and disagree.

He shrugged. "Susan did her homework, and I'm sold—" Susan grinned and he added, "—for now. Time will tell."

"Yes, it will," she said in a firm tone.

He hid a grin. "No one could disagree that the

man is underutilized; even he says so. By moving him into this office and putting him in charge of ad sales—"

"And classifieds," Susan chimed in.

"And classifieds," Mark obliged. "He gets the chance to earn his own wages, and maybe even a bonus."

Pat didn't look convinced. "I felt safer knowing he was in the lobby."

Susan pointed out, "Now he'll be even closer. In a way, he's gone from being security for the whole building to being security for our office. And Pat, the alternative was to let him go."

Pat glowered. "That's unfair!"

"Cold, hard facts usually are," Mark said. "He wasn't producing anything, sitting in the lobby. Susan's plan solves that problem."

Pat let out her breath in a loud puff. Finally she said in a grumpy tone, "I guess it's OK, then."

"Glad that's settled," Susan said. "We'd all better get to work. Pat, see if there's anything potentially unsettling on the mayor's agenda. Mark, do you want to talk to Ray?"

"Sure. I have an idea he's going to like the idea very much."

"Good. Meanwhile, I'll head over to the First Baptist Church for more information on the Bake-

Off. I think I'll make Sunday's commentary about the rumors surrounding the event this year."

"That'll get 'em reading!" Pat said, and left.

Mark looked at Susan. "When you start investigating this in earnest, I'd like to come along."

Susan looked incredulous. "Why?"

"Because, as you've pointed out, it's important that I understand how a reporter goes about the job."

"That's very big of you," Susan said.

"It's fair and that's what I do. So—"

Her lashes lowered halfway and she gave him a sultry smile. "Yes?"

His entire body tightened. *Easy, Treymayne. You don't want to go there.* "This editorial. How controversial do you think it will be?"

"We'll get some phone calls."

"What does that mean?" he asked, suspicious of her casual tone.

"Just that it's a hot topic."

He simply couldn't imagine that many people would care. He shrugged. "I think I can handle the heat. How are you going to approach it?"

Susan grinned. "I just want to tantalize them, to let them know what's coming from us as we investigate."

"Do you really think something will come from that?"

"Maybe, maybe not. It's a fishing technique, but it could shake something loose."

Mark gathered his notes, then reached for her thumb drive. "Do you mind? I'd like to review the details."

"Not at all. Please take it."

He pocketed the thumb drive. "Thanks. Susan, you did a good job with this." His gaze flickered over her. "A damn fine job."

Her cheeks heated, and she fought the desire to grin like a loon.

When he turned and left, Susan flopped down in a chair. Who would've thought charts and a very short skirt could cause such magic?

Remembering Mark's expression, she grinned. Poor guy. He didn't stand a chance.

Chapter
7

Next Monday, Mark picked up his cell phone from the cup holder in his Mustang and threw it into the backseat. Though it disappeared from sight, it continued to ring. And ring. And ring.

It was only seven in the morning, and that damn phone had been ringing ever since the paper hit the stands yesterday. "Who would care if there's an editorial about the Bake-Off?" he mimicked himself. " 'Who would read that?' "

The editorial had clearly caused a furor. He'd answered the first few calls, only to realize that the callers didn't want to hear any explanation or defense. They just wanted blood. "Susan, you owe me for this," he grumbled.

It had seemed such a good idea at the time, to stir up a "little controversy." But there was no "little" whenever Susan Collins was involved. There was only big and bigger.

Mark parked in his usual space and began to walk inside, when he caught sight of a tiny woman climbing out of a huge Chevy Caprice. Less than five feet tall, with a bleached-blond bouffant hairstyle half covered by a tiny hat, and dressed in a sober and sensible manner, she looked like a Martha Stewart yard gnome.

Her gaze locked on him and an expression of pure rage tightened her face.

There was no way in hell he was going to stand still and wait for *that* to catch up to him. He turned on his heel, strode to the front door, and made his way to the elevator. Once there, he punched the up button hard enough to make the dratted thing make the trip twice.

Just as the doors slid closed, the tiny woman shoved open the lobby door. The elevator creaked up to the second floor, and he entered the reception area as Ray was ending a call. Ray had begun his new job last week, and judging by the number of lines ringing, he was getting a baptism by fire.

Seeing Mark, Ray picked up a sheaf of papers and waved them even as he said into the phone, "Yes, Mrs. Blumenthal, I'll pass that on to—" Ray winced as the voice on the other end grew shrill. "Yes, Mrs. Blumenthal, I—" The caller burst into speech again. "I understand that, Mrs. Blumenthal, and I'm sure that— Yes. I know. Right, right. A retraction or an apology. I'll be sure your message is delivered and— Of course. Thank you for calling. Good-bye." He hung up the phone and grinned, his face flushed with excitement. "Whew! You sure got the town riled!"

"It wasn't me. It was Miss Collins, who seems to have a knack for that sort of thing."

"Whatever she's doing, it's got the town hopping."

"Hopping *mad*. I don't think that's a good thing," Mark said sourly. "Are all of those messages about the article?"

"Yup!" Ray patted the stack of neatly written slips. "Twenty-two complaints. I wonder if that's a record."

The phone rang again. Looking as happy as a hen with a worm, Ray lifted the receiver and said in a sunny voice, "Good morning, *The Glory Ex*—" A woman's crackling voice was heard on the other end of the line and remained in high gear for the rest of the conversation, punctuated by Ray saying in a soothing voice, "Yes, Mrs. Rawlings. I know, Mrs. Rawlings. I'll be sure and pass it on, Mrs. Rawlings."

Behind Mark, the elevator began to creak,

which was a sure sign that the yard gnome was on her way up.

Ray hung up the phone and handed a new message to Mark. "That makes twenty-three."

"Sorry you're having to deal with this."

"Are you kidding?" Ray's wrinkled face exploded in a grin. "This is the most fun I've had in twenty years!"

Mark chuckled. "Well, don't get too comfortable. There's a very tiny lady on her way up and she looked ticked."

"Tiny? With bleached-blond hair?"

Behind him, the elevator was shuddering to a halt.

"Yeah, she drove a huge Chevy. It's a wonder she managed to park it without hitting a tree; she couldn't see over the steering wheel to save her soul."

Ray winced. "That'll be a bad one. That's Miss Carpenter, the church secretary."

The elevator doors hummed as they prepared to open.

"I'm going to the conference room. If anyone asks, tell them I'm in meetings until four."

"Yes, sir!"

The elevator doors slowly creaked open just as Mark closed the door to the conference room.

He threw his stack of folders on the table, piled up the phone messages, and pulled Sunday's paper from his pocket. He hadn't bothered to read Susan's editorial, because who'd care about a little old Bake-Off?

But she'd been right. The *Examiner* had certainly garnered a lot of attention because of that one editorial. The question was whether or not it was *good* attention—something he should have asked before.

As he read, his brow grew lower. It was a good piece; it said enough but not too much. It didn't answer questions their limited research couldn't answer, so it mainly posed other, bigger questions. He'd never before appreciated how thorough and creative Susan was, but every word of the editorial had meaning and either suggested an outcome or clearly spelled it out.

When he finished, he leaned back in his chair and rubbed his face.

A knock sounded on the door. "Come in!"

Pat Meese shuffled in. Dressed in her usual high-waisted blue jeans and plaid shirt, her unmade-up face shiny from a morning scrub, her iron gray hair falling straight to each side, she'd have looked at home on a granola bar wrapper.

She grinned when she saw Mark with the

paper. "Good edition, wasn't it? Phone is ringing off the hook. Just like back in the old days, when journalists weren't pansies." She took a seat just as Susan came in carrying a bakery box and three coffees in a carrier.

She looked relaxed and—(damn it!)—excited, her jeans snug on her hips, her blue T-shirt emblazoned with HILTON HEAD across the breasts.

Not that he was looking at her breasts, though he had noticed that her nipples were visible through the thin material.

"Hi, guys. Having our meeting?"

"We are now," Mark said.

She held up a bakery box and wagged it temptingly. "I got one for everyone." Susan dispersed the coffees and creamers, then opened the box and positioned it in the center of the desk.

Pat slurped her coffee. "Ah! That's good." She then pulled the pastry box forward and began to dig through it. "I sure hope there's a bear claw in here somewhere."

Mark didn't touch his coffee. "Susan, your editorial certainly stirred things up."

Susan grinned. "Pretty cool, huh? Sometimes you have to kick the hornets' nest in order to count the hornets."

"You can get stung to death doing that, too."

Pat pulled out a caramel-crusted brown-sugar bagel. Around a mouthful, she said, "Good reporting, Collins. Proud of you."

"Hold on." Mark pointed to the huge stack of pink message slips that sat in the middle of the table. "You've riled the entire church. I know because all of them have called, and their own secretary is in the lobby right this moment, ready to tear one of us apart."

"That article is the truth, every single word. Besides, fishing is a time-old ploy. Someone is going to want to clear this up and they'll start talking."

Pat swallowed a bite of bagel. "Even if they don't, it's good for the paper to get some notice."

Mark picked up the stack of notes. "Here's the problem, ladies. Most of these notes are from people wanting to cancel their subscriptions. Our customers are angry. We *need* those customers."

"*Some* of our customers are angry. Not *all* of them."

"We can't afford to tick off even one." He rubbed his forehead, trying to wrap his mind around the issue. "Maybe we can print a follow-up piece, just to soften up the tone a little and—"

"No." Her chin went up, her eyes blazing. "I

stand by that piece, Mark. Every word is factual and I didn't exaggerate a single thing."

"I know you didn't, but—"

"No buts. Something is wrong with the way the Bake-Off is being run, and I've got a lot more than mere rumor. There have been a number of unusual circumstances, about the way it's being run, and the fact that not a single member of the committee would give me a quote—" She spread her hands wide. "What would *you* think?"

"How many people are on the committee?"

"Eight. When you consider the committee usually begs for publicity and that the success of the Bake-Off is tied to the event's attendance, you'd think they'd welcome some publicity—yet they've all avoided me. And when I caught sight of Pastor MacMillan in the Piggly Wiggly last night, he tried to hide behind the onion bin."

"He wouldn't talk to you?"

"Except to say that any statement regarding the Bake-Off would be made in the form of a press release. It's as if he thinks everything he says is up for legal scrutiny."

Hmm. That *was* odd. "Still, why get everyone upset? Shouldn't you just wait until you have something definitive before you write an entire opinion piece on it?"

"Not when the purpose of the opinion piece is to shake up some people in the hopes they'll start talking."

"That seems like an in-your-face way to do things."

"Mark, I didn't exaggerate, nor did I engage in random speculation. I printed the simple facts, and that is well within the ethical parameters of the op-ed page."

Susan stood, obviously frustrated. With a sharp glance his way, she picked up her coffee and went to stand by the open window, resting her shoulder against the wall. "Mark, this is where your lack of journalism experience becomes an issue. A newspaper doesn't stop investigating a story every time someone gets mad."

"But if our subscriptions go down, then—"

Pat made a rude noise. "Susan's right. You can't fold on this, Mark. Don't know if there's a story there, but it's good to get up some interest. People will talk."

"Which is what we want." Out in the foyer, the phone rang yet again and Susan smiled. "When you cover something that's controversial—"

"Or exciting," Pat interjected.

"Then the public buys more papers," Susan finished.

Mark thought it through, then finally nodded. "Okay, we'll wait it out and see where it goes. But I want a follow-up piece soon. If we leave the editorial hanging, it'll seem like empty conjecture."

"You got it."

Mark peered into the bakery box and selected a warm cinnamon bagel crusted with sugar, then flipped through the stack of notes. "Hmm. The mayor called three times."

"I'm sure he did," Susan said. "Whatever's going on, I wouldn't be surprised if he's in the thick of it." She looked out the window and sipped her coffee.

Mark ate his bagel and tried not to stare, but it was difficult. The morning sun streamed over her, warming the threads of gold in her red hair and gleaming off her creamy skin.

She was as smart as she was beautiful, and he was slowly learning to trust her.

Pat wiped her mouth on a napkin, wadded it up, and tossed into the wastepaper basket. "Well, guess I'd better get back to work. I need a good lead-in to an article, and it won't write itself."

"I'll help, if you'd like," Susan offered.

Pat's gaze narrowed. "I can write my own articles, thank you very much."

Susan's smile grew cool, but it remained in

place. "I know you can. Sometimes it just helps to have a fresh pair of eyes look at something."

"Did you learn that in college?" Pat said stiffly. "I don't know why anyone would bother to get a worthless degree. You can't learn how to do this stuff except through practice."

"That's not true, Pat," Susan said calmly. "While you're an effective and efficient reporter, formal education is an important part of becoming a better manager."

That was a good point. Mark watched Pat to see how she'd respond.

"I don't need no college degree. Don't want one, neither." Pat scowled. "You gonna fire me?"

"No! I'd hate to see you go; you add a lot to the paper. People know you and trust you. That's important."

Mark quietly added, "Of course, if you feel you must resign your post, we'd all understand. I'm certain Deloris Fishbine would take your job in a New York minute."

Pat started. "Deloris Fishbine is the city librarian!"

"She's told me many times she'd be more than happy to work part-time and fill your slot."

Pat's lips thinned. "Are you saying a part-timer person could do my job?"

"Nope. I'm saying that if you resigned, that's who and what we'd replace you with."

Pat glared at him, and he was sure she was mentally slaying him in ways that left his body unrecognizable.

Susan took a bagel from the box. "Pat, don't even talk about leaving. I need you. I'm still learning my way around. Heck, how many times a day do I ask you where to find this or how to do that?"

Pat looked slightly mollified. "Plenty."

"Exactly." Susan slid the pastry box toward Pat. "I'll beg if I have to."

Pat took another bagel. "I never said anything about leaving."

"Good, because I don't know what we'd do without you."

Pat sniffed, but it was obvious the words had touched her.

Susan added, "It would take a dozen Deloris Fishbines to replace you—not to say anything against Deloris, bless her heart."

Pat looked embarrassed and stood, awkwardly holding her bagel. "I guess I'd better go and get some work done." She gave a jerky nod and left, shutting the door behind her.

Mark leaned back in his chair. "Miss Collins, I begin to think I underestimated you."

Susan grinned over her coffee. "Thank you . . . I think."

"It's not a compliment if it's the truth. Though I might not agree with all of your methods, I have to admit that you always seem to accomplish what you set out to do."

"Why, thank you, Mr. Treymayne. I am overcome." Susan sipped her coffee, and he couldn't help but notice how elegant and delicate her throat was. He'd love to nibble down it to her collarbone, and then down to those round—

Susan reached across the table for the phone messages. "Shall I make a few phone calls?"

"Be my guest."

"I can't promise no one will cancel their subscription, but I can try."

"Fair enough." He leaned back in his chair and linked his hands behind his head. "So . . . what's on your agenda besides convincing all of our unhappy customers that we're not doing the devil's work here at *The Glory Examiner?*"

Susan sent him a glance from under her lashes, and decided that all men should wear glasses. They accentuated the square line of his jaw and framed his amazing eyes . . . she had to hide a shiver.

She realized he was still looking at her for an

answer to his question. What had he asked? Oh yes. "I'm going to schedule an interview with the head of the animal shelter to discuss budget cuts, so I have to prep for that."

"How so?"

"You have to do your research before an interview or you won't know what questions to ask. I have a copy of the mayor's proposed budget cuts, and some statements from his office as to why he doesn't feel the shelter is that important. I also have a copy of the shelter's annual request. Using these, I should be able to collect some good quotes and fill in a few holes in the article about why the cut is going to be so hard on the shelter." She finished her coffee and dropped the cup into the bin. "After I do the interview and make some of these calls, I'm going to do my best to land an interview with at least one member of the Bake-Off committee to tell their side of things."

"Do you think anyone will?"

"I don't know, but I'm going to try and keep trying."

Mark slanted a look at Susan. "I look forward to watching you interview someone."

"Thanks." *His eyes are so blue. I could drown in eyes like that. And for a man to have such thick lashes—*

"I suppose at some point we'll be attending the infamous Bake-Off?"

"Of course."

"I wonder if people will be shooting at us from behind the pound cake table?"

"If we're any good, they should be."

He laughed, and she grinned. There were all sorts of things she'd like to teach him, other than reporting. Hmm. Why not start now? For the last few weeks, since Mark had explained how dire the situation really was, she'd focused all of her energy on stabilizing the newspaper on her own terms, and not Mark's. Her noble intentions had gotten in the way of her first inclination after their passionate kiss in her office, which was to pursue it further. *Much* further.

That kiss seemed so long ago, yet she still felt the same stirring of . . . was it simple interest? Or something stronger? Whatever it was, it made her tingle from head to toe every time he was near. Even now, just seeing him sitting at the conference table, his tie slightly askance, his dark hair falling over his brow, his blue eyes framed by his impossibly sexy glasses, she was assailed with the desire to trace her lips down his strong jaw to his deliciously masculine mouth.

A trill of excitement washed through her, and

she put down her coffee cup and sauntered to the table. She perched on it, then leaned on one hand and smiled into his eyes. "So what about you, Treymayne? What sort of things can you teach *me?*"

For one startled second he just stared at her, his brows lifted in surprise. She almost expected him to pull away, but then his gaze flickered over her, lingering on her lips, her neck, her breasts . . .

Which were at eye level. The thought both alarmed and excited her. She'd meant to be seductive, but not brazen.

His gaze remained on her breasts, and her nipples hardened and peaked. Susan's face heated. *What in the hell was I thinking?*

She turned to slide off the table when his large, warm hand wrapped about her wrist and held her in place.

Susan's breath caught as Mark, his gaze locked with hers, slowly leaned forward. Bold as rain, he placed his warm mouth over one of her nipples. Through her thin shirt he laved the peak, and she gasped as a million sensations raced through her.

She arched against his mouth and sank a hand into his thick dark hair, her entire body quivering with a roaring dose of need.

His hands snaked up to her waist and he stood, sliding her across the table toward him—

Whap! A folder slid into a coffee cup and knocked it over, splattering coffee everywhere— the folders, Mark's arm, and across her shirt.

"Damn it!" He released her and began to save his folders, his mouth pressed into a thin line.

Embarrassed, Susan jumped off the table and fetched the bakery napkins. "I'll wipe up the desk. Are the folders ruined?"

He held the dripping folders over the trash can and carefully opened one and then the other. "The outsides are all that's really wet. There's a stained edge here and there, but otherwise, every-thing's fine." His gaze flickered over her. "Looks like you caught the worst of it."

She had, in more ways than one. Here she was, trying to be seductive, and instead she'd completely ruined the moment. Gone was the heat, the animal attraction, the sensuous promise. He must think she was the world's biggest dork. *She* did.

To cover her embarrassment, she shrugged. "I'm fine. A fresh shirt and I'll be good as new." She tossed the wet napkins into the trash can and went to the door to escape. "I'd better get to work—"

"Collins?"

She paused, one hand on the doorknob. "Yes?"

Was he going to ask her back in to finish their little flirtation? Or was he as embarrassed as she was? She was achingly aware of her wet T-shirt as it cooled over her left nipple.

He held up the bakery box. "Do you want the last bagel?"

Susan blinked. "Ah. No."

His face was as red as Superman's cape, and she realized that he was attempting to smooth the moment. "Then I'll take it up front to Ray. It was nice of you to bring these today."

It was sweet of him to try and make the moment easier, but part of her wished he'd been less able to coolly reason and more swept away.

Her heart was pounding, her knees quivering, while a low ache between her legs robbed her of all ability to think. Meanwhile, except for his high color, Mark looked remarkably collected. She doubted that *his* heart was still thundering in his ears.

"I— It was no problem." God, did she have to stutter?

Suddenly she had to get away, to the safety of her own office. "I'd better go and—" She turned and left.

Chapter
8

Dear Bob,

There's this guy at work and every time I see him, I wonder how he'd look without his shirt. I suspect he'd make a great model, but he doesn't wear the best clothes, so I'm not sure. All I know is I've got to see him without his shirt SOON.

Is this normal or should I get counseling? I don't know what it is, but I can't stop thinking about him.

Signed,
Confused and Curious

Dear C and C,

Honesty is the best policy. So just ask him to take his shirt off—tell him you think he'd look good. Most men take a compliment pretty well.

If he says yes, then you're off the hook. If he says no, pretend you were kidding.

There's a time for honesty and a time for not-so honesty.

Sincerely,
Bob

The Glory Examiner
July 24, section B2

Susan turned off her computer, leaned back in her chair, and rubbed her face with both hands. Though she'd tried her best, she still hadn't been able to gain an interview with a single member of the Bake-Off committee. But she *had* found the church's records online, including their budget and committee members for the last ten years. Perhaps she could get one of the past members to talk to her. It was a long shot, but it was all she had right now.

She picked up the folders and turned to put them into a drawer, when she caught the glow of the parking lot lamp. Startled, she glanced at her Lois Lane wall clock and blinked. It was almost eight. Now that she thought about it, she had a vague recollection of Pat stopping by to say something—had it been good-bye? She'd been so caught up in her work that she couldn't remember.

It had been a productive day and she'd been absorbed by it. It was all about the story—how to find it, what facts were obscured when you first observed it, how to track down all of the details that might or might not change your perception. It fascinated her. It was like fishing, and she was just starting to find the shortcuts and tips, and learning where all of the good "fishing" holes were.

She pushed back her chair and stretched her legs. Dad would be waiting— She grimaced. No, he wouldn't. He would be at the Bigger Jigger, probably on his eighth or ninth beer, too far gone to even notice if she came home or not.

She moved out from behind her desk and had just reached for her purse hanging on a hook by the door when a tall figure appeared in her office doorway. She gasped and jumped back.

Mark blinked, looking vaguely surprised. "Sorry. Did I scare you?"

Susan pressed a hand to where her thundering heart pounded against her breastbone. "Yes, you scared me! I thought I was alone up here."

He offered a crooked smile, his eyes crinkling adorably. "You were. I just came back to get a report I'd left on my desk."

She realized that he wasn't dressed in his usual preppy style, all button-down shirts and loafers. Instead, he was wearing comfortable, well-worn jeans that clung to his ass and made her mouth go dry. His hair was damp from a recent shower, judging by the smell of shampoo that tickled her nose, and he had a hint of a five o'clock shadow.

After work, Mr. Uptight and Right apparently transformed into Mr. Incredibly Sexy.

He leaned his shoulder against the door frame, a newspaper dangling from his hand. "You're working late tonight."

She rubbed her stiff neck. "I found some on-line records for the church."

His gaze sharpened. "Anything good?"

"I have lists of past committee members, so I'll start calling them and getting a sense of their history. I also have the budgets for the last ten years, though I haven't had time to go through them."

His eyes gleamed. "That's some good stuff."

"Thank you."

She didn't know what it was, the lateness of the hour, or that the entire building seemed dark except for the golden glow of her lamp, or if she was just more tired than she realized—but she suddenly felt . . . connected to Mark. As if they were unexpectedly in sync in some way.

Or were they? After their last embrace on the conference room table, she'd felt as if she'd been more engaged than he.

Easy, she cautioned herself. *Your libido is just out of whack. It's one thing to go for a guy who goes for you, another thing altogether to go after one who doesn't.* She cleared her throat. "So, did you find your file?"

His gaze seemed locked on her mouth and he slowly shook his head. "I haven't looked for it yet."

She nervously licked her lips.

His gaze flickered at her movement, and he shifted toward her.

Susan's heart fluttered as a shiver traveled over her. "I . . . I guess we'd better find it."

"Find what?"

"Your missing folder."

"Susan?" His voice was deeper, lower.

"Yes?" In her imagination, she stepped into his arms as he swooped her against him, his hands warm and seeking once again. She wanted another kiss. No, she *needed* another kiss.

He shook his head as if clearing it, then said in a husky voice, "Let me get that folder and I'll walk you down to your Jeep." He turned and entered his office. Flipping on the light, he found a folder neatly placed in a mesh basket on the corner of his desk. He scooped it up and tucked it under his copy of the day's *Examiner.* "Ready to go?"

Susan nodded, and as they made their way to the elevator, she eyed the muscular arms that showed to such advantage in his T-shirt. If she had arms that good, she'd wear tank tops every day.

The elevator door closed and the silence seemed to grow. Mark punched the lobby button a second time. "This is the slowest elevator."

Though she was feeling the same way, it sort of pinched that he seemed so ill at ease.

He shifted from one foot to the other, and she watched him in the polished surface of the elevator door.

He punched at the button again, his movements irritating her further. *You think you're the only one who wants to get away from this awkward situation?*

His gaze met hers in the polished door and he grinned. "That won't make it any faster, will it?"

"Nope." Susan turned back toward the door and watched him greedily, fascinated at the complex expressions that flickered across his face. Honestly, the man should have been a model. With such a great jawline and those piercing eyes—

His gaze lifted and met hers just as the elevator shuddered once . . . twice . . . and then jerked to a halt.

Mark frowned and punched the button again. "It's stuck."

"It happens all of the time. Here—" Susan stepped past him and punched the lobby button several times in a row. "Sometimes this'll unstick it."

"Not this time." His voice was directly behind her, and she realized that she'd touch him if she leaned back the tiniest bit. The air seemed to grow heavy and she knew without a word being spoken that he felt the same way.

She slowly turned and looked up at him.

Her breath stuck in her throat. Why was he looking at her like that? As if he was overcome with . . . with . . . desire?

The air thickened even more. His warm hand tightened gently over hers. "Susan?" His voice was soft and deep, so seductive that she couldn't breathe, yearning for—

No, she shouldn't think it. He didn't mean—

His lips grazed her ear, his warm breath sending shivers across her. "Susan? Your Dear Bob column . . . If you wanted me to take off my shirt, you only had to ask."

She closed her eyes as he trailed his lips from her ear down to the neckline of her shirt. She hadn't meant to write a Dear Bob column about Mark, she really hadn't. But it had been late and she'd been working at her desk alone and she'd been consumed with thoughts of him, and—well—it had happened. She was a bit surprised that he'd even seen it, because he never mentioned the column at all.

Apparently she'd been mistaken. Still, she couldn't quite regret it, especially with Mark nibbling on her ear in a way that set her entire body aflame, crazy for his touch. His fingers threaded through her hair, stopped by her hair band. She tugged the band from her hair, letting it spill around her.

"Yesss." He buried his face in her hair and engulfed her, pulling her against him so that his chest rested against her back, his thighs warmed her ass, and his swelling cock pressed insistently into the small of her back. She watched in the reflective door as he ran his hands over her arms, down to her thighs, then slipped under her arms to run back up her hips, her waist, and on to cup her breasts.

It was as if she had a private viewing of her own seduction. Her body quivered and she pressed back against him, gasping as his thumbs found her sensitive nipples. He continued to kiss her neck, his warm lips teasing her. She arched against him, her hands roaming behind her, finding his cock, and gently cupping his length through his jeans.

He moaned and turned her in his arms. At that, all restraint was gone. They kissed as if this was their one and only chance to be together, as if they were starved for the taste of each other. Within seconds she had his jeans unbuttoned and was pushing them down his hips, tantalized to discover he was neither a boxer nor a briefs man. Mark was no less adept at peeling off her jeans, though he left the scrap of lace that comprised her panties in place.

She helped him pull his T-shirt over his head. She gawked. He was as well muscled as she'd imagined, his shoulders broad, his chest hard, his stomach a testament to what must have been thousands of crunches. "Oh my," she breathed, running her hands over his abs.

He grinned. "I feel the same way about these." His hands molded to her breasts over her shirt.

"I'm not that well endowed." It was hard to speak clearly when sparks of pure lust shot through her entire body.

"They're perfect," he said fervently.

She started to reach for her panties, but he stopped her, holding her close, caressing her back. "Leave them on for now."

"But I—"

He kissed her. As he did so, he rolled her shirt

up, his fingers brushing erotically over her bared skin even as his kiss deepened, his tongue as insistent and demanding as his actions.

Dear Lord, get this man alone and undressed and he becomes powerful, aggressive, and passionate!

He broke their kiss only long enough to tug her shirt over her head. He recaptured her lips immediately as he expertly undid her bra with one hand and tossed it to the floor. The first brush of his bared skin and chest hair against her already sensitive nipples made her moan against his mouth.

He began to nip and caress his way down her neck, her shoulders, pausing to drive her crazy by sucking on first one, then her other nipple. She sank her fingers into his thick hair, arching against him, into his mouth. She caught a glimpse of herself in the silvery door, her head thrown back, her hair flowing, as Mark moved down her body, his broad shoulders and back blocking her nakedness as he kissed down her stomach to her hot pink lace panties.

Kneeling before her, he gently lifted one of her legs and placed it over his shoulder, then he began to kiss her through her panties, his tongue bold and forceful. She moaned. There was something so decadent about the fact that she still wore her panties. Something naughty and outrageous and oh so delicious.

He lifted the edge of the lace and slipped his tongue beneath it, finding her clit and making her writhe. She dug her hands into his hair. "No more! I can't take—*please!*"

Laughing softly, he tugged her panties down and she kicked them off. She reached for him, then hesitated. "Wait." She looked around the floor of the elevator, at their fallen clothing and the discarded folder and newspaper, and found her purse. She dug through it desperately, exclaiming in glee when she located a silver packet.

A condom. Mark winced. Good God, he was crazed to even think of having sex without a condom, but Susan reduced him to an unthinking mass of nerves.

She ripped open the package with her teeth and yanked the condom out, her face determined.

Mark laughed softly and pulled her to her feet. "Give that to me." He slipped it on, unrolling it as quickly as he could. Then he was lifting her, pressing her against the elevator wall, and pressing into her.

Susan clutched him to her with her legs, wrapping her arms about his neck as she pressed onto his fullness. She gasped as he slid home, calling his name as he thrust against her, his strong hands warm on her bare ass, moving more and more forcefully. They gulped their passion, their movements desperate and heated.

Mark knew only that his cock was finally where it belonged—deeply embedded in Susan. He moved faster, holding her firmly as he took her. Her head fell back; her lips parted as a shudder racked her body from head to foot. She gasped his name as she clutched him . . . and that was all it took. The world seemed to stop as his own orgasm shook him and he thrust into her one last time, letting her aftershocks drain him dry.

It took a while before he could think again. When he did, he slowly lowered her to the ground, holding her to him. He rubbed his cheek along her hair, savoring its softness, marveling at her smooth, taut body.

Once Susan could think, she wondered what one said to a man who'd just fulfilled every sexual fantasy she'd ever had. *Thank you for the incredible shagging*. She'd just screwed the living daylights out of her boss, and loved every second. Her body still quivered.

Mark stirred. "I suppose we should dress and try to get the elevator going."

She reluctantly began to dress.

Mark did the same, first removing the condom and tying a knot in the end of it. "That should do it." He caught her gaze and grinned. "If he gets out of here, we'll call him Houdini."

Susan had to laugh. "You're horrible." She zipped up her jeans and pulled on her shoes.

His grin widened. "I know."

She chuckled and fixed her hair, checking her reflection in the mirrored door. "OK. I can pass inspection in a dim room."

"How about me?"

"You look great." He had a glow about him, a sense of relaxed, swaggering well-being that told its own story.

She couldn't help but feel a little proud. She'd caused that look on his face, and the very idea made her grin so wide, it was a surprise her cheeks didn't hurt.

Mark looked at the elevator panel. "I suppose now we should put our energies toward getting out of this elevator."

"It usually begins working on its own in a few minutes. Try it again, only this time, hold the button for a while."

Mark pressed the lobby button, and after a deep shudder, the elevator continued its slooooow progression to the bottom floor.

Susan adjusted her T-shirt where it was twisted to one side, casting a cautious glance at Mark.

He caught her gaze and smiled, his expression calm and reassuring.

"So," he said casually, "how do you think Ray's working out as our receptionist?"

They maintained a steady flow of small talk out to the parking lot.

Mark walked her to her Jeep, where she tossed her stuff into the passenger seat, wondering if she should say something. But what? She didn't know how he felt and—

"You don't lock your door?"

She shrugged. "Sometimes."

"Is that wise? Someone could steal it."

"Mark, look at my vehicle. It's a 1998 Jeep Cherokee. Who would want it?"

He looked surprised, then burst into laughter. "I suppose you're right."

She grinned back at him. "Besides, it wouldn't take any time to break into it, even when it is locked. Watch." She locked the door and closed it. Then she rattled the door handle as hard as she could. When she stopped, there was a soft *click* and she opened the door. "See?"

"Good God! I'd get that fixed if I were you."

"Mark, unless flames are pouring from a car

this old, you don't fix it. If it leaks, it leaks. If it creaks, it creaks. You just enjoy its personality and quirks. In its own unique way, it's maintenance free."

He threw up a hand. "Don't even come near my Mustang."

She laughed. "It's a Jeep thing. You just don't understand."

"I understand plenty." His eyes twinkled. "I understand that you're a country girl and I'm a city boy. I lock everything."

Even your pants? Her cheeks heated at the wayward thought. *What's wrong with me? I should be content now.* But she wasn't. Instead, she felt a stirring of heat.

Afraid she might blurt out her thoughts, she forced a smile. "Well! Time to go!"

His smile flickered. "Oh. Yeah. It's late. I'll . . ." He shrugged, looking at a loss. "I'll . . . see you tomorrow."

"Of course. Bye!" She sounded so blithe that she almost grimaced. *Maybe next time you can add, "Thanks for the wham-bam! It didn't mean a thing to me."*

He walked to his car, parked a row behind hers.

Why couldn't she just be herself around Mark?

Why was it that every time things seemed interesting, she ruined it with a glib comment or a sharp "I gotta get outta here"? Not that she wanted to stay, for she didn't. A fun, passionate fling suited her just fine—she just wished she were more *dignified* about it.

Dispirited, she started her Jeep and slipped it into reverse. She looked in her mirror and caught Mark looking back at her, one hand on his open trunk.

The Jeep rolled out of the parking spot and she set her foot on the brake. It went right to the floor as if she'd pressed air.

Her eyes widened. The Jeep kept rolling back, straight toward Mark, who'd turned away to put something in his trunk.

Oh God, no! She stomped the brakes harder. The pedal went straight to the floor once again, this time even faster.

She jerked her gaze back to her rearview mirror. Mark's broad shoulders were centered in her mirror like a bull's-eye.

She slammed the palm of her hand on her horn.

Mark whirled around. His eyes widened, then with the speed of a desperate man, he jumped into his open trunk.

Bam! Bending metal and breaking glass sounded from behind her. *Mark! Where's Mark?*

She threw open her door and ran to the back. *Please let him be OK! Please, please, please—*

"What in the *hell* are you *doing?*" Mark climbed from the trunk, his glasses hanging from one ear, his shirt ripped at the arm, a scratch across one rock-hard muscle.

"My—my—brakes didn't work! I put it in reverse and then my foot went to the floor and—and then you were standing there and I couldn't—" She fought a sudden desire to burst into tears.

Mark gave a muffled curse and reached for her, but she sidestepped him. If he so much as gave her a concerned look, she'd shatter into a thousand pieces.

To keep her desperate hold on her emotions, she pointed to the Jeep. "I—I tried to stop it, but—" She took a ragged breath and closed her eyes. *Breathe, damn it! Just breathe!*

That helped. She opened her eyes to find Mark regarding her somberly. Then he strode past her and leaned into her open Jeep door.

She took the time to regain control over her scattered emotions. She'd thought for sure he'd been killed, or at the least badly hurt. She'd have never forgiven herself if he had. *But he's OK*, she told herself. *He's OK, and so am I.*

She bent to examine the damage to Mark's Mustang. One rear light was smashed and the bumper was buckled, and the rear corner was dented by the hitch on the back of her Jeep. She winced.

The sound of the Jeep hood being unlatched made her turn. Mark was leaning over the engine.

He opened the brake fluid reservoir. "There's no fluid."

"But I had it in the shop just two months ago."

He looked at where she'd been parked. "There's brake fluid all over the ground. A hose must have broken." He lay down on the pavement and made as if to slide under her Jeep.

"Treymayne, your shirt—"

"It'll wash." He wiggled under the Jeep until only his legs were visible.

Damn it, *she* should be the one under there. It was her Jeep and—

He wiggled back out, scowling, his hands black with grease.

She went to the back door of her Jeep and removed a roll of paper towels, yanked off a handful, and handed them to him.

He wiped his hands. "Someone cut your brake lines, Susan."

What? "How do you know the lines didn't just come unhooked?"

"Because they're sliced in two, straight as can be, not a jagged edge showing. *Both* of them." His jaw was hard. "Susan, someone tried to kill you."

Chapter
9

The next morning, Mark stood at his office window and looked down at the Jeep in the parking lot. A tow truck from Don's Tow and Mow had arrived and was now taking it from the lot. The sheriff's office had thoroughly gone over the vehicle, drawing the attention of nearly every damn person in town.

It was a wonder Nick managed to solve any crimes; as soon as he put up the crime tape, every person in Glory came by to gawk. The worst ones were Tundy and her Murder Mystery Club. They'd been loud in their disappointment that there was no body at the crime scene and were now pelting poor Nick with a hundred questions.

The entire thing was unsettling. *Damn it, Susan could have been killed.* It would bother him like hell if something had happened to her. He didn't even want to think about what might have happened if she'd driven that Jeep out of the parking lot.

He wasn't sure which bothered him more—the thought of her on one of Glory's crooked, narrow roads in a vehicle with no brakes, or her cavalier attitude about the whole situation.

She'd flatly refused to call the sheriff, saying she'd rather die than pull him from his home over such a trivial event. Mark had grumbled the entire way to her house, his bad mood increasing when they met Susan's father staggering up the front walk. Damn it, someone should be taking care of her, not the other way around.

First thing this morning, he'd called Nick. Hopefully the sheriff's involvement would make Susan take the incident more seriously.

While the accident itself had shaken her, he hadn't been able to impress upon her the seriousness of the event. She'd merely shrugged and said she didn't believe it was "all that," mentioning a time someone had rolled her yard with toilet paper after she'd written an article criticizing the high school band.

How could any of their very few and very unimpressive investigations tick off someone enough that they'd want to off the *Examiner*'s top reporter? He simply couldn't fathom it.

Sighing, he raked a hand through his hair. Susan Collins was as stubborn and unforgettable as a woman could get. It wasn't just her passion, though that was incredible, but her intelligence and wit and a dozen other things that he couldn't name. He was beginning to like her far more than was smart, a fact he'd realized because of his strong reaction to the idea that someone was trying to harm her. "What a complicated mess," he muttered.

Pat stuck her head around the corner. "I just need a few pictures and we're set; I've already written the story."

"What story?"

She came into his office, tucking away her old-fashioned reporter's notebook. "About the attempted murder."

He stared blankly.

"The Jeep? Susan? Your own reporter, for God's sake!" She shook her head in disgust. "I just got a quote from Don from Don's Tow and Mow, and someone definitely cut the lines and—"

"Pat, we can't print that story."

"Why not?"

"Because it's about us. We can't write the news and *be* the news, too. That's conflict of interest."

"Not if I write it. I wasn't involved like you and—"

"I'm *not* involved with Susan Collins."

Pat blinked. "Not with Susan, with the accident. The Jeep hit your car, didn't it?"

"Oh. Yes."

"What did you think I meant—" Pat's brows rose. "Oh. Why would you think I'd suggest that?"

Mark nearly slapped his forehead at his own stupidity. "Pat, we're not going to run this story."

Pat stiffened. "We have to—"

"No." He raised a hand for emphasis. "As far as I'm concerned, it never happened. Confine your reporting efforts to the stories you were assigned."

Pat's face turned nearly purple. "You can't just ignore what happened! We have to print it! It's our *duty* and—"

"What's our duty?" Susan came in, looking cool and collected in a pale green shirt and her usual worn jeans, her hair loose about her shoulders.

Pat quivered in indignation. "Our *accountant*"—she loaded the word with scorn—"says we're not going to cover the story about how someone tried to sabotage your Jeep."

Susan blinked. "What?"

"Conflict of interest," Mark said. "We can't be the news *and* report it."

"It's the biggest story yet!" Pat said in an outraged tone. She leaned forward, her expression earnest. "Just think of the papers we'll sell! An attempted murder right here in Glory!"

"That was not an attempted murder," Susan scoffed.

Pat gaped. "Was too."

"Was not. And if it was, it was made by the lamest murderer on God's green earth."

Pat stiffened, her face bright red. "Oh! You—you—I should have known you'd side with *him*!" With that infuriating statement, she huffed from the room.

"That went well." Susan closed the door and leaned against it. "Mark, we need to talk."

He frowned. "What happened to your neck?" Across one side of her neck, only visible when her hair moved, there was a deep pink streak.

She grimaced. "The seat belt from the Jeep."

"I didn't see that last night."

"It was dark. It's no biggie."

"Like hell." He moved from behind his desk and, with a gentle touch, tilted her head to one side. "Good God. Is there anything else I didn't see?"

She held out her right hand and turned it palm up. A bruise covered her palm.

"How did you get *that*?"

"I think I got it from hitting the horn so hard,

but I'm not sure." She shrugged. "Other than that, I'm just a little stiff. That's it."

"That's enough," he snapped, suddenly angry. "When we figure out who did this—" There was a place in hell for the bastard who'd cut her brake lines, and Mark was going to be sure the asshole landed in it.

Susan said in an impatient tone, "Now you sound like Pat."

"Except that I don't want to write about it."

"Mark, we *have* to report it."

He regarded her somberly. "Why?"

"It's our job. Let Pat write the story, but with no drama. I was never in any danger."

"Even bruised, you refuse to admit how serious this is."

"Uh-huh. By the way, about last night—" She took a deep breath, which strained her shirt and his control.

She's going to bring up our encounter in the elevator. Is she sorry it happened? I'm not. I'm damn glad—

"I really enjoyed our, ah, time in the elevator."

Phew. "I enjoyed it, too." *That has to be the understatement of the year.*

"But I know that you're not here long, and I want you to know that's fine."

"What do you mean?"

Her cheeks glowed pink. "I'm a mature woman and you're a mature man, and we both can enjoy our 'elevator time' without any ensuing drama."

How many times over the last few years had he made this exact speech: the I-don't-want-to-give-up-the-physical-part-of-our-relationship-just-yet speech. Probably a dozen, at least. But this was the first time anyone had made the speech to him.

She shrugged. "That's all I had to say. I just wanted to get that out there."

Jeez, what did one say? He finally settled on, "Thank you. I feel the same."

She brightened. "Do you?"

Actually, he didn't. Oh, he wasn't in love with Susan, though she was exactly the sort of woman a man could fall for. After Arlene's rampage through his heart, he had no interest in another long-term relationship.

Still, it didn't seem right to downplay what had been the hottest sex he'd ever experienced. The memories of the night before were so vivid that he'd gotten an erection just getting into the elevator this morning.

But could he admit all of that to her and not sound as if he was looking for something more? Probably not, so he'd just keep his thoughts to himself. Susan was right when she said he wasn't long for this town; the second the paper was on solid ground, he had a very fulfilling life to return to—one away from Glory, the newspaper, and Susan. "I think we should—"

A knock sounded on the door.

Susan opened it, and the sheriff strode in.

"There you are," Susan said. "Glory's finest."

Nick grinned. "Hey, Susan. How are you?"

"Perfectly fine, as I was just telling Mark."

"Good," Nick said. "I would like to talk to both of you."

"Have a seat." Mark gestured to the chairs grouped by the window.

Susan crossed to a chair but didn't sit. "Nick, tell Mark this is not a big deal and no one tried to kill me."

"Just sit down," Mark instructed. "Let the man talk, will you?"

Susan sniffed but sat.

Nick took the chair beside hers. "Is your boss always like this?"

"Most of the time." Susan stretched out her long legs and crossed them at the ankles. "He's uptight, just like Clark Kent. Sorta looks like a Clark, too."

Nick chuckled. "Well, Clark and Lois, tell me

what's happening here at *The Daily Planet* that might have someone riled enough to cut Susan's brake lines."

Susan and Mark exchanged glances. "Susan stirred things up Sunday with an editorial about the Baptist Bake-Off, but I can't imagine anyone would want to harm her over that."

"People mad?"

"Hopping. Lots of threats to cancel subscriptions, but none that were personal that I remember."

Nick looked at Susan. "You agree with that?"

"Yes. No one made any threats against me at all."

Nick scribbled something in a small notebook. "I heard some people were upset about the op-ed piece, but—" He shrugged.

Susan replied, "I didn't accuse anyone specific of anything. I just suggested someone should ask why the Baptist Bake-Off has changed leadership for the first time in twenty-two years."

Mark frowned. "Twenty-two years?"

"Yup. Pastor MacMillan's had the same committee chair the entire time, until this year. That's a long tradition to break."

Nick wrote something else down. "So no direct threats."

Mark shrugged. "I don't expect to be invited over to dinner to certain houses anytime soon, but that's it. Susan, you?"

"Not a one. In fact"—she smiled smugly—"I got some good leads from it. A few people have offered to talk to me off the record."

"Who?" Mark demanded.

"I can't say."

Nick shook his head. "You secretive types. Any other stories you're working on that could be raising people's ire?"

"Nope," Susan said. "Which leaves our supposed murderer with no motive—yet another reason to think this was just an act of random vandalism."

Nick's expression grew serious. "I don't know, Susan. Someone did cut those lines. It wouldn't hurt you to be a bit more cautious than usual."

Susan opened her mouth and Nick held up a hand. "Before you start arguing, I'd like to point out that I haven't had my morning coffee and I'm likely to get cranky real fast."

She gave him a reluctant grin. "I suppose I can wait."

"Deal."

Mark sometimes forgot that Susan had worked for Nick for years before she'd come to the *Ex-*

aminer, but the two shared an easy, comfortable camaraderie.

"Thanks." Nick looked at his notes. "Here's what I have so far. The Jeep was in the parking lot. The worst thing that could have happened was that you might bump into another car—at a whopping five miles per hour or less. It didn't even set off the air bags. No one was trying to kill anyone with that caper. *However*, just because whoever this was sucked at it, or perhaps was merely trying to scare you for some reason, doesn't mean he or she might not try again—and make a more serious effort next time, too."

"*That's* what I'm talkin' about," Mark said. "You have to take this seriously."

Nick's cool gray gaze flickered to Susan. "He's right about that. You need to be on alert."

Susan grimaced. "What am I supposed to do? Hide under my bed while they try Part Two of their Evil Plan to give me a really, really bad day? What will their next attempt be? Rig a lightning rod to my toe while I'm asleep?"

Nick chuckled and stood, tucking his notebook under his arm. "However you feel about it, wiseass, I'm going to investigate and *you* are going to keep your eyes and ears open, just in case."

She shrugged. "Fine. I'll do anything if it'll make the two of you stop badgering me."

Nick looked at Mark. "That's as good as we're going to get."

Mark sighed. "I was afraid of that."

"She's stubborn as heck."

Susan plopped her hands on her hips. "She's also right here, in hearing range."

Nick clicked his tongue. "Touchy little thing, isn't she?"

"You have no idea."

Susan put her hands in the middle of Nick's back and propelled him to the door. "Out! How can you sheriff from this small room? All of the bad guys are out there."

He laughed and opened the door. "Fine. I can tell when I'm not wanted."

"That's not true, or you wouldn't have come here in the first place. Go bother someone else with your theories and investigations."

Nick quirked a brow. "Does this mean I'm un-invited to poker night?"

"Of course not. It's your week to bring the beer."

"It's always my week to bring the beer." Nick gave her a hug. "Promise you'll keep an eye peeled."

"For you, I'll peel them both."

Nick said his good-byes and left.

"Well," Susan said in a sunny voice, "it's time to get back to work. I'll tell Pat to go ahead and write the story about the vandalism done to my Jeep. We have to print something; too many people have stopped by the crime scene."

Mark sighed. "OK. Give it a good quote, at least."

"Oh, I will." She flashed him a grin as she walked toward the door. "I'll complain that I was hoping the insurance would total it out, but noooooo." She winked and left, and he watched as she crossed the hall to her office and settled in.

He tried to work, but every time he glanced up, she seemed to be doing something suggestive: biting her soft bottom lip, bending over to pull a file from a drawer, tucking a silky strand of hair behind one ear. Everything she did made him think of the elevator and it was driving him crazy.

Susan's phone rang. She listened for a moment, her gaze flying to meet his. "Yes, I will! Of course. How much did you say? Wow!" She listened a while longer, her eyes sparkling. "May I bring someone else with me? No, no. Just Mark Treymayne, Roxie's brother. He does our accounting. OK. I will. See you soon. Bye!" She hung up and grabbed her purse, her eyes sparkling with barely contained excitement. "Let's go!"

He was on his feet and following her out the door, his car keys at the ready. "Where are we going?"

"That was last year's Bake-Off chairperson. She says she's tired of all the misinformation and she's ready to talk, but only off the record. My hunch was right—there's a lot more to the story! Last year's proceeds went missing, and it was over thirty thousand dollars!"

Chapter
10

"Where are we going?"

Susan buckled her seat belt. "To see Widow Rawlings. She lives in the white house beside Indian Springs Elementary School." She rubbed her hands together. "I *knew* we'd get a break in this story!"

Mark turned the Mustang out of the parking lot. "Your ploy worked."

"Yes. And we only had *one* cancellation of the paper, and that person reinstated it this morning."

"So we didn't lose any customers?"

"Nope." She grinned at him. "Admit it was a brilliant idea."

He slanted her a look that told her not to press her luck. "It was an OK idea."

Susan chuckled. "Mark, admit it."

"We'll see how things pan out."

She sighed happily, then pulled her notebook

and a pen from her purse. "I'll ask her if there's ever been an audit of the Bake-Off proceeds."

"I can't believe they made over thirty thousand dollars last year."

"I do. It's far more than a simple bake sale. They do classes and sponsor women's church groups from all over the state. It's a very big deal. Last year, one of the bigger churches from over in Greensboro brought two chartered buses of ticket-paying, class-taking, bakery-sale-buying women. All in all, over four thousand people attended."

"I had no idea it was so big."

"Why do you think I keep pushing the story?"

He caught her astonished gaze and realized he had no good answer. "I suppose I just thought you didn't have anything better to pursue."

She cocked a brow.

His neck grew hot. "It's not like there are a dozen stories competing for attention."

"I'm not desperate for news, Mark. There's plenty going on around here if you'll take the time to look for it."

His gaze flickered to his rearview mirror and he slowed to turn.

She frowned. "This isn't the right road."

"I know. I want to see a little of the countryside."

"OK." She regarded him for a moment, noting how his hands were so steady on the wheel. She liked a man who knew who he was and how to do things, and she sometimes wondered if Dad had ever been like that. According to some of his older friends, he was once an accomplished carpenter. Though he sometimes offered advice on her home improvement projects, his general observations were never accompanied by more specific instructions.

Mark asked, "What set you on this story, anyway? Just the change in leadership?"

"That and one other thing. When they changed the chairperson to someone off the board, I did a little research and looked up the articles we'd written on the Bake-Off in the last few years. Every year, after the sale, there's always an article on the proceeds and where they will be spent—except last year."

"Never mentioned?"

"Not even hinted at. And it's a big deal for the church. They always posted a sign in front of the church that said THANK YOU FOR YOUR GENEROSITY! in large red letters." She frowned. "I couldn't remember them doing it last year. And after I thought about it, I was sure they hadn't."

"That's interesting. I wonder if—" Mark looked in the rearview mirror and frowned. "Hang on."

"Wha—"

He swerved severely and yanked the car off the road onto the shoulder, dust kicking high into the air.

Susan clung to her seat, coughing a little. "What's wrong?"

Mark undid his seat belt and threw the door open. "I've had it with those—"

The rest of the words were lost as he marched back to a van parked almost directly behind them. Susan undid her belt and got out of the car, walking up to the van just in time to hear Mark demand, "Don't tell me that! You've been following us since we left the newspaper, and I want to know why."

Susan could just make out the reddish curls of the driver: Ah, Tundy, from the assisted-living center. Susan leaned over and sure enough, PINE HILLS ASSISTED LIVING CENTER—WHERE JUST LIVING ISN'T ENOUGH was emblazoned on the side. So, Tundy and her Murder Mystery Club had been following them. That was interesting.

"Why, Mr. Treymayne," Tundy said in a placating voice. "I don't know what you're talkin' about. Me and the girls and C.J. here were just out for a nice ride—"

"That's right!" piped up Clara, leaning out the

window behind Tundy. Clara had apparently just had her hair done, for a profusion of white curls were carefully frosted into a helmet around her wrinkled brow. "We're just drivin' along mindin' our own business, when you screeched to a halt and almost made us have an accident. You really should get that tail light fixed."

Angular and tall, Rose Tibbons, the ringleader of the club, poked her head around Clara from the backseat, her bright red wig crooked. "Treymayne! What in hell do you think you were doing, driving like that? I know your mother, young man!"

Mark crossed his arms, his expression grim. "If you hadn't been following me so close, it wouldn't have mattered how I stopped. You were tail-gating."

Tundy puffed out her cheeks. "Tailgating? Mr. Mark, you know me better than that! I never drink and drive."

Mark had opened his mouth to retort, but this stopped him.

Susan hid a grin. "Tundy, tailgating also means you were following far too close."

"*Way* too close," Mark added. "When I looked in my rearview mirror, all I could see was your van grille and headlights."

"Oh. That's because we were trying to write

down your license plate. We hadn't filled in that line on your dossier yet—"

"Dossier?" Susan asked, reaching for her reporter's notebook. "What dossier?"

Tundy's round cheeks turned bright red. "Nothin'! There's no dossiers! Never heard of 'em!"

"But you said—"

Clara leaned forward, her bottle-thick glasses magnifying her pale blue eyes. "Fine, you caught us. We *were* following you. But only because we want to catch whoever is tryin' to kill Miz Susan."

C.J., who'd been looking out the window, turned at this. "It wasn't me."

Rose scowled. "No one said it was."

"OK. Just thought I should mention it." He turned back to the window.

Clara sighed. "We didn't mean to bother you. We're just sleuthing Miz Susan's case."

Rose agreed, "We'll find the killer or die with you."

Susan noticed Mark was having trouble not laughing. "Thanks," she muttered to him before she faced Tundy and her gang. "I hate to think of you all wasting your time on a small case of vandalism, which was all it was."

"No, it wasn't," Rose stated. "Don from Don's

Tow and Mow told us your brake lines were cut. That's a murder attempt if I ever heard one."

"So we're going to follow Miz Susan," C.J. said, "And if she gets killed right in front of us, we'll know who did it."

Mark nodded. "That's a heck of an investigative method."

"You can't beat a van full of eyewitnesses," Clara said sagely.

Susan wondered if any of them could even pass a basic vision test. She snapped her notebook closed. "Mark and I'd love to stay and chat, but we're off to visit Widow Rawlings." It was better to put their destination out there, or the Murder Mystery Club would begin to suspect all sorts of weird things.

Tundy's gaze sharpened. "Is she a suspect?"

"Nope. She's been feeling ill and Mark's mother made us promise to stop by and visit her."

Susan felt Mark's approving gaze.

"Miz Treymayne do like playin' lady of the manor," Tundy agreed. "Did she make you bring soup? She always made me take soup to sick people, which was a pain, because it spilled in my car. To this very day, my car smells like onions."

"We didn't give her the time."

"Smart move."

"About this following thing, Tundy." Mark looked hard at her. "I know a bad idea when I see it, and this is one."

Rose snorted. "Mark Treymayne, don't you lecture Miz Tundy about knowing things. Why, look at you, going all over town with Miz Susan here, both of you smelling like roses and weddings, and neither one of you knowing it."

Susan stiffened. *Smelling like roses and weddings?* She didn't dare look at Mark. "I don't know what you're talking about, Rose. Mark is my boss, so of course he and I work together."

"He don't hang about Pat like he does you," Rose pointed out.

C.J. looked up and said in a remarkably lucid tone, "He don't watch her ass the way he watches yours, either."

Susan turned to look at Mark, whose neck was a telltale red. "You've been staring at my ass?"

Rose snorted. "He stares like he's never seen one before."

Mark held up a hand. "I'm not going to discuss this anymore. If you want to talk, it had better be about why you're following us and why I shouldn't call the sheriff and put a stop to it."

Tundy sighed. "Gang, I guess the gig is up. Mr. Mark ain't goin' to let us off the hook. Guess we'll all just *go home* and let him and Miz Susan be. Yup, you'll *never* see us again 'cause we're going *back to the center* and *take a nap*—"

Susan burst out laughing. "Tundy Spillers, you are the worst liar I've ever seen! You aren't planning on going back to the center at all."

Clara looked disappointed. "That's too bad. I really need to pee."

"Me, too," C.J. said, peeking over Rose's shoulder.

"Didn't you all go when we went to the gas station?" Tundy demanded. "All of you went in!"

"We didn't have time to use the restroom," Clara said. "We were busy getting these." She held a pack of Red Hots.

"They make your tongue red." C.J. stuck his out to demonstrate. "But they don't help you much if you need to pee."

"In fact," Clara said, "because I had to guzzle so much root beer to put out my mouth fire, I'd say the Red Hots made me have to pee worse."

Tundy looked disappointed. "Guess we won't be following you anymore. We've got to get to a facility."

"Good thinking," Mark said.

Tundy put the van in reverse, then pulled out onto the road.

Susan looked at her watch. "We'd better get back on the road or we'll be late."

As she returned to the car, she sneaked a peek back to see if Mark really was checking out her posterior.

She caught him in midgawk.

He grinned unrepentantly. "If I'm going to get blamed for it, I might as well do it."

She patted her rump. "I'm just glad it's worth checking out."

He chuckled. "Let's go before the club comes back and tries to discover all of our secrets." He went to her door and opened it for her.

She enjoyed his old school manners. There was something incredibly sexy about a man who was comfortable enough as a man that he didn't have to bully his way into your life; he just opened the door and stood back.

It wouldn't do to like it too much, though. Once Mark had the paper back in the black, he'd return to his fancy accounting practice in Raleigh.

And that was the way it should be. Or the way it had to be, anyway. If there was one thing she'd learned from working so closely with Mark over the last few months, it was that he had a big city view of life, one that didn't fit well in a small town like Glory. Oh, he might get along great with most of the residents, and he might look comfortable sitting at his perfectly clean desk at the paper, but the truth was, he would soon tire of living in a town where things were so slow that citizens were forced to start up Murder Mystery Clubs just to stay busy.

That was a good thing for her to remember. While she was content to live in Glory for the rest of her life, Mark wasn't. It was an excellent reason to keep their relationship at the heavy flirting level.

She snuck a glance at him as he turned the car back onto the road, his movements sure and damned sexy. It was a pity that her greatest goal—to turn the newspaper around—was also the thing that would send him racing back to Raleigh. If she didn't love the paper so much, she might be tempted to slow her plan down a little and savor him a bit more. But this job was her dream-come-true and she wouldn't compromise it for anyone.

With a bit of a sigh, Susan settled back in her seat and reopened her notebook. "I suppose we should come up with some interview questions for Mrs. Rawlings. Any ideas?"

Chapter
11

An hour later, Susan and Mark emerged from Widow Rawlings's house and climbed back into the Mustang. For a long moment, they sat in the car, staring straight ahead.

"Wow," Mark said. "I did *not* see that coming."

"Me, neither."

He frowned. "Do you think she's telling the truth?

"Yes."

"Me too."

Susan shook her head. "Who'd have thought such a crime could go unreported like that?"

Over thirty thousand dollars missing, and when the board members noticed the gaps in the deposits and planned to meet to request an audit, they were summarily informed they'd been replaced.

Mark rubbed his chin. "I can't believe no one came forward and said anything."

"They trusted Pastor MacMillan, and he assured them that he would personally see to it that an audit was done—"

"Which wasn't."

"Not that Widow Rawlings knows about. But, to be fair, she hasn't been on the committee this year and all of their meetings were closed."

Mark frowned. "You think an audit *was* done?"

"Who knows? Pastor MacMillan assured the old board members that if the money was indeed missing, as it appeared, that every penny would be returned."

"And they just believed him."

"They have so far. That's why none of the other ex-board members have come forward to talk to us."

"All that money gone, and no one can explain it."

Susan nibbled on the end of her pen. "Embezzlement is the obvious answer, and yet . . . who? Widow Rawlings didn't have an idea."

Mark shook his head. "We don't have enough to go with a story."

"Not yet." She sighed. "The pastor is a fixture in this town. A lot of people have been sad to think of him retiring."

"Even my mother thinks he walks on water.

The new pastor doesn't have a chance. She's already called him an 'upstart' and 'pretentious,' and she hasn't even met him yet."

Susan tucked her pen and notebook into her purse. "This story is huge. It'll cause such an uproar!"

"I hate uproars."

She sent him an amused glance. "You really aren't cut out for the news biz, are you, Clark?"

"Probably not."

Susan leaned her head back against the seat. "We can't print this story without two more sources corroborating it, but now that we know what questions to ask and who to ask . . ."

Her brows knitted and her blue eyes fixed unseeingly straight ahead. Mark could almost hear the wheels turning in her head.

He drove back to the newspaper office, letting her think. Her instincts had been right once again. Perhaps it was time he began to trust them. He glanced at her, noting that she was now biting her lip. He shifted uncomfortably in his seat. God, he loved it when she did that. It made him think of—

"Clark?"

He gave a reluctant grin. "Yes, Lois?"

Her smile was as bright as the sun breaking

through a rain-drenched sky. "Thanks for coming with me."

"It was good to see how you guys operate. When I first arrived, I thought that by reading a few articles, I knew enough to make decisions for the paper. I'm beginning to see I was mistaken."

"*You?*"

He regarded her with a flat look. "Sarcasm doesn't become you. But, I probably deserve it. I guess I was a little arrogant when I started."

"A little?"

"Hey, I've already admitted you were right. You're not getting anything more from me today, unless—" He shot her a direct look that let her know exactly what "unless" he was talking about.

She blushed, looking adorably pleased.

Mark pulled into their parking lot and turned off the Mustang just as someone came jogging down the street.

Susan recognized the woman immediately. "Well, well, well. I guess the mayor is in a meeting, since his secretary-slash-girlfriend is out running."

Mark assessed the woman jogging toward them.

Susan didn't much like Robin Wright—few women did—and with reason. Robin collected men the way a hunter collected trophies. Susan

wouldn't be surprised to find that Robin decorated
the walls of her lake house with the stuffed underwear of all the men she'd conquered, mounted on
wooden plaques like deer heads.

Robin was jogging in her usual scant short
shorts and a jog bra that barely held her augmented assets, with her dark hair pulled up in a
ponytail that swished sexily as she pranced down
the street.

Susan started to make a comment to Mark and
saw his gaze locked on Robin.

Aware she was being watched, Robin slowed
her pace but bounced even more, so that it truly
seemed as if she might escape her top. As she came
level with Mark and Susan, she flashed a smile directly at Mark and said in a purring voice, "Hello,
Treymayne!"

Susan bit her tongue against the "Tramp!" that
tried to escape.

Mark lifted a hand but didn't say anything, no
doubt because his tongue was now tightly wrapped
around his tonsils.

*If there is any justice in this world, Robin will fall
and get a full-body road rash.*

Susan got out of the car, slamming her car
door a little too hard, hoping to jostle Mark from
his reverie. He followed her, pausing only to lock

the doors, his gaze still on the performance being played out before them.

Robin jogged on, looking perky and annoyingly healthy, leaving Susan aware that both of her breasts wouldn't equal one of Robin's munificent mammaries. She simply didn't understand the male psyche. Here she was, supportive and intelligent, capable and reasonably attractive, yet Mark was panting over a fake like Robin Wright. *At least he looked at my ass today.*

Well, Robin had just better back off. Mark was her flirtation, damn it! Simmering, Susan walked to the newspaper building beside him.

Just as they reached the door, she grabbed his hand, yanked him into the bushes, and planted the most heated, passionate kiss she could on his astonished mouth. With a groan, he grabbed her close and indulged her in the longest, sexiest, most desperate kiss she'd ever experienced. Hands seeking, breath mingled, they clung to one another, pushing aside clothing in a desperate way, tasting and testing, tempting and trying. If it hadn't been for the sound of a car pulling into the parking lot they might have gone further.

Susan suddenly realized that Mark's shirt was almost completely unbuttoned while hers was twisted at the waist.

As they began fixing their clothing, Mark sent her a quizzical glance. "Not that I'm complaining, but what was *that*?"

"It was a reminder."

"Of what?"

"Of the elevator."

His blue gaze locked on her. "You think I need a reminder?" He slipped an arm around her waist and yanked her close. "Every time I get into that damned elevator, I remember our time in it. Every. Single. Second." He kissed her nose and released her. "Now fix your hair. The band is coming out."

Oddly pleased, she did as he'd told her.

Susan finished righting her clothes. Mark did the same, straightening his glasses as he sent her a grin that told her it wasn't over yet. "Ready, Collins?"

She tucked a strand of hair behind one ear. "Ready, Treymayne."

He glanced around, then stepped out of the bushes. He pulled Susan into the building and they quickly made their way to the elevator. Susan noticed that his hand trembled a bit when he punched the up button.

Suddenly the entire day seemed brighter, warmer, and far more exciting.

Chapter
12

The next week, Mark watched as Susan did her best to get the former board members to talk, but to no avail. Even Widow Rawlings refused to answer more questions, seeming worried that someone might find out that she'd spilled the beans on the much-loved Pastor MacMillan. According to her, she'd said all she was going to say and that was that—and if anyone dared use her name or quoted her directly, she'd sue them all.

Mark had to give Susan credit; she hadn't rested since their interview with Mrs. Rawlings, even managing to pursue other stories at the same time. She was exhibiting a delightful tenacity that left him aching for a taste of far more than her reporting skills.

At this morning's weekly meeting he noticed that she seemed thoughtful, as if a new idea had occurred to her overnight. He'd hoped she might say something, but he was left to wonder what was going on in that fascinating mind of hers.

The day dragged on and on for Mark. Every time he turned around, he saw Susan. She was on the phone, laughing and talking in a way that made him wish he was on the other end of the line, or sitting at the computer, nibbling the tip of a pen in a way that made him think of other things she might nibble. Everything she did— no matter how innocent or unaware—sent him on an imaginary journey that always ended the same way.

He even faked a lunch appointment just to get a break from his own imagination. When he returned, Susan was at her newly repaired Jeep.

As he got out of his car, Mark watched her slip a hand into her jeans pocket and fish out her keys. The movement lifted her T-shirt and gave him a flash of her flat, tanned stomach. His senses went into overdrive, his heart thudding hard against his ears. *She has to be a runner to be in such great shape.* He realized she was looking at him curiously, so he quickly asked, "Where are you off to now?"

"To the county animal shelter. I have to follow up my interview with the shelter director about the coming budget cuts." Susan reached into her purse and pulled out a camera and checked the battery life. "It's difficult to get in touch with Mitzi. She's a volunteer so her hours are unpredictable."

Mark eyed the camera. "Is that ours?"

"Nope. The paper's camera is vintage. It needs film and the batteries have to be changed every ten or so days."

"We need to fix that."

"Yup. Until then, I'm using mine." She sent him an amused grin. "I thought a cute puppy shot would be good for the front page."

He didn't look impressed. "You'd better be careful or you'll end up coming home with a pet."

"Not a chance in the world. I don't have room for a pet. Besides, my dad is allergic." Or claimed he was, anyway. In all of the years Susan had taken care of Dad, she couldn't think of one time he'd sneezed except when he'd had a cold. But that was Dad. Susan suspected that because he couldn't control the big things—like his drinking and how to keep a job—he was fanatical about controlling the little things, like whether they had a dog.

"Hmm." Mark looked skeptical. "I'd still be careful if I were you. The bleeding hearts who run places like that are natural con artists. They know how to work your weak areas, appeal to your over-grown sense of sympathy."

"My sense of sympathy is fine. The only cute

and cuddly thing in my home is a picture of a puppy."

"Not the traditional hot dog, baseball, and apple pie type of gal, eh?"

"Oh, I'd say I qualify. Not to brag, but I *do* own the fastest bass boat in the county. In fact, I'm going out on it tomorrow afternoon if I can get away from the office."

He grinned, which crinkled his eyes in the most endearing way. "I'm impressed. You are all of it—baseball, hot dogs, and apple pie. In fact—" to her shock, he leaned forward, his cheek against hers as he said in a low voice—"you sort of taste like pie."

Shivers raced through her and she jerked away, sure he could see that her nipples had just perked to attention. Somehow, someway, she had to make her heart stop shivering to a halt every time he touched her.

She nervously tucked a strand of her hair behind one ear. "Must be my vanilla bean lip gloss. Works every time."

His smile dimmed. "Every time? How many times have you used it?"

That wasn't quite the way she'd meant it, but she couldn't find a graceful way to retract the statement. She shrugged. "It's my secret weapon.

Everyone in town knows about it." Which was true because Teresa sold it at the Stuff and Fluff, the only hair salon in town.

"How many *men* know about it?"

"Hundreds. Now, if you'll excuse me, I have an article to write."

He crossed his arms and leaned against the door, cutting off her access to her vehicle. The movement pulled his sleeves tight on his bulging biceps. "No," he drawled, "I don't think I will let you leave. Not yet, anyway."

She tried not to look at his arms; she really did. "What do you mean, no?"

"Admit I'm the only man who has tasted your lip gloss in the last month—no, *two* months."

Was he *jealous*? The thought was tantalizing. Men talked to her, and laughed with her, and frequently asked her opinion on this or that woman they knew . . . but they never got jealous of her.

She suddenly realized that Mark's gaze was locked on her mouth. Though he stood casually, tension emanated from him.

She shoved a hand into her pocket and cleared her throat. "This lip gloss question is rather complicated, since I've worn it since seventh grade."

"Vanilla?"

"No. I just found that in the last year."

His gaze narrowed. "So how many men have benefited from your vanilla lip gloss?"

Hmm. If she told the truth and admitted he was the only eligible male she'd kissed in anything but a platonic way, she was basically admitting that she was as near desperate as a single woman could get.

On the other hand, if she lied and told him that she'd kissed several men, she would come across as a loose woman. She shrugged. *Better a happy hooker than a desperate spinster.* "Fine. Other than you, fifteen men have tasted my lip gloss, and they all liked it."

Mark's eyes widened. "*Fifteen?*"

Too many? "Well," she temporized, a bit thrown off by his shocked expression, "twelve if you don't count men over the age of my uncle Richmond."

"*Twelve?*"

He didn't look any less shocked, so she found herself adding in a rushed voice, "OK, OK! Four if you don't count the ones too young to leave their mothers."

He burst into laughter, deep and rolling. Grinning, he asked, "So how young were these boys?"

"Five and six. They were selling cookies and they each gave me a hug and a kiss on my cheek for each box of cookies I bought." She gave a sheepish grin. "I bought a lot. They were peanut butter."

His expression softened into a smirk. "Oh. *Those* kinds of kisses."

"Anything else you want to know, Clark? Because if not, I have a story to chase down and you're in the way."

"You haven't finished your story here."

"What story?"

"The one that explains the other four men who've tasted your lip gloss."

She tossed her head. "Right. Four."

He eyed her narrowly, his smile slowly growing. "Know how I can tell when you're lying?"

"How?"

He chuckled. "You lift your chin like this." He angled his chin at an impossible level.

"I do not! I had my chin perfectly level and—" She clamped her mouth closed when she realized her chin was angled exactly the way he'd suggested.

He laughed. "See?"

She tried, but she just couldn't be mad at a man whose eyes crinkled when he was teasing, and her answering smile slipped out before she could stop it. They stood there grinning like loons, nothing between them but air warm with humor and approval.

Susan found herself looking at his mouth, which curved so appealingly. He had a beautiful, masculine mouth—firm yet sensual. She'd been mentally rekissing him ever since she'd kissed him in the shrubs. The problem was, if she started kissing him, would she ever want to stop? Or, worse, if she started kissing him, would *he* stop it?

Normally he seemed cool, calm, collected, and far too in control, but she was learning that one touch, one look, and she could ignite his flame. Yet it wasn't enough just to set him afire. She wanted something more . . . tangible. She just didn't know what.

Was this how Lois Lane had felt? Befuddled and yearning at the same time? She wanted him to kiss her and touch her and . . . well, all of it. But she also feared that closeness and hated to think of how it would end. For it would. In Susan's experience, all relationships, with the exception of pure friendship, had a finite end. It was just a question of when.

She snuck a glance at him from under her lashes and wished she hadn't. He was smiling, clearly amused by her.

She tilted her head to one side. "So, Treymayne, if I bring back some unbearably cute puppy pictures, will you use them on the front page?"

"If you think it'll sell papers, yes." He quirked a brow. "But I'd like something in return."

He looked so serious all of the sudden, and he'd never looked more like Clark Kent. *Darn it, I like this guy.*

She blinked, her smile fading. *Where in the hell did that come from? I don't want to like him. It's one thing to be attracted to a guy; that can be contained. But liking him is a whole other road, one I don't want to get stranded on.*

A man like Mark would never be happy in Glory. He'd been up front that the second the paper was in the black, he'd be hitting the road, and she didn't blame him one bit.

Though she loved the town, she knew its limitations. There was no movie theater, only one decent restaurant, and, worst of all, everyone knew everyone else's business.

At one time, she'd never thought she'd be happy here, herself. Circumstances—and concern for her father—had kept her here as surely as if her feet had been cemented to the ground. At first she'd been frustrated, but as time went on, she'd made her way, found good friends, and seen a little of the world around her. Not much, but enough to know that happiness wasn't a place but a decision one made about one's circumstances in life.

She supposed she could have been bitter like a few of the town's residents. But she wasn't a bitter sort of person. She'd worked instead on fashioning a place for herself. Now she loved living in Glory and couldn't imagine being comfortable anywhere else. This was home.

"Susan, I'll tell you what . . ."

She jerked her gaze to his, noting that his blue eyes were shimmering with laughter.

"I'll trade you: the puppy picture on the front page for a favor."

"What's that?"

"Sell an ad." She stiffened, and he added quickly, "Just one."

"I thought we'd agreed to try my way for two months. It's only been two weeks."

"This isn't about that. I'm curious as to how difficult it'll be to sell ads here. In Raleigh there's a lot of competition—three newspapers, a trade magazine, entertainment rags, the Internet, billboards, you name it. Here there's just the *Examiner*. Besides, I've been taking the time to learn your side of the business. It wouldn't hurt for you to experience mine."

She leaned on the hood of her Jeep as she considered this. "If I sell one ad—and I'm not saying I will—will you promise to not make snarky comments when I put a puppy picture on the front page?"

"Not even one?"

"Not one."

He nodded. "Done. But you have to do it within the next day."

She nodded and looked around at her options. Across the street, Mayor Harkins was standing on the sidewalk in front of City Hall, arguing with Robin, as usual. Also as usual, Robin's leather skirt was too short and her shirt too tight over her fake breasts. She looked madder than a hornet, which was nothing new, either. She was dating that loser, Mayor Harkins, so how else could she look?

Beyond them old Pastor MacMillan was approaching, no doubt to offer his sage advice. He was the closest thing Glory had to a marriage counselor. Susan eyed him for a moment, wondering if she should ask him for an ad. But she knew it would be a wasted effort.

She glanced at Mark. "If you want to see something funny, watch what happens if I walk toward the pastor."

"He runs?"

"Like a rabbit chased by a fox." She gazed around at the nearly empty town square. "Who to choose?" She caught sight of Jeff Brockaw climbing out of the low-slung Jag that he'd just parked at Glory National Bank.

Aha! She waved her arm and yelled, "Yo, Jeff!"

Jeff turned, a satchel in his hand, probably deposits from the airport. "Hi, Susan!" he called back, a dimple appearing in one cheek.

Jeff was startlingly good-looking with his chestnut hair and golden eyes, but he didn't affect her the way Mark did, which was a pity. She sometimes had the impression that, if she hinted she would like it, Jeff was willing to take the relationship to a new level. Unfortunately, all she felt for him was friendship. *Why can't we pick and choose when that happens? Life is just not fair.*

"Is that the supposed bestseller guy?" Mark asked, his back as stiff as his tone of voice.

"Yup."

"He's taller than I thought."

There was no disguising the disappointment in Mark's voice. "What's that got to do with anything?"

"Nothing," Mark said.

Bewildered, Susan turned back to Jeff and cupped a hand over her mouth so she could yell back across the town square. "Jeff, are you still doing that fly-in at the airport next month?"

He nodded. "Why?"

"Want an ad in the paper?"

He didn't hesitate, God bless him. "Sure! Couldn't hurt."

"Same info as on the flyer?"

"That'll work."

"Great! Half a page?"

"Sure."

"I'll send you a proof by e-mail."

He waved and went on into the bank.

Mark shook his head. "You kill me. I've called twenty businesses in the last two weeks and not one bought an ad. Ray's sold eight and you corraled a half-pager without trying."

"Probably because you tried too hard to sell them."

"I did not!" He raked a hand through his hair, mussing it adorably as he reluctantly moved away from her Jeep. "Guess there'll be a puppy picture on the front page."

"Which you'll love."

He laughed. "I didn't promise *that*, but I won't mock it."

"Good." She turned and unlocked her door. "Better go. The mayor seems determined to cut the city's budget to the bone, even if it means getting rid of some necessary services like the animal shelter."

"From the short time I've been in this town, I've noticed that the mayor is a bonehead."

She chuckled and tossed her purse into the passenger seat. "Harkins got elected for one reason, and one reason only."

"Blackmail?"

"It's even more pathetic than that. Every year he runs unchallenged, and every year he wins." Susan glanced back at old Pastor MacMillan, who was now talking in an animated way to the mayor and his girlfriend, who both looked glum.

Mark's gaze followed hers. "Maybe we could use the paper to roust up some interest in running for office. It might make a good exposé if— Uh-oh."

Susan turned back to Mark but his gaze was over her head, focused on the other side of the parking lot. "That's Dot Weaver," he said, indicating a woman who was bustling toward them, an anxious expression on her round face, her fakely-black hair almost plastered into a bob. "She's one of Mother's friends and the biggest gossip you've ever met." He sent Susan a glance. "You might want to escape before she gets here."

"You don't need to tell me twice." Susan

hopped into her Jeep, started it up, and rolled down the window. "Bye, Mark! See you later."

He waved her on. "Go ahead, visit your cute puppies. Don't even think about me, here, wasting away as she talks and talks and talks and—"

"If you hurry, you might make it to your office before she even reaches the elevator. I bet if you give Ray a fiver, he'll tell her that you're in a meeting."

He was already turning away, digging for his wallet as he went. "I know I have five bucks somewhere."

But Dot Weaver was no fool. She hiked her dress to her knees and scurried after him, jiggling the entire way. She reached the door at almost the same time he did.

Susan giggled when Dot grabbed Mark by the arm and caused him to let go of the door. The woman immediately began talking as fast as her lips would allow.

Susan grinned as Mark sent her a comical you-see-what-I'm-dealing-with-here look before he disappeared into the building, reluctantly following Dot.

Susan headed for the animal shelter. It was out of town, along the road that led to the Pine Hills Assisted Living Center, and she drove the route with the ease of familiarity, the air whipping her hair from its band.

It was odd, but she couldn't shake the thought that behind his glib words, Mark had been a little down. Not that it should matter. Honestly, she couldn't be expected to check his emotional temperature. He had friends . . . Or did he?

She frowned as she turned down a long country road lined by slat fences on one side and shaded by large oaks. She hadn't seen Mark out with anyone—male or female—since he'd arrived. Maybe he was still licking his wounds over his divorce. She didn't know much about it except that Arlene had been a wild child looking for someone to support her "fun" habits, according to Mark's sister. Roxie's theory was that once the novelty of being married wore off, Arlene had started jonesing for excitement.

In contrast, Susan knew how to savor, and even relish, simple things. Things like puppies. Not that she wanted one herself, of course, but she could appreciate the draw.

" 'Don't bring one home,' " she mimicked Mark. Ha! If he knew Dad's opinion on animals in the house, he'd never say that.

But of course, Mark didn't know her dad; very few people outside of his aging drinking circle really did. Over the years, Dad had isolated himself, and unless Mark became a patron of the Bigger Jigger, or was the son of one of Dad's old high school buds who frequently provided rides when the whole crew was too toasted to drive, it was highly unlikely they'd ever meet.

That suited Susan just fine. She didn't want to explain her dad or his problems to Mark. People always assumed that all her dad had to do was decide to quit drinking, and that would be that. They didn't understand that it would take more than a mere decision. He'd have to admit his problem and then seek medical help, and he wasn't willing to do either.

Heart heavy, she sighed. *I'm getting maudlin. I need a puppy hug worse than I thought.*

Good thing she was on her way to get a fix. With a sigh, she turned into the animal shelter drive and parked the Jeep.

Chapter
13

"I can't believe this." Susan turned her car down the tree-lined road that led to her house. "I'm a sensible woman and I never make decisions based on emotions. I know the cost of that better than most." She pulled into the driveway and parked, then turned to look at the puppy sleeping on the front seat of the Jeep.

"That can't be comfortable, Krypton," she said, trying his name on for size. The shelter's staff, obviously strained beyond their limits, had dubbed him Frank, which was ridiculous for such a stately puppy.

Well, he wasn't *always* stately. Right now he was on his back, paws in the air, sound asleep. His tail and ears hung over both sides of the seat, his soft pink belly and privates exposed for the world to see.

"Must you show the naughty bits?"

He opened one eye and looked at her from up-side down, gravity making it appear as if he was grinning.

"You have no modesty. Not even a little."

His tongue lolled out, along with a strand of drool.

"Lovely. I throw my principles to the wind, pay to bust you out of the brig, risk being mocked by Mark Treymayne, and *this* is what I get."

The puppy stirred, blinking sleepily as he slowly rolled onto his stomach. He yawned so widely that she giggled.

"You'll break something if you don't stop that." She rubbed his ears and he grunted, snuffling at her hand. "You're just *too* cute."

Susan undid her seat belt and threw open the door. "Ready to see your new home? It's a nice place and I'd like to keep it that way, so expect some rules." She found his lead and hooked it to his collar. "Time to meet the fam." She dreaded Dad's reaction. He didn't like most changes, and this was a big one.

Susan collected the bag of toys she'd bought at Mitzi's Pants and Purrs pet store and stood back from the door. Krypton hopped from the seat to the drive and, after a few tugs, started up the walk-way. She let him sniff the flowers and the border, and even lick the stone frog that she'd put by the periwinkles.

"What the hell is that?"

She looked over her shoulder at Ethan, who had walked up to the fence and was eyeing Krypton with wonder.

Susan walked/pulled Krypton over. "This is my new puppy."

"That's not a puppy. That's a colt. Or maybe a small donkey."

"It's a St. Bernard. He's only twelve weeks old."

Ethan's brows rose. "What on earth possessed you to get a St. Bernard?"

"He sort of chose me."

Laughter shone in Ethan's eyes. "Someone suckered you into it, didn't they?"

"No!" She hugged the bag of toys tighter. "I know *exactly* what I'm getting into. I-I wanted a dog for company."

"Uh-huh."

"Wait and see." She turned to go to her house but stopped short when the lead wouldn't go any farther. Acutely aware of Ethan's eyes on her, she tugged on the lead, but nothing happened. She wound her hands in it and yanked, but it felt as if it was tied to a tree.

Frustrated, she looked back and saw Krypton sitting in the middle of the drive, looking like a fat bear, his legs splayed with his puppy belly seeming to hold him upright.

Ethan burst out laughing. "That's some dog!"

"He's a rock."

Krypton's tail wagged and he stood, sauntered to her Jeep, and relieved himself on the back tire.

Ethan whistled. "That's about a gallon. When he gets serious, you're going to need a shovel."

"And a wheelbarrow." She sighed. "Do you know anything about St. Bernards?"

"Only that they get huge, eat a lot, and drool. Oh, and in the movies, they'll bring you a flask of brandy when you're lost in the mountains." He eyed the dog with interest. "Think you could train him to bring flasks? That'd add some spice to poker nights."

"I am not going to train my beautiful puppy to carry a flask," Susan said stiffly. "I just hope I can convince him to make his mountains out here and not in the house."

Ethan reached over the fence and rubbed the puppy's ear. "He's a cute one. What did you name him? He looks like a Butch to me."

"Nope, I named the cutest puppy ever Krypton."

"Krypton? The bad stuff Superman was allergic to?"

"No, that's kryptonite. Krypton was the planet Superman came from."

"Oh, yeah." Ethan looked at Krypton, who looked steadily back, panting heavily, a strand of drool hanging from his bottom jaw. "Well, he's a cute thing."

"I just hope Dad thinks so." She tugged on the lead. "Come on, Krypton, time to meet the old man."

It took her ten minutes to get the puppy into the house. He had to smell and pee on every flower and blade of grass.

The drapes were pulled and Dad was stretched out in his chair. He saw her and started to rise. "Is it dinnertime already?"

She unhooked the lead and placed it on the table by the front door, then went to open the curtains, Krypton snuffling behind her.

"What's that?"

Dad's voice was sharp, so she met it with a sharp one of her own. "My new dog."

"I'm allergic to dogs."

"No, you're not. That's just something you say to keep from having one in the house."

Dad pushed the ottoman out of the way and

stood, hanging on the chair arm as he found his balance. He was still wearing a T-shirt and pajama bottoms. He squinted at the dog.

Krypton sat and stared back, his head tilted to one side as if trying his mind-control skills. *Don't even try*, Susan thought. *Dad's not the kind to—*

Dad's eyes widened. "Wait a minute! That's— that's one of those dogs that carries a brandy flask!"

What is it with you men? She said primly, "They use St. Bernards as rescue dogs in the Alps."

Dad eyed the dog with newfound interest. "Think we could teach your dog to carry a flask—"

"*No.*"

Dad put his hands on his hips, his old pajama bottoms crinkled and worn. She bet he had four new pairs in his dresser, all unopened. He refused to throw out any of his clothes until they were unwearable.

To Susan's surprise, Dad reached forward and tentatively rubbed Krypton's ear.

The dog just continued to sit, panting, looking as relaxed as if he'd been there his entire life. "I bet he would carry a flask if we asked him, wouldn't you, boy?"

The puppy's tongue lolled out one side and Susan would have sworn he grinned.

Susan had to smile. "Dad, I have to get to work.

Do you think you could watch Krypton until I get back?"

Dad rubbed his chin. "I don't know. What do I have to do?"

"Take him outside each hour, so he'll learn to go there and not on my new floors."

Dad looked leery. "Anything else?"

"Make sure there's water in his new dish. I'll feed him when I get home."

"That's it?"

"Don't let him out without his lead. I don't want him to run into traffic."

Krypton yawned widely and lay down, as if to say running was completely out of the question.

Dad eyed him approvingly. "He doesn't have much energy, does he?"

"Mitzi said Krypton was very laid back."

"Seems to be." Dad bent down and looked Krypton in the eye. "We need a better doggie name for you."

"Dad, he's my dog. You can't just rename him."

He blinked at her. "What? Oh, right. What did you call him again?"

"Krypton. After the planet where Superman was born."

"I like Ricky better."

"Well, he doesn't. We had a long talk about

it in the car and he agreed Krypton was a fine name."

Dad chuckled. "He's a talker, is he? Well, if he said that, then it must be so."

"Thank you for watching him."

"No problem! It's good to be able to do something for you, for a change. Watching the pup will be fun. In fact, I was thinking of going down and playing some pool later on with the guys." Dad tilted his head as he looked at Krypton. "He's mighty big. Do you think he'll fit in that basket on my bike? I'd like to take him to—"

"*No*. He's not to go anywhere. You're going to have to stay here." At Dad's crestfallen expression, she added, "When I get home from work, I'll—"

Her cell phone rang and she pulled it from her purse. "Hello? Yes. Oh, hello! Ms. Woods, I appreciate your calling back. The reason I'm calling is— Yes, I understand, but— Oh! Sure. That would be perfect. In twenty minutes? Will that work? Good. See you there." She hung up.

Dad was eyeing her with interest. "Work?"

"Yes. The organizer for this year's First Baptist Bake-Off." Susan almost rubbed her hands together in glee as she smiled at her father. "When I come back, I'll drive you down to the hardware store and Krypton can meet your friends."

Dad sighed, obviously reluctant. "Meanwhile, I have to stay here?"

"Krypton needs you."

As if to affirm this, the dog's tail thunked on the floor.

A reluctant smile touched Dad's scruffy face. "I suppose we can take a nap together, if things get too slow."

An unexpected sparkle of hope danced through her. Maybe this would help Dad stay sober. She gave him a quick kiss. "Thank you. I've gotta go. I'll call in a while and see how you two are doing."

"OK. Just don't call too often. You'll wake us."

Susan called the office, but Mark was on the phone, so she left word with Ray that she was on her way to Micki & Maud's to meet with Jessica Woods. Ray took the message, said he'd send Mark toward the diner as soon as he hung up.

Ray was a much better receptionist than Pat, who rarely answered and often hung up right in the middle of a sentence. At least that seemed to be working out. Best of all, Ray seemed happier. The poor guy must have been lonely down there in the lobby.

Susan parked in front of Micki & Maud's and made her way inside. The small diner was bustling with noise and people, a decided change ever since Micki's daughter had come all the way from New York to run the kitchen. Connie was a certified Cordon Bleu chef, and wow, had she added something to the menu.

Micki wasn't always happy with Connie's selections, but even she had to admit that the customers were pouring in. Susan had even seen people from some of the nearby towns make the trek to Glory just to try Connie's legendary peach cobbler.

Susan thought Connie's lively presence added just as much to the little diner as her extraordinary cooking skills. Though the diner was plain—linoleum floors, a long laminate counter, a scattering of diner-style tables and chairs, and a line of booths along one wall—it bustled with Connie's creative energy.

"Hi, Connie!" Susan sat at the long counter. "Coffee, please, with cream and two sugars."

"French vanilla, hazelnut, or Micki's Original?" Connie flashed a wicked grin and brushed a dark brown curl from her forehead with the back of one hand. "Or a latte double whip?"

Susan groaned. "Don't tempt me. I've put on ten pounds since you came to town. Aren't you due for a vacation soon?"

"And leave Mom to ruin the place?"

"Ruin?" Micki, white haired and sharp as a tack, came breezing through the kitchen door, picked up a pan of dirty silverware, and headed back. "I ran this place just fine before you came, and I'll run it just fine without you, missy!"

Connie chuckled. "Mom's mad because the Asheville paper did an article on my peach cobber."

Susan's smile slipped. "The *Citizen-Times* came here?"

"Yeah, word's getting out. Pretty soon we're going to have to expand this place."

"No, we're not!" Micki stuck her head through the window separating the kitchen from the diner. "Where would we go?"

"I don't know. Maybe Asheville."

Micki's gaze narrowed. "Micki & Maud's started in Glory and it'll *stay* in Glory!" She turned back into the kitchen.

"Mom doesn't like that idea," Connie said.

"I can tell. I thought you two were getting along better."

"We were. She was starting to embrace some of the newer menu items, I agreed to let her keep making Micki's Meat Loaf Madness, and it was working out. But then the paper came and didn't ask Mom one single question—only me. Made her mad." Connie frowned. "The reporter did sort of cut her out."

"That must have hurt."

Connie nodded. "She's put her all into this restaurant. I don't know what—"

The door opened and René walked in looking fine in his fireman uniform. The deep blue complemented his mahogany skin, his black hair was close cut and curly, and his eyes were the most gorgeous green.

He brightened when he saw Susan and ambled over to the counter. "I should warn you, *ma chère*, I'm feeling lucky this week."

Susan grinned. "You say that every week. And every week I prove you wrong."

He chuckled. "Not this week. You'll see."

Connie leaned on the counter and smiled. "René, I hear tell that every time you go to Susan's poker game, you lose your shirt." Her gaze flickered across him. "Rumors like that make me want to take up poker."

His smile widened as his gaze took in Connie's pixielike charms. "Not *every* time. But close!"

Susan sipped her coffee. "René can't bluff worth a bag of beans."

"I can too," he protested. He caught Susan's

teasing gaze and laughed, a warm, delicious sound that rolled as melodiously as his Cajun accent. "Susan Collins, bring your money to the table. Let Uncle René relieve you of that burden." He winked at her and headed to a small table in the back, where Steve Jenkins sat waiting.

Connie watched him go, admiration in her brown eyes. "If I ever burst into flames, send that man to rescue me. That Cajun accent . . . ooh la la. It's sad that Katrina hit New Orleans, but it washed one of the loveliest fish upstream to Glory."

"He still misses it, but says there's nothing left for him to go home to." Susan sipped her coffee. "I wonder if there's more to the story."

Connie's gaze sharpened. "A woman, perhaps?"

Susan shrugged. "I'm not sure."

"All I know is that I need to learn to play poker. It's not fair that every eligible man within twenty-five miles is in your garage, rain or shine, come Wednesday night."

Right. They came to her house, but when the game was over, they all went home. It suddenly struck Susan that being surrounded by eligible men without having one to call her own was a very sorry state of affairs. Connie had already dated at least two of them and was working on a third.

But then, Connie knew how to flirt. Maybe she'd share some of her mad flirting skills?

The door opened again and Mark came in. Dressed in his usual khakis, blue button-down shirt, and loafers, he could have been a model for an L.L. Bean catalog. That heady combination of intelligence and rugged sexiness turned Susan to mush.

Connie apparently agreed. She leaned across the counter to say in a low voice, "If René doesn't come around soon, I just may have a shot at your boss man."

"He's not your type."

"I don't have a type. I just like *men*." Connie eyed Mark like she was judging a side of beef. "I'd like to have me my own accountant. I'd put him to very good use."

"Oh? And what would you do with him?"

Connie's eyes twinkled. "I'd make him do my taxes in the nude."

Susan choked on a laugh just as Mark reached the counter.

Connie grinned at him. "Hello, handsome. What can I get you?"

He slid onto the stool next to Susan, and an instant hum of low excitement began to warm her stomach.

Mark nodded to Connie. "I'll have a cup of coffee, please."

Connie tucked a curl behind one ear and dimpled cutely. "No latte? Espresso? Double-whip mocha?"

"Just plain coffee."

Connie glanced at him from under her lashes as she handed him a cup. "You're one of those guys who like things straight up, aren't you?"

Susan had to bite her tongue at Connie's teasing tone.

Mark chuckled. "You could say that."

Connie started to answer, but her mother rang the bell in the kitchen window. "Order up!"

"That's my cue." She winked at Mark. "I'll be back."

Mark grinned, which made Susan stiffen. Connie needed a bucket of cold water to calm her overactive libido.

Mark mixed creamer in his coffee. "Where's this woman we're to meet?"

"We still have ten minutes. She's coming from Asheville."

He drank some of his coffee. "How did the animal shelter interview go?"

"Great!" She hurried to change the subject. "About this interview—"

"*And?*" His blue eyes quizzed her. "Did you get duped into taking home a puppy?"

"Nope." Though Krypton might be a puppy in looks, he most definitely was not a puppy in weight.

Mark regarded her steadily. "Really? Because someone *might* have called the newspaper office and left a message about the free vet checkup that came with your puppy adoption."

Damn Mitzi Ketteringer and her frickin' efficiency.

Susan smiled weakly. "Busted."

"Hey, I like dogs. Used to have two."

"What happened to them?"

"I lost them in the divorce. Even when you're glad the divorce is happening, you lose things you never expect to. Dogs. My favorite easy chair. The coffeepot that made the *perfect* coffee." He looked down at the cup in his hand. "Although this is pretty close, so I shouldn't complain."

"I don't know much about divorce. I've broken up with a man or two in my time, and I dated a guy in Asheville for a long while, but—" She shrugged. "He owned a grocery store."

"You dumped him?"

"After I caught him in bed with one of his cashiers."

"Ouch."

"No. I could have married him and *then* found him in bed with a cashier."

Mark's gaze darkened. "You're right. It's easier before you get married. I was a fool. I married a woman who gave out every signal that she was irresponsible, immature, and wild."

"You thought you could tame her?"

"I thought I could at least housebreak her." He chuckled, but there was a hint of sadness to it. "You can't make another person change."

Susan sighed. "No, you can't."

He sipped his coffee. "What kind of puppy did you get?"

"A St. Bernard."

He choked on his coffee. "No!"

"I know, I know. You warned me. But for some reason, the phrase *I was wrong* gives me the hives."

"I've noticed. I have the same allergy."

"Maybe it's contagious."

He laughed. "Maybe."

She shifted on her seat, aware that his broad shoulder was brushing hers. "I suppose I should give you the scoop on Jessica while we're waiting."

"Shoot."

"She's a counselor in Asheville, but she takes her grandmother to church here every Sunday and somehow got roped into being the chairwoman for the Bake-Off this year."

"Why did you arrange to meet her here?"

"No one can keep a secret in the presence of Connie's incredible peach cobbler."

He quirked a brow. "Is that going on the newspaper's expense account?"

"Of course." Susan flipped open her purse and pulled out a folder and placed it on the counter. "The background information on Jessica Woods is the usual—where she's from, about her job as a counselor, all of that stuff. And here"—she pulled out another, far thicker folder—"is the information on the Bake-Off, along with past articles we've done."

He looked through the folders, amazed at the information she'd collected. Good God, all of this for a church bake-off?

Susan flipped through her notepad. "I have several questions already. If you think of any as we go, feel free to ask. It's important that we really listen to what Jessica says and how she says it. Sometimes you get more clues from the *how* than you might think."

Mark nodded. She was absolutely fascinating when she was serious.

Her brows knit. "Traditionally, someone from

the church board fills the position of chairperson, yet this year they called in Jessica. She's really nice and I know she'll do a good job, but why didn't they use one of their regular organizers?" She frowned. "It's as if I keep finding more pieces to the puzzle instead of matching the ones I already have."

"I don't see why—"

The door opened and a tall, elegant blonde walked in, her hair pinned in a bun, her business suit appealingly short-skirted. She drew the eye of every man in the room—except Mark.

"That's her," Susan said under her breath, hopping off her stool and heading for the blonde.

While Jessica was certainly attractive, all Mark could think about was how Susan's ass looked in her snug jeans as she crossed the diner.

Susan brought Jessica over and introduced him, and the three of them found a booth where they could discuss the Bake-Off. Over the course of the next hour, Mark was given an entirely new picture of Miss Susan Collins. Even he, a complete novice, could recognize good investigative work when he saw it, and she'd done her homework well. She knew the history of the event, the players involved, and had already seen the possibility for a number of stories.

Jessica Woods was hopelessly outmatched. She was obviously trying not to say anything controversial, thereby proving Susan's theory.

When Susan's insistent questioning shook Jessica until she accidentally let slip that she'd undertaken the chore of chairperson only because her grandmother had forced her into it, things got a bit tense.

"I'm sorry, but I can't answer all these questions. I'm the chairperson for this one year and—I don't know anything about past years."

"Surely they gave you records and—"

"No. No, they didn't. And let me tell you, I complained long and hard about that, too. My grandmother's been a member of this church for over fifty years. She and I have always been close and when she asked me to do this, I agreed." Jessica sighed. "I've regretted it ever since. There are no—"

"Jessica! What do you think you're doing?" Lucy Carpenter's clipped tone broke into their conversation.

Mark instantly recognized the small woman, her blond hair piled on top of her head in the most improbable set of ringlets off-setting an almost wizened face, stood glaring at Jessica. The older woman's face clearly showed irritation and suspicion, her tiny frame almost aquiver with indignation.

Jessica lifted her chin. "I'm talking to some friends."

Lucy's gaze narrowed. "You were told not to speak to the press."

"For heaven's sake, it's a—"

"Perhaps I should call your grandmother. It would upset her greatly to know you're not doing your duty."

"That's low, Lucy, and it would be a lie. Besides, Gram is over ninety and she doesn't need the excitement."

"Neither do we." Lucy cast a hard gaze on Susan, then Mark. "Come, Jessica. Since you're in town, you might as well stop by the church and go through the program."

For a moment, Mark thought Jessica might refuse, but with a sigh, she collected her things and stood. "I suppose I had better go. It was nice meeting you. Sorry I couldn't be of more help."

"Help? Help with what?" Lucy asked sharply.

"Let's go." Without looking to see if the older woman followed, Jessica swept out of the diner. After a tense moment, Lucy followed.

Susan closed her notebook. "That was interesting. We have enough to do a preliminary article now, and that's all I was shooting for."

Mark paid the bill, leaving a generous tip.

Susan looked at the clock over the service window and began to grab her things. "If I hurry, I can get it ready for tomorrow's paper. Are you going back to the office?"

"I still have some tax entries to make."

She nodded and hurried out of the diner, Mark following.

His gaze dropped to Susan's ass as she strode down the sidewalk to the *Examiner* building. Who'd have thought that being the Chief Financial Officer for a small-town newspaper could have so many fringe benefits?

But so far, the best one had been seeing Susan work her magic. Whatever was happening with the Bake-Off, Susan would figure it out.

Chapter
14

Susan turned her face to the blissfully warm water and let it cascade over her body. It was later than usual for her, but Krypton had awoken her at six, begging to go out, and when she'd returned to bed, it had taken her an hour to fall back asleep. Still tired, she'd then slept through her alarm.

She'd dreamed about Mark. Again. It was becoming a habit and she didn't like it one bit. This time he'd been here in her house. They'd been laughing and talking and then she'd led him up the stairs, one kiss at a time.

She grabbed the shampoo and vigorously scrubbed her hair. "You need to grab that man by the collar and get this out of your system," she announced.

Krypton came to see what all of the commotion was about, sticking his head into the shower and licking one of her legs.

She giggled. "Stop that!" She shooed him away

and rinsed her hair, then turned off the water. Today, she would do just that: grab Mark by the collar and—

Her phone rang.

Her hair wrapped in a towel freed an ear and she grabbed the phone.

"Susan?" Mark's husky voice warmed her head to toe. "You need to get down here."

"To the office?"

"To the town square. I think I found a story for the paper."

"Wh—"

"Just get here. I'll be waiting." He hung up.

She tossed her phone on the bed and raced to dress.

"Well, I'll be."

Mark heard Susan's murmured comment as he walked up beside her. She stood in front of City Hall where two long tables had been set up, a number of people milling around them. The tables were covered in bright yellow plastic, and someone had hand-lettered a large sign that read LEMONADE ONLY $1 A CUP, TAX DEDUCTIBLE. He recognized Tundy Spillers's unnaturally red hair as she unpacked several large coolers and ordered anyone who happened to stop by the table to help her set out some napkins. "The Murder Mystery Club is up to something."

Susan's eyes gleamed. "They always are. Whatever they're doing, they've already drawn a crowd. I see Deloris from the library, the mayor, and old Pastor MacMillan." She rubbed her hands together. "C'mon, Treymayne. Let's see what Tundy and her gang are up to."

He followed her, just as curious as she was. The Murder Mystery Club had come into being at the Pine Hills Assisted Living Center when the new activities director had required all members of the center to be a part of a weekly activity or organization. Clara, C.J., and Rose had created the Murder Mystery Club. Rabid *CSI* fans, Rose and Clara spent most of their time watching TV and lusting after Gil Grissom. When they weren't doing that, they were out searching for a mystery to solve.

Mark followed Susan toward the tables, noting that the usual suspects had collected around the two tables. Clara was sitting in her wheelchair wearing a powder blue dress, a pink shawl around her shoulders.

Nearby, Rose Tibbons was dressed in her usual Lady Bird Johnson–style red wig, her bright white tennis shoes planted firmly on the ground. Tall, bony, and dressed in a bright flowered muumuu, she cut an imposing figure as she towered over her companions.

C.J. stood by, smiling vacantly. The old man tended to drift in and out of awareness of where he was and with whom, so Mark was never sure if he was an active part of the Murder Mystery Club or if he just tagged along for the fun of it. Roxie, who visited with the group once or twice a week, said that C.J. was showing signs of improvement now that he was a part of the club.

Tundy was dressed in her trademark pink velour jogging suit, busily pouring lemonade from a pitcher into an array of glasses, splashing as she went.

"Looks to me like a normal old lemonade stand. Maybe they're trying to raise money for something," Mark suggested.

"I don't know." Susan flashed a grin his way. "Let me buy you a glass of lemonade."

They approached the tables, Pastor MacMillan breaking off in midsentence to hurry away. The guy looked exactly the way every Hollywood casting director thought a preacher should—he was tall, gray-haired, with a kindly expression.

As Mark watched, the preacher hopped into the church van and left. "Sheesh. He is serious about avoiding you, isn't he?"

Susan shrugged. "I'll just have to figure out what's going on without his help." She ordered two lemonades for them, C.J. collecting their dollars.

Mark drank his lemonade. "That's pretty good. It even—"

"Thanks!" Clara held out a rubber gloved hand. "I'll take that!" She almost yanked the empty glass out of Mark's hand, settled it on a tray that rested in her lap, then wheeled her chair to a stack of boxes. She dropped the glass into a slot, tugged a notepad from her pocket, scribbled something on it, ripped the paper off the pad, and then dropped it into the glass.

Susan's eyes widened and she whispered to Mark, "What was that all about?"

Mark shrugged. "Who knows? This morning Ray caught them hiding behind the big sign at Micki & Maud's Diner, taking pictures of everyone who came and went."

"What for?"

"I think the word 'dossiers' was mentioned. Ray was rather upset about it, too."

"One of the club members mentioned dossiers when you accosted them after they followed us to Widow Rawlings's house." She mulled this over. "Wait a minute. Who are they making dossiers of?"

"Ray asked that and they got all secretive and then changed their story."

"To what?"

"Tundy said they were really just scoping out 'victims' for their annual candy drive."

Susan chuckled. "They're a lively group."

"Miserably so. I don't think Tundy's been a calming influence, either. In fact, I think she keeps them stirred up."

Susan sipped her lemonade, watching as C.J. helped Deloris Fishbine with some change. "I hope someone will take the time to stir me up when I'm older."

Mark's eyes crinkled behind his glasses. "I think you're more the stirring type than the stirree."

"Could be." Susan grimaced at her glass of lemonade. "A bit sour."

"You expected sweet? From this gang?"

"You have a point."

Susan leaned against the table and waited until Rose wandered near. "So, what's the purpose of this lemonade sale?"

Rose brightened. "We're going to open our very own CSI lab in my bathroom," Tundy called out, and Rose left.

Clara wheeled up to add, "Rose is going to use mine when she wants to shower."

Susan turned to Mark. "This could be a great story."

"Especially when the EPA shuts them down."

"Screw the EPA," Clara said stoutly. "I refuse to register my guns!"

"That's the ATF, not the EPA." Susan frowned. "When did you get a gun?"

Clara sniffed. "Well, I did have one, but Mr. Fostwith—he's the director of the center—said he wasn't comfortable with residents having them, as some are likely to use them when there's no banana pudding or the hot water's not as piping as they like it."

"Sounds reasonable."

Clara nodded. "I'd never use a piece to demand banana pudding, but there've been times when the hot water wasn't so hot and I felt like popping a cap in someone's ass, so I suppose he has a point."

Susan caught Mark's incredulous stare. "Clara, I'm glad you gave it up quietly."

"I tried to hide it, but that darn Nurse Becky is a smart one. She found my stash, and that was that."

Mark seemed fascinated. "I know I shouldn't ask, but where did you hide your gun?"

"Why, in my underwear drawer, of course! It

might not deter an experienced man like you, but it would give pause to some of the pimply faced kids they hire at the center." She cackled. "I put a few thongs in there just to keep 'em guessing!"

Susan chuckled. "I bet you do."

"And they're not going to mess with our lab, either. We need it to solve crimes, like figuring out who tried to kill you, Miz Susan."

Susan sighed. "Clara, no one tried to kill me. It was pure and simple vandalism."

Clara looked disappointed. After a moment, she said, "You know, I've never heard of a vandal doing damage you can't see. Vandals like to break windows and such. *That* would be vandalism."

Mark frowned. He'd never thought of it that way, but . . . "Susan, she might have a point."

Clara beamed. "I'd make a crack investigator, wouldn't I?"

Rose came to stand beside her. Since Clara was fairy-sized, even when she wasn't confined to a wheelchair, Rose's tall, bony height was exaggerated and she looked like some sort of large, gangly bird. "What do these two want?" she asked, her voice sharp with suspicion.

"They just came for some lemonade, like the others," Clara said in a placid tone. "I told them about our CSI lab."

The hint of a smile softened Rose's face. "That'll be the cat's meow. We'll really be able to solve us some cases, then!"

"We'll have fingerprint powders and a microscope and chemicals for telling what brand of lipstick a murderess might be wearing. All sorts of things!"

"Clara," Susan said gently, "Nurse Becky might be mad if you and Rose store chemicals in your bathroom."

"Wait until we get us a dead body to process!"

"I'm pretty sure that would be illegal," Mark said.

Rose scowled. "That's government for you. Always taking this away and making that hard to do."

C.J. roamed nearby, counting the glasses. "There are only twelve clean glasses left."

Clara's face fell. "Only twelve? We could sell twice that much just in the next hour."

Mark shrugged. "You can wash your glasses at the newspaper office if you'd like—"

"Hold it!" Tundy was suddenly there, glaring at Susan and Mark. "Are you botherin' my gang?" She leaned down to Clara and said loudly, "Remember who they are!"

"Who they—" Clara blinked. "Oh, right! The *media*."

Mark couldn't have looked more confused if they'd accused him of being an Eskimo. "What's wrong with being the media?"

Susan had to smile. "Don't you know? We're *evil*." She looked at Tundy. "Speaking of evil, how'd that personal ad work for you?"

Tundy brightened. "Not as good as your 'Dear Bob' mention. Once't that ran, I got six answers! Two were from perverts and one was a Russian guy wanting his green card, but the other three look promising. I'm meetin' one of them tonight for coffee at Micki & Maud's."

"Excellent!"

Mark held up a hand. "Wait a minute. Why is being a part of the media considered 'evil'?"

Susan glanced at Tundy. "Mind if I answer that?"

"No! Go right ahead. I need to count our funds."

Susan turned to Mark. "We, the media, are always trying to trip people up. We investigate and force people to tell the truth and—" She turned to Tundy. "Wait a minute. We do exactly what your Murder Mystery Club does."

"Yeah, and no one likes us, either," Tundy agreed.

"Nope," Rose said, looking rather pleased. "Why, the mayor bought his glass of lemonade and talked to everyone at the table, but he wouldn't even look at us."

"That's OK." Clara grinned, her false teeth blazingly white. "I short-changed him two bucks on his twenty."

"And I spit in his glass when no one was looking!" C.J. added with evident glee.

"That's my man!" Tundy said, patting C.J. on the back.

Mark laughed. "If you all want to wash the glasses in our break room, feel free."

"No," Tundy said firmly, holding her hand up and yanking on a rubber glove. For a moment, she looked like an evil doctor from a cheesy B movie. She plucked Susan's empty glass and placed it on the tray in Clara's lap. "If we wash the glasses, how will we keep track of how many we've sold? We don't want to do no harm to the IRS by cheatin' them out of their money."

Rose harrumphed. "I don't believe we should give money to the U.S. government. What have they done for us?"

"Yeah." Clara nodded so hard her glasses

flopped on her nose. "What's the government done for us?"

Susan was pretty sure all three of the residents from the Pine Hills Assisted Living Center were living off their Social Security checks and were heavily dependent on Medicare, but she wisely held her tongue. "If you run out of glasses, there are some Styrofoam cups in our break room. You're welcome to them."

There was an odd silence as Clara, Rose, and Tundy looked at one another.

Finally, Clara shook her head. "No can do. Our glasses are uhm—" She looked appealingly at Tundy.

Tundy looked at the few glasses left on the table. "They're prettier than Styrofoam ones!"

"But you're running out—"

Tundy waved her hands. "OK, you've both had your lemonade. Move aside so other people can have some."

Susan looked around. No one else was waiting in line, but with a droll look at Mark, she said good-bye and promised to come take a picture of the group for the newspaper, which made them all happy.

Mark crossed the town square toward the newspaper building.

"What in the heck was *that* all about?" Mark asked.

"I don't know, but they're up to something. Did you notice they were all wearing gloves?"

"They probably got them from the lunchroom ladies at the assisted-living center. Seriously, Tundy and the Murder Mystery Club have about as much chance of getting involved in a real crime as Micki & Maud's has of getting a Michelin rating."

"They uncovered Doyle's blackmail scheme."

"By accident, not through their superior sleuthing skills, no matter how Clara and Rose tell it."

Susan couldn't shake the feeling that there was something odd going on. "I don't know. They're up to something and I can't imagine what they're doing with a lemonade stand. It has to be more than a mere fund-raiser." Susan frowned. "Do you think they're trying to collect fingerprints?"

"What?"

"With the glasses. They were wearing gloves, and they refused our offer for Styrofoam cups."

"It's possible, but . . . what good would that do? You'd have to match the fingerprints for them to be of value, and they don't have the resources for that."

"Maybe they don't know that. Whatever they're doing, I'm going to find out."

She shot a sidelong glance at Mark and decided he didn't need to be included in her every move. Soon she'd be the sole editor of the *Examiner*, and it behooved her to hone all of her skills, especially those that could detect a story. Besides, she was beginning to enjoy Mark's company a bit too much. It was endearing that he'd been so excited when he'd called this morning, and even more so when he'd joined her at the lemonade table and actively participated in digging for information.

She wasn't used to this feeling of partnership that was slowly forming. For now, at least, they had the same goals—but once those were gone, nothing would tie Mark here.

Her chest felt hollow and she had to force a smile when Mark opened the door of the office building. *I need to focus on my job and not on him.*

With renewed determination, she decided to discover what it was that Tundy and her Murder Mystery Club were up to—even if she had to buy lemonade every day for a month.

Chapter
15

Dear Bob,

My new puppy has chewed his way through two rugs, a decorative pillow I bought from an Asheville boutique, and the bottom leg of my dining room table. I've tried to discipline him, but he just yawns and goes to sleep.

What should I do? I want to keep this puppy, but my house is starting to look like a war zone.

Signed,

Doggone Tired

Dear Tired,

Get thee to the library and check out one of those *Dog Whisperer* videos pronto! Cesar Milan is a brilliant man. And very hot!

Sincerely,

Bob

The Glory Examiner
August 13, section B3

"Where are you going, Mark?" Roxie smiled at her brother. "Heading to the Bigger Jigger for a beer?"

Mark buckled his seat belt. "I need to return Susan's thumb drive."

"Right now? It's almost eight."

"She might need it before tomorrow." It was a lame excuse to see Susan and he knew it, but he hadn't been able to catch her alone all day, though he'd tried his best. She'd been somewhat elusive, though he'd managed to sneak in another conversation or two.

She always participated with enthusiasm, but he would have rather had kisses over mere conversations. But that was not to be; except for a week ago when she'd yanked him into the bushes and planted one on him, she hadn't initiated a single kiss. *Damn it, she seemed aloof all of the sudden. I don't think I've said or done anything to tick her off . . . or have I?*

The question had nagged him all day, until he'd finally decided there was only one way to find out: he'd have to ask Susan.

Roxie crossed her arms and rested them on his open window. "Mark, what's going on? You left Mother in midsentence."

He shrugged. "Just feeling restless." *Hungry* was more accurate.

"Is it your work? Maybe you need to go back to Raleigh for a few days."

"I'll go as soon as I get the newspaper running in the right direction."

Her expression softened. "I can't thank you enough for doing that. I know you have your business in Raleigh to run and—"

"Nonsense. It's been fun." It surprised him to realize that was the truth.

Roxie looked curious. "Mark, do you like living here in Glory?"

"It's OK, I guess. Do you?"

"For the time being." She smiled, her expression sweet and happy. "Nick and I have something special. I want to see where it leads."

A pang of envy hit Mark. "I'm happy for you two. I keep expecting you to announce a date."

"Mother hates him," Roxie said happily. "She hasn't said a word to him in a month."

"He's lucky." Mother was a much better enemy than friend.

"So am I." She eyed Mark a moment, her smile fading. "What about you? Are *you* happy?"

He narrowed his gaze. "Don't start on me."

She sighed. "Fine. I won't. By the way, Tundy came by looking for Nick and she seemed pretty upset."

"What happened?"

"I don't know, but she said she shouldn't have to find the po-leese in an emergency, that they should find her."

"Did she call nine-one-one?"

"No."

"His office?"

"No."

"So how's he supposed to know there's an emergency?"

Roxie grinned. "I didn't ask and she didn't tell."

"You and your don't ask, don't tell policy. Whole conversations disappear that way."

"It's nice," Roxie agreed.

"It'd make you a lousy reporter."

"I leave that to you and Pat and Susan."

"Not me. Pat and Susan are the pros." He was just starting to realize what that meant. "Susan put together a PowerPoint presentation and . . . Roxie, she is sharp." He explained Susan's plan.

Roxie's eyes sparkled with amusement. "You'd better watch out. If people find out that all it takes is a PowerPoint presentation to change your mind, you'll be in big trouble."

"It wasn't just the PowerPoint. It was more the entire package."

"Oh ho! Was it now?"

"Yes, but not the way you think." Actually, it was exactly the way Roxie thought, but he wasn't about to admit that. There were certain things one did not discuss with one's sister. "Numbers never lie."

"Uh-huh. I think you're growing soft—" She threw up a hand when he started to protest. "That's not a bad thing. We could all use a little softening now and then." She moved away from the car. "If you see Nick, let him know Tundy's on the warpath. He should be at Micki & Maud's, swapping stories with old Sheriff Thompson."

"Will do." Mark left and was soon on his way to Susan's house. He wondered if she'd be glad to see him. Probably not.

A loud horn brought him from his reverie as he turned onto the road leading to Susan's house. He glanced in his rearview mirror, sighed, and pulled to the side of the road.

A large white van followed suit. As he exited his car, Tundy leaned out the window. "Mr. Mark, have we got a story for you!"

"Really? What's happened?"

Clara leaned forward and said in an excited voice, "Someone broke into Miz Tundy's apartment at the assisted-living center!"

"You're kidding!"

"Nope," Tundy said proudly. "Trashed the whole place."

Mark frowned. "Did they take anything?"

"Not that we could see. I think someone's intimidated by our investigate skills and is tryin' to throw a wrench our way."

Rose crowed, "We're hot on the trail and the perps know it! I bet it's the same guy who tried to kill Miz Susan."

"But no one's tried to harm Susan in over two weeks. I think she was probably right in saying it was just vandalism."

"Psssht," Tundy hushed him. "If that's true, then why did someone break into our supplies and try to scare us off? By the way, if you see the sheriff, tell him we got evidence."

Rose nodded. "We dusted the entire room and got over forty sets of prints!"

"Some were ours," Clara said.

Mark frowned. "You dusted for prints? But that's a crime scene—shouldn't you leave that to the police?"

"We're criminal investigators, too. We've got the tools." Tundy's smile faded. "The problem is, we need the sheriff to run these prints through that FBI fingerprint data bank."

"Nick's at Micki & Maud's. Roxie just told me."

"Why in the hell didn't you tell us that before! Time's a wastin'!" Tundy revved the engine and they were off, the tires spitting gravel.

It was a quarter after eight when Mark pulled up to Susan's house.

He walked up the drive toward the stone path that led to the porch, realizing as he neared the garage that the bass boat was gone, along with Susan's Jeep.

Suddenly, he couldn't shake the feeling that something was wrong. *Someone cut her Jeep brakes. What if something else has occurred?*

A flicker of worry traveled down his spine. Surely she hadn't gone fishing alone. Surely she—

WOOF! A huge bundle of fur hit him square in the chest and sent him flying. When he regained his bearings, he realized he was flat on his back in a petunia patch, a huge puppy sitting on his chest, tongue lolling to one side. "Good God," Mark muttered. He pushed the puppy off, rubbing his chest as he sat up.

The dog looked at him. "You're huge!" Mark told him.

Krypton wagged his tail so hard, his butt wagged with it.

"Looking for Susan?"

Mark looked up to see Mr. Collins standing on the porch wearing a ratty housecoat and apparently not much else. Mark scrambled to his feet and brushed the dirt from his jeans. "Good evening. Sorry to disturb you. I came to see Susan, but I don't see her Jeep."

Susan's father rubbed his unshaven jaw, blinking blearily. "I was asleep, but your car door woke me."

"Sorry about that." Mark crossed the walk to the porch. "How are you doing, sir?" He held out his hand.

"Fine. Fine." Squinting as if the streetlight hurt his eyes, Mr. Collins shook Mark's hand and then shoved Krypton inside. "I don't usually take a nap in the evening, but I was up late last night working on—something for Susan."

Mark nodded, catching a strong whiff of soured beer. The first time he'd met Mr. Collins they'd been at a high school ball game and Susan had been a cheerleader. Mr. Collins had rarely come to the games, but he'd come to this one. He'd arrived with two or three other men, all reeking of beer and shouting hellos to Susan whenever the crowd wasn't roaring at the game. He'd felt embarrassed for her, though she'd never shown anything other than pleasure that her father had come to see her cheer.

Mark wondered if she'd been embarrassed but too proud to show it. She had more than her fair share of pride, that was for sure. Just try and help her do something and she'd prickle up like a porcupine.

Mark leaned against a pillar on the porch while Susan's father lowered himself into one of the two rocking chairs, very slowly as if a sudden move might make something break.

"Do you know where Susan is?"

Mr. Collins blinked sleepily and scratched his stomach. "Isn't she here?"

Mark had to hold off his irritation. "No. And it's late, after eight. Does she usually stay out this late when she goes going fishing?"

"No, not that I know of. Course, I was passed out, but—" He caught Mark's expression and flushed. "I mean, I was asleep. I didn't hear her come in, if she did."

The flicker of worry flamed bigger. "Was she by herself?" Mark asked.

Mr. Collins waved a hand. "Lord, no. She never goes anywhere alone."

Mark had to still his irritation. *If this was my daughter, I'd be worried.* "Who did she go with?"

Mr. Collins shrugged. "Couldn't tell you. But that girl has more men friends than you can shake a stick at. If she went somewhere, you can bet some man went with her." As if aware how this could sound, Mr. Collins shot him a hard look. "*Not* that she's loose, mind you."

"I didn't think you—"

"She's not. She's a good girl. One of the best. In fact, I don't know what I'd do without her." Mr. Collins's bottom lip quivered, his watery eyes looked suddenly as if they were swimming in tears. "She's a good girl and I—"

"She's incredible," Mark said hastily. *Susan lives with this every day and never said a word.* He didn't know much about alcoholism, but it might explain why Susan was so determined to do things on her own, and why she'd never invited Mark to her house. He hadn't thought of it before now. This was the way she'd lived . . . and perhaps the way she'd survived.

His heart ached as he looked at the scruffy, unshaven man before him. It explained a lot of things. "Where does Susan usually fish? Perhaps I should check on her."

"Why would you do that?" The old man stretched out his legs and crossed his ankles. "She'll be fine. She always is."

A deep anger stirred Mark's worry. "If you don't mind, I'll just go and check on her."

"On the lake? How? You got a boat?"

"No, but I can check the ramp where she parked her Jeep and go from there." Hell, he'd *swim* the damn lake if he had to. "So if you'll tell me where she usually goes, I'll—"

A car pulled up and parked behind Mark's Mustang. The door flew open and Lucy Carpenter emerged. She was dressed in an olive green poly-ester pantsuit that would have been trendy in the 1970s, and her bleached-blond hair was piled on her head like a huge cinnamon bun. She marched across the lawn as another person climbed hastily from the passenger seat and almost ran to keep up.

She stopped just short of the porch. "I've come for Susan!" the older woman said in ringing tones trembling with hate that would have sounded overacted on a Shakespearean stage.

Her companion caught up with her, a younger man who looked like a surfer dude with blond hair and green eyes. "Hi, I'm the new pastor, Scott Lawrence. I don't believe we've met."

Susan's father wiped his hand on his house-coat and then extended it to the preacher. "Nice to meet you." He sent a wary glance at the blond woman. "Lucy, I don't know what Susan's done to rile you, but I'm sure she'd apologize if she was here."

"Ha!" Lucy said, throwing her head back for emphasis. "You're going to pretend she's not here!"

"She's *not* here," Mr. Collins said. "She went fishing."

"And we're getting worried," Mark added grimly.

Pastor Lawrence frowned. "Should we call nine-one-one?"

"Nah," Mr. Collins said. "She's just late, that's all. No telling when she'll be back."

The pastor looked uncertain, so Mark said, "I'll make sure she gets home safe."

Pastor Laurence nodded and added in an apol-ogetic tone, "Sorry we bothered you so late in the evening. We just had a church meeting and emo-tions sometimes run high. Miss Carpenter and I will just go." He took Lucy's elbow. "Let's get back in the car and—"

She yanked her arm free and approached Mr.

Collins. "Look here, Collins. I came to see your daughter and I'm not leaving until I do, so you'd better go and get her!"

Mark glanced at the new pastor, who gave an apologetic shrug. "She was determined to confront Susan. Perhaps it would be better if it happened here rather than in church Sunday."

Lucy rounded on the pastor. "I thought you came here to support me!"

"I came to keep you from doing something you'd regret."

Disdain oozed from her voice. "Had Pastor MacMillan come with me, *he* wouldn't have lamely stood by and let that *drunk* tell us what's what!"

Mr. Collins's face crumpled as if someone had slapped him. "I'm no drunk!"

"Ha! Everyone knows you are. I used to feel sorry for Susan, having to deal with your lazy, no-good ass, but no more. She's gone too far, and I'm paying the price with—"

Scott put a hand on the secretary's arm. "Mrs. Carpenter, you can't hold the newspaper responsible for rumors when all they did was write an article that raised some fairly simple questions about our Bake-Off."

Lucy's face turned red under her makeup. "Ever

since they started asking questions, people have been whispering and suggesting ugly things about Pastor MacMillan!" Her small eyes narrowed. "It's been *hell* and I won't put up with it any longer. I want a retraction—or *else*."

"Or else what?" Mark asked.

"Or . . . or . . . or . . ." Lucy stamped a heel. "I demand a cancellation of my subscription and a *total* refund."

"I'm the financial officer for the paper and I'll be happy to take care of that tomorrow. Right now, I need to find Susan. She went out in her fishing boat and hasn't come back."

Scott looked concerned again. "Do you think something's happened?"

"I don't know, but I am on my way to find out."

"I should go with you."

"Thanks, but I think you've got other things to do right now. If I need help, I'll call the sheriff."

Scott nodded and turned back to Lucy. "We'd better go."

"I am not le—"

"Yes, you are," Scott said in a steady voice. "We're going back to the church office to discuss this. I'm sure there's something we can do to smooth things over."

Lucy obviously wanted to argue, but the fact

that Susan wasn't available left her with no recourse. It took the pastor another minute or two, but he eventually got the furious church secretary back in the car and drove away.

"What a mess," Mark muttered. Susan had certainly stirred things up. He'd never again doubt the power of the press.

"You're wasting your time looking for Susan," Mr. Collins said, giving a mighty yawn. "She's just having a good time fishing while—" His gaze flicked to the street beyond, and he smiled. "Yep, there she is now."

Chapter
16

Mark turned as a car door slammed. Susan, drenched head to foot, was saying good-bye to someone as she collected fishing gear and life vests from the back of the car.

Leaving Mr. Collins behind, Mark headed out to help, but she'd finished and was waving off her ride before he reached her.

She didn't look pleased to see him, but he was happy to see her—and not just because her wet T-shirt was hugging her curves in a very titillating way. She could have been hurt or drowned. His heart sang a joyous song that he refused to examine. "What happened?"

"Someone drilled a hole in my boat."

His happiness stuttered to a halt. "*What?*"

"Yeah, I felt the same way," she said sourly. "That bass boat's a cherry. Or was, until someone drilled through the hull." She scowled, her hair plastered back from her face, her pale skin gleaming under the streetlight. "I'll have to get some fiberglass and patch the damn thing, and then there's the gel coat to worry about and—"

"I don't give a damn about your boat."

She looked startled. "That thing is a Gambler, one of the best ones they make! I saved for three *years* to buy it and now—" She went on, but he couldn't listen.

He was just so glad she was standing there, able to storm at him, her long red hair plastered to her neck and shoulders, her wet eyelashes spiked around her blue, blue eyes. He wanted to grab her up and hold her, to bury his face in her neck and tell her how happy he was to just see her.

But her father stood watching from the porch. "Where's your boat?"

"Swamped, but safely tied up at the marina." She walked toward the house and pulled her wet hair to one side. She wrung it out on the lawn, great fat drops trickling to the grass.

There was a huge bang as, from the inside of the house, something large thudded against the screen door.

Mr. Collins shook his head. "Your dog is going to break that door."

"Just let him out," Susan said.

"Heck no. He'll just want to lick you, and he's

liable to catch something from that dirty lake water you're wearing."

"Thanks," Susan said with a sardonic glance. "I'm sure he appreciates your concern."

"I'll go and feed him. That will settle him down." Mr. Collins went inside and they could hear him talking to Krypton.

Susan dropped her tennis shoes on the lawn, where they landed with a splash. "What are you doing here, Treymayne?"

"Me? Oh. I ah, I came by to . . . to return this." He fished the thumb drive out of his shirt pocket.

"You couldn't have waited until we were in the office?"

He shrugged. "It's a good thing I came. Lucy Carpenter showed up before you returned and she was hopping mad."

"Lucy?"

"She says people are talking about Preacher MacMillan because of all the questions you've been asking around town. It took both me and the new preacher to talk her out of confronting you here in your own yard."

"Hmm. That's very interesting."

"You don't look surprised."

"The only thing that's surprised me today is my

boat sinking right out from under me. We didn't notice we were taking on water until we were out in the middle of the lake."

"Good God! Are you sure you're OK?"

She shot him a look brimming with irritation. "My boat is underwater—so no, I'm not okay!"

He threw out his hands. "Easy, I was just trying to figure out what happened."

She grimaced. "I know. Sorry. It's been a long day. We went out—"

"Wait. Who's 'we'?"

"Doc Wilson. He and I fish together once in a while. Anyway, we went out to our favorite cove and were just setting in when we noticed water lapping at our feet. At first I thought it was the plug, though I checked it before we lowered her into the water."

Damn, it was hard to think when she was close by. With her hair slicked back, he could see the line of her face clearly. Even drenched head to toe, she looked as sexy as most women who'd spent hours on their appearance.

The porch door slammed as Mr. Collins reappeared. He shuffled to them, stopping just short to eye Susan's drenched state with a shake of his head. "Did you save the fishing rods?"

She jerked a thumb toward the pile of equipment by the road. "Yeah. Two cushions floated away, though."

"Those'll be expensive to replace." He shook his head. "You just missed Mrs. Carpenter."

Susan smiled wearily. "So Mark was telling me. That's the best news I've heard all day."

Mr. Collins frowned. "It wasn't good for me or Mark here. We had to listen to her." He glanced around. "How bad is your bass boat?"

"It's submerged in Lake Hope."

"What did you do?"

She sent her father an exasperated glance. "I didn't *do* anything. Someone drilled a hole in it."

"Why would they do that?"

"I don't know, but it pissed me off."

Mark realized Susan's words were more clipped than usual. "You think it's our murderer?"

"Do you have to call him that?"

"Until you prove it otherwise, yes."

"Well, he still sucks at it."

Mr. Collins's brows lifted. "Murderer?"

Mark shot him a hard glance. "This is the second time your daughter has been the victim of foul play, Mr. Collins. Someone cut her brake lines a few weeks ago, and now that person's drilled a hole in her fishing boat."

"*But*," Susan added, "whoever it is, they are

really bad at it, so you don't need to worry that I'll die anytime soon."

Mr. Collins rubbed his chin. "That Lucy Carpenter was pissed off. Think she might've done it?"

Susan's eyes narrowed. "Whoever it is, messing with my bass boat means *war*."

"That's my girl," Mr. Collins said approvingly.

"Doc had just found a great fishing hole, too."

Her father blinked, suddenly looking older and confused. "You usually go fishing with old Sheriff Thompson."

Susan gave her father a tired smile and patted his arm, her voice softening. "I told you I was going fishing with Doc this morning, remember?"

"I must have been sleeping when you told me." He gave an uncertain chuckle. "I sleep like a log sometimes."

Susan's shoulders drooped as if she were exhausted.

Mark turned to Mr. Collins. "I think a pot of coffee is in order. Mind if I make some?"

"No, no, son. Go ahead—"

"Mark," Susan began, "there's no need for you to—"

"It's as much for me as for you." He slipped his arm around her shoulders and led her toward the house.

"Mark, seriously," Susan said. "There's no need to make coffee. I need to put the life vests away and—"

"I'll get them on my way out. You just want them stored in the garage, right?"

"Yes, but—"

"Is it locked?"

"No, but—"

"Then what's wrong, Collins? Afraid my coffee's too strong for you?"

She gave him a flat stare. "I'm not afraid of anything. I just need to get that equipment inside."

"Yeah. It might get wet."

A reluctant smile tugged at her mouth.

Having scored his point, he reached for the door, but she was quicker, grasping the door and holding it for him instead. Her gaze met his, challenging him in every way.

He winked.

Her cheeks pinkened and she turned on her heel and led the way to the living room, Krypton trotting up to greet them.

Mark looked around and silently whistled. "Wow. Someone's been watching HGTV." Everything was new, modern, and bespoke quality. Well, everything except the broken-down lounge chair by the fireplace. Mark had a suspicion why that particular piece occupied the center of the room like a shabby throne.

Krypton ran in behind them, licking whatever fingers he could reach and wagging his huge tail. Mark watched as the dog flopped on the rug before the fireplace and completely covered it. "Good God, he's getting big."

Susan smiled, rubbing the dog's ear. "He's a wee, tiny thing, aren't you, Krypton?"

The dog gazed adoringly at Susan as Mark headed out of the room. "I'll make some coffee," he said as he went.

"Yes, please!" Susan said fervently.

Mark was impressed by the kitchen's granite countertops and professional appliances. After a brief search he found the coffeemaker, which looked like something one might see on the space shuttle. Then he found the coffee and creamer in a convenient cupboard, right where he would have placed them himself.

He heard the murmur of voices from the living room but made no effort to listen to the conversation. Susan wouldn't appreciate him knowing or seeing more than he already had.

His stomach growled and he realized he hadn't had dinner. It was unlikely that Susan had, so he found some soup and bread and enough ham and cheese to make sandwiches.

Moments later, he had the soup on the stove, sandwiches made, and the coffee ready. *Not bad for a bachelor man.*

He heard Susan's voice. "Go to sleep, Dad."

Her father's answer was indistinguishable, but Susan answered, "I know. It'll be OK. I promise."

Mark's throat tightened. The child was the parent. It saddened him to hear the matter-of-factness in Susan's voice. How long had it been so? He tried to remember Susan in high school and found his images of her were of a self-sufficient, coolly regal girl who had no time for anyone or anybody.

He poured two cups of coffee just as she walked into the kitchen, Krypton padding behind her. Sometime in the process of putting her dad to bed, she'd stopped to change into a dry T-shirt and jeans. Her damp hair was tied with a bright green band, and the faintest hint of color was back in her cheeks.

Mark handed her a steaming cup. "How's your dad?"

She held the cup in both hands, cradling the warmth as Krypton went to sniff the stove, then settled down across from it as if on guard. "He's gone to bed. He hasn't yet slept off—" She looked away.

"He seemed tired," Mark said noncommittally. "So do you."

"It's nothing that a good cup of coffee won't fix." With a strained smile, she crossed to the stove. "Whatcha got cooking?"

"A little soup and I made some sandwiches. Thought you could use something warm to eat after being dunked."

She looked surprised. "Thank you. It . . . it smells delicious."

His heart ached as it dawned on him how alone she was. She gave the impression of being surrounded by friends and of possessing an active, successful life—well, she *was* successful and she *did* have a large number of friends. But he wondered how many of them were aware of her father's condition, of her responsibilities, and how she'd shouldered the burden of his total care, all without complaining.

He found some bowls and dipped out some soup, then put it on the plate with the sandwiches, and placed them on the counter. Krypton watched with an air of long suffering.

Mark eyed the dog. "Don't even think about it."

The dog sighed and dropped his head to his paws, looking as forlorn as could be.

"Aww, poor baby," Susan said.

"Baby? He's a horse."

She grinned. "He may be a horse, but he's *my* horse."

"Good thing I didn't send you to the prison to do a story. You might have adopted an inmate."

She chuckled. "You wouldn't have been able to walk away from this puppy, either. He knows how to look pathetic. Check his expression now."

Mark glanced down at the dog, who sadly met his gaze, though he never raised his head. Mark had to fight a grin. "That's desperate."

Krypton wagged his tail weakly.

Mark shook his head. "Pathetic."

Susan bent to pat the dog, whose tail began to wag in earnest. "Poor baby puppy. So misunderstood. Tell mean Mr. Mark that you're a good dog, the very best ever."

"Go ahead, pander to him," Mark said dryly. "He's incorrigible."

She rubbed Krypton's ears, making the dog blissful.

Mark pulled out a stool at the granite counter. "Here. Have a seat."

She sat and hugged the coffee cup to her, shivering a bit. "What an evening."

He pushed her soup closer and sat on the stool beside hers. "Here, it'll warm you up." He waited until she'd eaten a few spoonfuls of soup, a bit more color returning to her face. "Is the boat salvageable?"

"The engine's ruined, but the rest of it's waterproof. It'll just take some time to repair." She took another swallow of soup. "Thank you for making this. It's just the thing. I should take a hot shower, but I'm too tired."

Mark was silent a moment, eating his sandwich. "I really believe this is another attempt on your life."

"I don't believe that. Everyone knows I'm a good swimmer."

"I didn't," he said promptly.

She raised her brows. "I was on the school swim team and we won regionals that year."

He should have known that. "I didn't really pay attention to much in high school."

"Yes, you did. I never saw anyone more attentive to our cheer squad than you."

Mark had to grin. "I was young, foolish, and didn't understand the concept of quality."

"Uh-huh." She took a bite of her sandwich, her expression reflective. "Why would anyone want to kill me?"

"Maybe they just want to scare you." He went to refill their coffee mugs. "It sure feels like it to me. When I arrived and you weren't here—" He shook his head and placed the mugs in front of their plates. "Who would want you dead or harmed or scared off or whatever is going on?"

"The only controversial piece I've written lately is about the Baptist Bake-Off."

"Lucy Carpenter is angry, but she doesn't seem the sort to drill holes in a boat or scoot under a Jeep and cut the lines."

"Yeah, she's more the knife-you-in-the-shower type. Subtlety is not her strong suit. Still, I can't think of anyone else who might be mad enough to do something like that."

He sipped his coffee. "By the way, I ran into Tundy and the gang on my way here, and someone broke into her apartment at the assisted-living center."

"Oh no! Was anyone hurt?"

"No one was injured. But what's interesting is that they think the same person who cut your brake lines is responsible for the break-in."

"How did they come to that conclusion?"

"I don't know, for they don't have a shred of evidence, yet in an odd way it makes sense. Someone in town is upset and they're letting us know."

Susan mulled this over. "It's possible, I suppose. They have good instincts; the Murder Mystery Club has uncovered far bigger mysteries than this one."

"I don't give a damn about mysteries, so long as you're safe." He collected their empty sandwich plates and carried them to the sink.

"There's no one else who would want to scare me." Susan sent him a glance from beneath her lashes, aware of how nice this was, sitting in her cozy kitchen and chatting with someone who seemed genuinely worried about her.

She was glad Mark was here. She wished Dad had been more sober, but that was probably too much to ask. She searched Mark's face for some sign of pity or condescension, but all she found was concern and determination.

She took another spoonful of hot soup, feeling stronger by the minute. If Mark hadn't been here when she returned, she would have dealt with Dad, then taken a shower and maybe, much later, finally eaten a sandwich. It felt good to be taken care of.

"So who would have drilled a hole in my boat?" she mused.

"Maybe someone from out of town? Someone who didn't know you could swim?"

"Like who?"

"Hmm. There's the new pastor."

Susan laughed. "He might be the sexiest pastor ever, but he's no killer."

Mark's jaw tightened. "You think he's sexy?"

"Every woman in town does," she said matter-of-factly.

"What do you all do? Meet and discuss men?"

"Nothing so formal but that sort of covers it. We share our intel." She grinned. "That's how I know he's a pretty upright guy. Besides, he has no motivation. What did someone have to gain by drilling a hole in my boat?"

"I don't know," Mark said grimly, "but if I find out, I'll make sure he never does it again. I'll—" He clamped his mouth closed, his lips almost white.

She sipped her coffee, uneasy with his obvious concern. She wasn't used to having someone worry over her, and she found it flattering yet unsettling.

Not that she needed someone to take care of her; she'd been on her own for too long. Besides, she couldn't ask anyone else to put up with Dad. That was her job and not one she'd willingly dump on someone else's shoulders, especially someone she cared about. It was a good thing Mark wasn't long for Glory. As much as she hated to admit it, she could easily get too used to having him around. She cleared her throat, trying to dislodge a ball of sadness.

Buck up, Collins, and get it over with. "Mark, thanks for making dinner." She got off her stool. "Guess I should get in the shower. I really appreciate that you stopped by."

Krypton lifted his head and then rolled to his feet, shambling off toward the living room.

Mark had his coffee cup halfway to his mouth, but at her statement, he replaced it on the counter.

Susan stretched and yawned. "It's been a long day."

"Yes, it has been." He slid off his stool and shoved a hand into his pocket. His arm rippled with muscles at the small effort, and Susan's mouth went dry. "Here. Before I forget."

He held out her thumb drive. As she reached for it, he closed his big hand over hers. "Susan, I—"

A sound came from the front of the house, and Susan's heart sank.

Mark frowned. "What was that?"

She pulled her hand free, dropping the thumb drive on the counter as she headed for the living room. "That was the screen door."

Mark followed silently. Krypton stood by the front door, wagging his tail in vain hope. He sighed and lumbered to his pile of blankets and began gnawing on a toy.

"Your father left?" Mark asked.

She nodded mutely, worry shadowing her eyes. "He hasn't been feeling well today and I'd hoped—" She turned her face away, but not before he caught the faintest downturn of her lips.

"Will he be back tonight?"

"Probably not. Once he's gone—" She shrugged and forced a smile. "That's OK. It means more hot water for my shower. Thanks again for coming, Mark." She opened the screen door and held it there.

As he walked through, he looked down into her face, her blue eyes so clear, her red hair starting to dry and curl about her face. Mark lifted a hand to her cheek. "I hate for you to be alone."

She moved away. "I'm not. I've got Krypton for company, and if I get lonely, I only have to make a phone call. I'm not a hermit, you know."

He forced a smile to match hers. "I'll get your

286 KAREN HAWKINS ~

life vests and fishing equipment from the sidewalk where you left them."

He collected the pile of fishing rods, tackle, and life vests. As he gathered the last one, he turned back toward the porch. She was still holding open the screen door, a wistful expression on her face.

That did it. He carried his burden to the porch and stacked it neatly to one side of the door. Then he slipped an arm around her waist and yanked her close. Without giving her time to protest, he covered her mouth with his and kissed her. The banked passion that simmered between them roared to flames, and it was several moments before he lifted his head and gulped air. "God, you drive me crazy."

Her eyes warmed with laughter. "I don't mean to."

"You're not going to make me believe that." He leaned closer, resting his forehead to hers. "Just how big is your shower?"

Her gaze never left his. "Umm . . . it's normal sized—"

"Big enough for two?"

Susan's mouth went dry. She craved Mark's touch. Twice this evening he'd almost brought her to tears with his calm tenderness. He was such a good guy, and she found that wildly attractive. Here was a man who, if he said he'd be somewhere, would be there. A man who could cook a meal when he saw you needed one. A man who listened and didn't judge. The sort of man one could fall hopelessly head over heels for—if he was planning on staying.

But this man wasn't. He'd been very clear about that. All he promised was a temporary haven in the storm.

A more sensible woman would stop this right now. But she was tired of being sensible. Right now, she just wanted to *feel*.

She slid her hands up his arms, his skin warm beneath her fingertips. It was time to do something purely for herself, something that would wipe all of her cares out of her head.

She slipped an arm around Mark's neck and said in a sultry tone, "I'm not sure my shower's large enough for us both, but I'm willing to find out." With a smile, she took his hand and led him inside and up the stairs.

Chapter
17

She led him to her room, where he got a blurred impression of muted colors and a huge, beckoning bed. Mark swung her into his arms, pushed the door closed, and carried her to the mounds of pillows and blankets.

He yanked his clothes off as she found a condom in her bedside table. He donned it with hands shaking with eagerness.

As she quickly undressed, each inch of silken skin she revealed made him more crazed for her.

He sank into the bed beside her, his foot hitting something on the floor on his way. He looked down. There on the rug were a pair of sexy red high heels. He lifted them, dangling them by their straps. "Are these yours?"

She nodded. Reclining upon the mounds of pillows and blankets, she looked like a Greek goddess, all seductive hollows and white marble skin. "I have a lot of shoes like those."

"I've never seen you wear them."

Faint color touched her cheeks. "I suppose I should. I just don't enjoy the sort of clothes that go with them."

His grin was wicked. "Then maybe you shouldn't wear anything with them."

Her eyes widened as he slipped the shoes on her feet, marveling at the delicate curves of her legs. She was so beautiful; these fools in Glory had no idea what a jewel was in their midst.

She laughed softly and stretched out one leg, her calf flexing sexily. His cock tightened even more and he captured her foot and placed a kiss to the delicate hollows around her ankle. She shivered and sighed his name. Then he pressed kisses on the inside of her calf, the hollow of her knee, and higher still. He caressed the inside of her thighs, savoring her warm skin beneath his lips.

When he reached her silken center, the red shoes came down to rest on his back. He gently pressed a kiss between her thighs, making her gasp and arch against his mouth. God, she tasted sweet! He teased and tempted, swirling his tongue over her as she writhed in passion.

He could tell she was close to release so he pulled back, wanting to savor it with her. He lifted himself over her and pressed the tip of his hard cock against her, looking deep into her eyes.

Her face awash with passion, she squirmed against him, begging him. It took all of his strength to hold off, but he did, tasting her neck and face, capturing her mouth with a deep, searching kiss as he slowly, so slowly, lowered himself into her.

Instantly her tight wetness grasped him, and Mark had to fight his own passion as well as hers. Never had he felt such a wanton wetness. His body went rigid with desire as he forced himself to move inside her with a slow, relentless tempo.

She gasped and came against him, clutching him between her thighs, her shoes pressing into his back, sparking fire through him. He groaned, forcing his body to maintain the slow speed.

Susan was soon moaning again, thrashing against the pillows, her dark red hair streaming over them. Mark slipped his arms beneath her shoulders, sinking his hands into her soft hair as he drove deeper into her. She gasped—then passion overtook him and he came deeply inside of her.

Mark awoke from his brief doze and blinked sleepily, his memory instantly returning to the shared shower followed by another passionate romp in this bed. He smiled and reached over—

She was gone. He rolled to his elbow, frowning. Where—then he saw that the bathroom door was open, and he heard the shower running.

He got up, exploring the unabashedly feminine room with interest. He wasn't sure what he'd expected, but this wasn't it. There was a crystal and silver chandelier, while a chair held an open book and a soft throw. He paused before a movie poster. "Lois Lane." He grinned. "Of course."

"And what's wrong with Lois Lane?"

Susan stood in the doorway wearing a towel turban and a purple silk robe that clung in all the right places.

He eyed her appreciatively. "Wrong with Lois Lane? Not a damn thing."

She grinned cheekily. "Good. I hate having to throw a man out of my bed before a good cuddle." She crossed to the bed, hopped onto it, and patted the cover invitingly. "You up for it?"

Strangely enough, he was. He sat beside her, slipped an arm about her waist, and slid them down to recline on the mounds of pillows. "Do you sleep with all of these?"

"Sometimes. I like to have them all around me like a pillow cocoon."

He chuckled. "Is your bed partner allowed inside your cocoon?"

"If he's earned it." She rested her turbaned head against his shoulder, smelling very sweet and sexy. Instantly his body stirred to life.

This was nice. Better than nice, in fact. He'd had passion galore in his marriage, but not much else. Without that something else there was little left as the passion cooled.

In retrospect, the relationship had been doomed to failure from the beginning, but that hadn't stopped his heart from being spectacularly flayed.

After Arlene had left, he'd never thought to find that heady rush of pure, unadulterated desire again. He hadn't, until he'd met Susan.

Which was why she was safe. So long as they had this frantic lust burning between them, his heart would know better than to become engaged. No one touched a hot stove twice.

"Mark, when do you have to go back to Raleigh?"

"Soon. Corporate tax season is just starting to gear up."

"Oh." She traced a lazy finger over his chest. "Roxie says you love your job."

"I do, especially once we started acquiring."

"What's that?"

"We take over businesses that are failing." He grinned wolfishly. "Sometimes I feel like a pirate in a suit."

She chuckled. "You look like one now." They were silent a moment and then she said, "Mark? Can I ask you something?"

"Sure." He snuggled in deeper beside her, breathing in her scent. Damn, he loved how she smelled.

She looked him straight in the eyes. "Where do we go from here?"

Alarms sounded in his peaceful state. "What do you mean?"

Her blue, blue eyes fastened on his. "Even though you're leaving soon, it seems a waste to just let this—" She gestured toward the space— and lack thereof—between them. "—go to waste."

"I suppose we'll just have to make the most of it."

"I thought the same way myself, at first."

"At first?"

She nodded, her expression uncertain.

"And now?"

"There's a problem. I'm afraid I could come to like it."

His heart sank. It would be so easy to say

something ambiguous, something nonthreatening. It was on his tongue to do so, when he met her candid gaze and blurted the truth. "Susan, I'm not staying in Glory. I have a company waiting for me in Raleigh." In addition to corporate taxes due in six weeks, he was scheduled to present two seminars in various states to recruit new team members, and brief the board of directors. "Maybe you could come to Raleigh sometimes. There's no reason why we can't still see each other." *At least while it lasts.*

She sat up, her expression inscrutable. "When will you leave?"

"A month, maybe two if I can swing it."

"And after that?"

"Maybe I could come here on weekends, and you could come there once in a while." He ran his hand down her silken arm. "It will be fun."

"Maybe. I'll have to think about it." She climbed from the bed, her long legs displayed for a moment before the robe settled around her.

His smile faded. "What are you doing?"

"Getting dressed. You should go, too. Dad will come back soon."

Mark watched as she pulled yoga pants and a top from a drawer and hastily donned them, giving him a tantalizing look at her back and ass. She was a wonder, all lean and supple, and he desired her more now than he had an hour ago. She was an incredible partner and they'd made passionate love, bumping their heads and elbows in their hunger to be as close to each other as they could.

"Susan, come back to bed."

She pulled the towel from her head and long ropes of wet hair fell about her shoulders. "I don't think so."

He moved to the edge of the bed and swung his feet to the ground. "You want more than just . . . this."

"Yes." She paused in drying her hair with the towel. "I want things I can't have. I want to know that this is going to last. That this isn't just a weekend event for you and nothing more." Tears glistened in her eyes. "No, it's even more than that. Mark, I want to know that you'll stay with me forever."

He froze. "That's a lot."

"I know it is. I could lie and pretend I don't want that, but I'm not that kind of girl. I thought I could be; that I'd just take this relationship one day at a time and enjoy it, but—" She shook her head, a pained expression on her face. "Mark, I can't. So we need to stop this before it goes any farther."

"Susan, it . . . it takes time to make that sort of commitment. I don't know if I'm ready for—"

She held up a hand and managed a shaky smile. "You don't need to say anything more. I understand. It takes caring. And you don't have that. Not for me, anyway."

"It's not like that—"

"It is for me." She sat on the edge of the chair. "Mark, I can't do this and not fall for you."

"What's wrong with that? If we keep seeing each other, then maybe—"

"You aren't going to stay in Glory."

He frowned. "No, but why can't we—"

"Because I can't leave Dad. I'm all he has."

Mark hadn't expected the conversation to get so serious, but he supposed he should have. Susan was funny and intelligent and steadfast. Suddenly, the question was not if she was enough for him, but if he was enough for her.

He wasn't really sure.

Slowly, he stood. "I guess I'd better go, then."

He dressed silently, his limbs heavy. They walked down the stairs in silence.

He wasn't the sort of man to offer more than he had to give, and if she couldn't accept that— He sighed as he walked through the door. "I'm sorry, Susan."

She managed a smile. "Me, too. See you at the office."

She shut the door and left him on the porch, standing in the cool night air and wondering why his heart ached as if someone had kicked it.

Chapter
18

Dear Bob,

The Baptist Bake-Off is coming soon, and I'm entering my coconut crème cake. My friend "Thelma" has competed for several years and has been telling me to enter for some time, but now that I have, she's mad, saying I'm just trying to steal her thunder.

I want to keep Thelma as a friend, but I want a ribbon, too. She must have a dozen of them and it's time I had one of my own.

What should I do?

Signed,

Cakeless in Glory

Dear Cakeless,

Sounds to me like your friend has a classic case of the Red Ass. You could either ignore her complaints and enter, or you two can find different categories so you're not going head-to-head. By the way, I'd be glad to eat a piece of your cakes and make a recommendation as to which would fit in which category. Just bring them by the *Examiner* office!

Signed,

Bob

The Glory Examiner
August 21, section B3

On Thursday, Mark parked his Mustang and climbed out, looking at the newspaper building. He stood for a long while, noting that Susan's Jeep was parked in its usual spot. That was the only usual thing about Susan nowadays. Since last week she'd been distant, and he absolutely hated it.

He *missed* the old Susan. The one who was comfortable in every situation she faced; the one who'd argue with him at the drop of a hat, and told him exactly what she thought and when. That Susan had been replaced with one who spoke when spoken to, answered any question he put to her, but never initiated one of her own. The whole thing made him feel lonely, somehow.

He shoved his hands into his pockets and turned away, feeling lower than low. How had it come to this? He wasn't a person who made decisions lightly or—

"Mr. Treymayne!"

He turned to find Tundy waving at him from the Murder Mystery Club's lemonade stand. Without anything better to do, he wandered toward her.

As soon as he reached the table, Clara

wheeled up in her chair. "Did you hear about the excitement?"

"No." The table was empty except for three lonely glasses of lemonade.

"I heard about it," came Susan's voice behind him.

She was looking fresh and cool, the breeze teasing a strand of hair from her ponytail. She avoided his gaze as she answered Clara. "I heard Robin Wright yelling that she was going to sue every one of you if she had to."

"Pah." Clara waved a dismissive hand, her fingers sparkling with the Home Shopping Network's finest cubic zirconia and fake emerald rings. "That woman was just mad we wouldn't sell her no more lemonade."

"Why wouldn't you?"

A crafty look settled over Clara's face. "Can't tell you. It's a secret."

"Would you sell *me* more lemonade?"

"Nope."

"What about me?" Mark asked.

"Nope. You neither."

"You guys have a lot of secrets, don't you?" Susan said.

Clara couldn't have looked happier. "More

than any other club in town! Even the Kiwanis!"

Rose, who'd stalked by carrying a box of files, nodded. "Damned Kiwanis think they run the world. Well, *ha!* They don't know half the things we know."

"Oh, I doubt that." Susan leaned against the table, arms crossed over her chest as she shrugged. "But even if it's true, there's no way you could have as many secrets as the Baptists."

Clara stiffened. "I bet we do."

Rose dropped her box of files, plopping her hands on her angular hips. "I *know* we have more secrets than the Baptists."

"Maybe not the Catholics, though," Clara added in a fair tone. "They've had longer to collect secrets than we've had."

Rose thought about this. "Plus they have all of those vaults under the Vatican. Saw a show about that on TV."

"I saw that, too," Clara said. "We might not have as many secrets as them, since we don't have the same storage capacity."

Mark hid a grin, but Susan merely shrugged, obviously unimpressed. "Yeah, well, the Baptists have *real* secrets."

Clara gripped the arms of her wheelchair. "We do, too!"

"Yup." Rose nodded. "More than most people know."

"Like what?" Susan asked, looking suspicious.

Clara and Rose exchanged glances. "Well . . ."

Rose shook her head. "You can't."

"I know," Clara said glumly. "But maybe we can tell her about last night?"

Rose brightened. "That's not a secret."

"Nope. Since Tundy filed a police report on it and all."

Mark could almost feel Susan's interest bloom.

"What is it?" she urged Clara on.

The older woman beamed. "Rose got broke into just like Miz Tundy's!"

"What?"

"Yup." Clara's blue eyes were ablaze with pure happiness. "They broke into the window of Rose's bedroom at the assisted-living center and tore the place apart while we were in the dining room having tapioca!"

"Tore the room apart? As if they were looking for something?"

"Yes, sirree! Turned out all of the drawers and pulled the mattress off the frame and ripped everything out of the closet and—" Clara suddenly waved across the parking lot. "Yoo-hoo! Pastor Lawrence! Want some lemonade?"

The new pastor, who'd been speaking with old Pastor MacMillan, waved and indicated he'd be there soon.

Rose leaned closer to Clara. "Do we want the old pastor to have some lemonade?"

Clara frowned. "I don't know. Ask C.J."

"C.J.!" Rose called. "Come here!"

C.J. was helping Tundy align the three glasses of lemonade on the corner of the far table, but at Rose's call, he came up to her, a wary gleam in his eyes. "Yes?"

"Do we need to sell lemonade to the old pastor?"

He blinked, his white eyebrows arched in surprise. "How would I know?"

Rose snorted her agitation. "You have the list, silly!"

"Oh. Do I?" He pulled a small notebook from his shirt pocket and opened it. "I do, don't I? Who were you asking about again?"

"The old pastor."

"Right." He thumbed through what appeared to be a list of names. Susan was leaning so far over the table trying to see it that Mark feared she might fall.

"Nope!" C.J. slapped the notebook closed and replaced it in his pocket. "We've already got the old pastor's pr—"

"C.J.!" Tundy forced a fake smile and bustled the old man off, looking like the Energizer Bunny in her hot pink sweat suit. "Come along! Other side of the table! Gotta spread out the help, you know."

"Yes, but I was just saying that we've already got old Pastor MacMillan's—"

"I know, I know." Tundy shot a harried glance at Susan. "We *all* heard you, C.J. Now take that big ladle and stir the lemonade. Gotta keep it fresh!"

"But the old pastor—"

"He don't need any more lemonade," Tundy said in a voice that brooked no resistance.

"Oh! OK." Apparently mollified, he crossed to his directed position, took the ladle, opened the top of the cooler, and began to stir the lemonade.

"What we need," Clara said, "is the new pastor to come and get his lemonade." She lifted a hand and called, "Yoo-hoo!"

He waved again but continued his conversation.

Susan had been right; they had to be collecting prints. But why?

Susan smiled. "About this break-in?"

"Who told you about that?" Tundy demanded.

Clara and Rose looked guilty.

"I believe there was a police report filed?" Susan said smoothly.

"Uh. Not yet." Tundy sniffed. "I didn't want to place one, you know, but the director of the center said we had to. Damn fool idea, too. Nothing was taken."

"Nothing?"

"Nope," Rose said. "Though I think they were after my dentures."

"Why on earth would anyone want your dentures?" Clara demanded.

"They're good dentures! Doc Rosenblum made 'em herself, and she promised they're as good or better than the ones you can order off the late-night TV."

"Doc Rosenblum knows her way around dentures," C.J. added from where he stood by the cooler, unexpectedly lucid. "She did mine, too." He used his tongue to pop his dentures out, then popped them right back in. "Never had more comfortable ones in my life."

Mark wondered if he'd ever get that sight out of his mind.

Susan said, "I could see where dentures might be valuable, but these people . . . whoever they are . . . they had to be after something more valuable. Otherwise they would have just broken into Doc Rosenblum's office and gotten more than one pair."

Clara, Rose, and Tundy stared at her.

After a moment, Clara siad, "I'll be damned. I never thought of that."

"Me neither," Rose said. "Humph."

Tundy cocked a brow at Susan. "Maybe you're right. Maybe they were after something else."

Rose piped up, "I think they wanted the dentures *and* our dossiers."

"Me too," Clara agreed.

"Dossiers?" Mark asked. "What dossiers?"

Tundy made a noise like a strangled cat. "You two! Don't be blurtin' out our secrets!"

Clara blinked. "We didn't. We didn't tell Miss Susan a thing about our dossiers. How we had them on every person in town, or how we had pictures of them all, and how we were ferreting out their private information by going through their trash and getting their pri—"

"*Clara!*" Tundy bellowed.

Clara looked sheepish. "Sorry."

"Oh, the dossiers," Susan said in a breezy tone. "I've already heard about them."

"A few people know," Tundy admitted sourly.

"You and Mr. Treymayne here. Oh, and Deloris Fishbine. I don't know how, though I have my suspicions." Tundy eyed Clara narrowly, who stared into the sky as if beholding a forgiving angel. After a disgruntled minute, Tundy added, "Miz Pat knows, and the mayor's girlfriend, that Robin Wright woman, knows. C.J. blurted everything out when she got all huffy because we didn't want to give her one of our lemonades."

Susan suspected that even more people knew what was going on with the Murder Mystery Club but wisely didn't say that aloud. "I wonder how Pat figured it out."

"*I* didn't tell her," Tundy said.

"Neither did I!" Clara said stoutly.

"I didn't mention anything to anyone, either," Rose added.

They all looked at C.J., who was humming a tuneless song as he stirred the lemonade, his hips swishing as he danced a bit.

"Damn it all, this club has got to get some decorum!" Tundy stated. "We can't be gabbing our top secrets all over town!"

Susan nodded sympathetically. "It's tough keeping a secret." She pointed to the box of files at Rose's feet. "I take it those are the dossiers."

Rose nodded. "Every last one."

"Do you think whoever was searching your room might have been looking for them?"

"Why would they look there? We don't keep them in my room. We keep them— Ooof!" Rose glared at Tundy. "You smacked my back."

"Sorry. Saw a fly." Tundy turned to Susan. "Whoever searched Rose's room turned it inside out just like they did mine."

Susan said, "It sounds like they were thorough."

"Cut a hole in my mattress big enough to put your head in," Rose affirmed.

"Next time they might go for C.J.'s or Clara's room. . . ." Susan said thoughtfully.

Mark had to hide a grin when Tundy's eyes widened. He cleared his throat. "Tundy, would you let Susan and me see those dossiers of yours and do a little sleuthing of our own? Maybe we could find out why someone wants those files so badly."

Rose shook her head. "Hell no, we won't let you have the records! Why, you'd print up a story about some nonsense, and then someone would want someone dead—"

"Whoa!" Mark interrupted. "What on earth are you talking about?"

Clara pointed a beringed finger in his direction. "Don't tell us how this scenario works. *We've* seen the shows. We know what's going to happen: how the second a journalist gets involved, some-one starts gettin' killed."

"It happened on *Columbo*," Tundy said, "and *Murder, She Wrote*; *Rockford Files*; *Barnaby Jones*—all of 'em!"

"Even on that *Magnum, P.I.*," Rose added.

"Wooee, he's a hottie!" Clara fanned herself.

"So don't even ask for our dossiers," Tundy concluded. "We don't know if we can trust you, and even if we could, we don't want to be the cause of no murders."

Mark frowned. "Tundy Spillers, you know me and you know you can trust me."

"I know you a little," she said grudgingly.

"You know me a lot. You were my sister's maid for two years!"

"True."

"And then you lived with me and my mother when you came to take care of her when she was sick."

"Which was the hardest job I ever had." Tundy looked at Clara. "After taking care of cranky old Mrs. Treymayne, you three are a piece of pie."

"I know," Clara said. "She used to visit us at the home and it drove us all crazy. Her daughter Roxie is nice, though."

Rose agreed. "But her momma, whew. She was a piece of work. We used to hide in the broom closet if we saw her coming."

"I liked the broom closet," C.J. added from the lemonade cooler, a wistful tone in his voice.

"We all did," Rose agreed.

"That was a good closet," Clara added. "Smelled like lemon wax."

"Besides," Tundy said, eyeing Mark, "you haven't always been a good judge of character. Look at that woman you married."

Beside him, he could feel Susan stiffen. "I'm a much better judge of character now."

Tundy turned to Clara and said in an undertone, "Arlene had a pretty face, but whew, she was hard as nails. She had the biggest fake boobs I ever saw, and she a little bitty thing, too. It's a wonder she didn't tip over and fall face-first when she walked, 'cause she sure had huge—"

"Tundy, I think that's enough." Mark tried not to look Susan's way. He could just imagine the disgust on her face. "My past marriage is just that—in the past."

"Besides," Susan chimed in, "we really want to hear more about those dossiers. May we just take a quick look at them to see what you have that someone might be looking for?"

Clara sniffed. "We can solve our own mysteries, thank you very much! Why, that's what a Murder Mystery Club *does*, is solve mysteries."

"That's right," Rose said, looking down her beak of a nose at Mark. "What sort of investigators would we be if we handed our secret information over to someone the first time he asked?"

"Especially," Tundy added in a dark voice, "to people like *you*."

Clara blinked. "People like Miss Susan?" She leaned toward Tundy. "Are we against redheads? 'Cause if we are—" She glanced up at Tundy's own red hair and then over to Rose's red wig and gulped. "We're in a heap of hurt."

"No!" Tundy said, looking offended. "I mean the *media*. They work for the newspaper, remember?"

"Oh." Clara looked at Susan and Mark with a wistful expression. "I sort of like havin' my picture in the paper."

"And we love having it there," Susan said without missing a beat. "In fact, if you're interested, I'd love to put you all on the front page selling your lemonade."

"The *front* page?" Rose patted her crooked wig while C.J. said, "Hot damn! I like bein' in the paper!"

"I don't know about that," Tundy said. "This here's our undercover operation and I don't think we should—" She caught Susan's gaze and clamped her mouth closed.

"Undercover?" Susan asked gently. "The lemonade stand? What information were you collecting here?"

"No! I didn't say 'undercover.' I meant to say ah, under, ah, under *butter* operation."

Clara blinked behind her huge glasses. "Tundy Spillers, that doesn't even make sense."

Rose shook her head. "Nope. Not a bit."

C.J. scratched his head. "Under butter? We don't have any butter here."

Tundy grimaced. "C.J., just forget it. I was trying to find a way to explain our situation to the newspaper folks."

C.J.'s face cleared. "Ah! Just tell them we're selling lemonade to get people's fingerprints for their dossiers—"

"C.J.!" Clara, Rose, and Tundy snapped almost in one voice.

He jumped. "*What?*"

Mark and Susan exchanged glances. For one delicious moment, all was forgotten between them except the story. Mark welcomed the return to their old ways with enthusiasm. Susan's theory

had been correct; the club was collecting fingerprints and more on the entire town.

"Damn it, guess the cat's out of the bag now,"
Tundy grumped.

Susan nodded. "Yup. Might as well tell us
everything. We're going to find out one way or
another."

"You're relentless," Tundy said with grudging
admiration.

"I try," Susan agreed.

"Can I tell her?" Clara asked in a chipper voice.

Tundy sighed. "Go ahead. We've been worn
down. I . . . Oh, look! The new preacher's leaving.
We can't let that happen. C'mon, Rose, put on a
glove and grab a glass. We gotta get his prints!"
Tundy and Rose hurried off.

Clara looked around as if expecting to see men
in trench coats peeking from nearby trees. Satisfied none were there, she turned back to Susan.
"Promise you won't print this in the paper? At
least not until we're finished with our investigation. We don't want to spook any potential murder suspects as may be lurking about town."

"I promise."

"Good! It's hard to tell the good guys from
the bad guys, so we thought we'd just investigate
everyone."

"I see," Susan said, nodding.

"That way when a crime is committed, we'll already have all of the preliminary work done." Clara reached under the table and pulled out the plastic file box Rose had been carrying, then flipped it open to expose an array of pink and blue folders.

"Pink and blue?"

"Pink for women, blue for men."

"Of course," Mark muttered.

Clara grabbed the first folder and flipped it open. "This one's on—" She squinted at the page. "Ethan Markham."

"That's my neighbor." Susan looked surprised.

Clara smirked. "We know." She placed the open folder on the lemonade table. "Here we have a basic info sheet, including name, address, work, family info, education—anything we can find out." She flipped a page. "And then here we have a photo and—"

"Wait." Susan looked closer. A picture of Ethan had been stapled to a piece of paper. "He's bending over his bike. You can't see his face."

Clara chuckled. "Me and Rose took that picture. Thought we had one with his face, too, but when we got home we couldn't find it, so we used this one instead." She picked up the paper and held it a few inches from her face, squinting through her glasses. "That's OK, though. We'll recognize him from this angle."

She handed it to Susan, who looked at it and handed it to Mark. He frowned. "No one would know this was Ethan."

"I would." Susan plucked the paper from his hands and placed it back in the folder. "What else do you have here?"

"Birth and marriage records. We got copies just by sending in requests online."

"You didn't!"

"Not for everyone, of course. Depends on what state they're from. And then we got phone numbers, addresses, and names of kids and kin and such. Finally, we've got financial records, like bank and pay deposit stubs."

"How did you get those?"

"Went through their trash, of course."

"That was fun," C.J. said. "I like going through people's trash."

"And," Clara continued, pointing to a card stapled inside each folder, "now we've got fingerprints. Of course, we had a bit of a problem knowing if we had left or right ones, so we just stuck them in wherever."

Susan looked at the fingerprint card. Ethan's

name was printed in shaky block letters across the top. Below it, a set of fingerprints had been painstakingly pressed onto the card. "According to this card, he has two thumbs on the right side."

"Does he?" Clara peered at the card. "Hot damn!"

Mark cleared his throat. "Pardon me, Miss Clara, but what good are those fingerprints? I mean . . . do you know how to match them?"

Clara brightened. "Sure do! We bought a crime scene kit off the Internet and it came with a DVD that shows everything! We know how to take prints, how to put them on the cards, and how to match them. Although—" She looked over her shoulder, then bent forward to whisper, "The next time we solve a murder, when we need these prints read, we've decided we'll turn 'em over to the FBI and let them do it for us."

"I bet they'll be happy to know that."

"Yup! And they can sort out that right/left thing." Clara chuckled. "It's amazing what technology can do these days. Why, the other day on *CSI*, their scientist man figured out what color and type of lipstick a woman was wearing just by adding an eyedropper of something to a vial."

Susan patted the older woman's hand. "Clara,

I don't think all of those tests and stuff they show you on *CSI* are real."

Clara sniffed. "Of course they're real! Why, if they lied about something like that, they'd get sued by someone."

Susan could tell from the way Clara's face had turned fire truck red that the older woman didn't agree. She merely said, "Boy, that Gil Grissom is sexy, isn't he?"

Clara's face cleared like the sun appearing from behind the cloud. "He sure is! I'd do him in a heartbeat." Her smile dimmed a moment. "It's sad he left the show, though."

"I think he'll be back."

"I hope so." Clara tapped the dossier in front of her. "If I was a crook, I'd be afraid these days, they've gotten so good at figuring things out. Not like the old times, when crooks like Dillinger used to be able to pull off capers and get away with it."

Mark frowned. "Wasn't Dillinger shot and killed in front of a movie theater by the cops?"

"That's what he *wanted* people to think."

"Really?"

"Of course! He's in a criminal protection plan somewhere. At one time, I thought he might be living in the assisted-living center. There was a

J. D. Illinger who was being transferred in, and I just knew—" She shook her head sadly. "But it wasn't."

Susan couldn't help asking, "What gave it away?"

"The breasts. She was Jane Denise Illinger." Clara shrugged. "One of those odd coincidences. Unless—do you think they might have given him surgery?"

"No," Mark said baldly.

Clara looked disappointed. "Probably not."

Susan looked at the box of files. "Clara, could you let me borrow your files just for a few nights?"

"Tundy wouldn't like it. Since someone started breaking in on us, she sleeps with those things under her be—" Clara clapped a hand over her mouth, but Tundy was still across the square.

"Could I take just a few? I used to work as the county dispatcher, and I may know a few things you could add to these folders to make them more complete. I did all of the paperwork for the sheriff's office for years."

Clara frowned. "You'd add good stuff?"

"Oh, yeah. Lots of good stuff."

"Hmm. I don't suppose it would hurt if you just took a few. But you can't tell Tundy. I like her and she's a fine van driver, but good gosh, she's bossy. Sometimes Rose and I sit out in the garden just to get a breather from her now and then."

"No problem!" In just a few moments, Susan had appropriated a good dozen of the folders, and she and Mark said good-bye to Clara and headed to the newspaper building.

"What are you going to do with those?" Mark asked.

"Someone wants them badly enough to break into the assisted-living center to find them, so I'm going to go through each and see what's really going on."

"And then?"

"And then we'll see if we need to write another shake-the-hornets'-nest story."

Mark groaned. "I was afraid you were going to say that."

She smiled, and though she wanted to slip her arm through his, she didn't. For her own peace of mind, she'd tried to establish some distance between her and Mark since their talk and so far, she'd succeeded. What she hadn't been able to do was erase the sense of loss that dogged her like a rainy day. It was funny how he'd become such a big part of her life in only a short few months, and yet he had. Far more than she wanted him to know.

She hurried past him, saying over her shoulder, "Don't worry, Mark. If the hornets come to sting, I promise to protect you."

Chapter
19

Dear Bob,
  Can a person die of a broken heart?
Signed,
Lost

Dear Lost,
  Yes.
Signed,
Bob

                    The Glory Examiner
                 August 28, section B3

Susan closed the top folder, then rubbed her face with both hands. The Murder Mystery Club actually had something going with the "dossiers." With a seemingly haphazard collection method, they'd managed to gather an incredible amount of information in just a few weeks. In the last six days, Susan had taken time to confirm the veracity of as much of the information as possible and found it surprisingly accurate.

If these dossiers were a good example of the rest of the batch, there was no telling what had led to the break-in. Though Susan now knew more about her neighbors, she hadn't seen a thing that seemed inflammatory. At least not in these.

She sighed and pushed her chair back from her desk, stretching her arms overhead to ease the tension in her shoulders. If she'd learned anything from the folders, it was that she'd never throw out another receipt without shredding it first. She might burn her shredded paper, too, just in case the Murder Mystery Club decided to tape some of her receipts back together. You never knew how far that crew would go. She glanced up at the clock. It was almost nine; time to go home. Lately, she'd found it harder and harder to do so, even with Krypton's welcoming presence. Something now felt missing. Something—some*one*—she'd never had.

Her heart ached at the thought. It was so painful seeing Mark here, day in and day out, while trying to pretend she was fine. She *wasn't* fine. She'd started to care for him. It was a good thing she'd stopped that nonsense right in its tracks.

Pat's flat-footed walk sounded in the hall, then the older women stuck her head in the door. "Still here, eh?"

"Dedication is my middle name."

"Humph." Pat's gaze fell on the pink and blue folders and her mouth pressed into a straight line. "Those are the dossiers! How did you get those?"

"Clara gave them to me."

"Does Tundy know?"

"Not yet."

Pat looked slightly mollified. "Oh. I thought maybe Tundy was playing favorites. She refused to let me even peek at 'em."

"I wonder how many other people know about these?"

"Most of the town, I'd think. I saw Lucy Carpenter at the library this morning—"

"She sure spends a lot of time there."

"I see her going in there almost every day. Anyway, I heard her tell Deloris that if the Murder Mystery Club ever came snooping at her house for a so-called dossier, she'd slap a lawsuit on them so fast it would make their head spin."

"A lawsuit? For what?"

"I dunno. She didn't say."

Hmm. That was interesting. Susan pulled out her notepad and began paging through it. "Something odd is happening in Glory. Which is a good thing, I suppose, because between the vandalism on my Jeep and boat and the attempted thefts at the assisted-living center, we've worked up a good string of stories."

Pat beamed. "We have, haven't we?"

"Your piece on my boat was masterful. I particularly liked the headline—'In the Lake? Big Mistake!' "

"Why, thank you. I appreciate that." Pat glanced at the Lois Lane clock on the wall and made a face. "Guess I'd better go. I want to stop by Micki & Maud's for a roast beef to go, and they don't do carry-out after nine."

"OK, thanks, Pat." Susan waved her on. "I'll see you tomorrow."

Pat hurried off. A moment later, the ping of the elevator sounded and she was gone.

Susan rose from her desk and reached for her purse when—

Crash! A paper-covered rock landed on her office floor among the shattered glass. Susan jumped and made her way to the window. In the parking lot below she could hear Clara say, "Damn it, C.J., you weren't supposed to break the window! Just knock on it gentle like."

Tundy yelled, "Get in the van! We're haulin' ass!"

Of course, with Clara's wheelchair, it took them a five full minutes to make their escape. Susan had to laugh at their arguments. Once they were gone, she carefully fetched the rock and undid the paper.

She read the note, her humor disappearing. For a long time afterward, she sat staring out her broken window. Then she reached for the phone.

```
        The Murder Mystery Club
   invites you to a party tomorrow,
        this Thursday at 7 P.M.
      at Micki & Maud's Diner.
      Don't RSVP, just show up.
    There will be lots of surprises.
           Cookies after.
```

"Did you get one of these?" Roxie held out the invitation written on notebook paper in thick Sharpie pen.

Mark glanced up from where he'd placed a shirt in his suitcase. "Yes."

"The meeting is tomorrow." Roxie sat down on the edge of his bed. "I wonder what Tundy and her gang are up to now?"

"Who knows?" Mark folded a tie and placed it beside the shirt.

"Are you going?"

He shrugged.

Roxie looked at him for a long moment, then got up and shut the door and locked it. Then she went to the radio and turned to the jazz station.

"What are you doing?"

"Making sure Mother doesn't listen in." Roxie's eyes were grave and considering. "OK, we have privacy. So spill."

"Spill what?"

"You've been a total mope this last week, and now you're packing. What's going on?"

"Nothing." Mark zipped the case closed. "All done. I have enough clothes in my overnight case for the next day or two and then I'll be out of your hair." *And out of Susan's life.*

"Mark, you haven't answered my question."

"Because I'm not going to."

"You might as well. I can just get the answer from Susan, you know."

"I didn't say my leaving had anything to do with Susan."

"You haven't said that it doesn't."

He sighed. "Look, I agreed to stay long enough to make sure the paper was on the right track, that's all."

"And is it?"

"It's getting there. Readership is up, thanks to the more aggressive reporting Susan and Pat are doing–"

"Susan's accidents helped that."

"Some. So has the Bake-Off controversy. I wish we could figure that one out." He shrugged. "Susan will do that. When she does, let me know, will you?"

"No, I won't. You can ask her yourself."

He picked up his suitcase and placed it on the floor, his chest so tight he felt as if a huge weight rested upon it. "Roxie, I can't stay. That's all there is to it. The paper's in better shape than ever. Just listen to Susan; she knows what she's talking about. Because of her, not only is readership up, but so are ad sales. Ray is a natural."

Roxie put her hand on his arm. "Mark, she's just as miserable as you."

Which didn't make him feel any better. "She'll be fine. She has several hundred friends. I know because her father told me so."

Roxie made a face. "That man is a jerk."

"He's all she has."

"She could have more, Mark."

"Not from me." He sighed and sat on the edge of the bed, facing his sister. "Look, Roxie, I know you're trying to help, but it's not meant to be."

"Then why are you both so miserable?"

"Because sometimes it's harder to lose what *might* be." He couldn't wait to get back to Raleigh. Once there, he was sure he'd sleep again, something he hadn't been able to do lately. He was exhausted and cranky.

Seeing Susan almost every day didn't help one bit. Every time he looked at her, he burned with desire tinged with the sad knowledge that they weren't meant to be. She stayed out of the office more now, but they couldn't avoid each other all of the time, and when he did run into her, he was stung with desire. Not just stung, but stabbed, sliced, and diced. He wanted her, and he wanted her now.

But he couldn't have her, because he couldn't afford to pay the price. It was that simple and that difficult.

He raked a hand through his hair. "She's a Glory girl, Roxie. She's not going to leave."

"So stay here."

"I don't belong here. I have my business and a life in Raleigh."

Roxie lifted her brows. "A *life*? All you do is work, work, work, and then work some more."

He frowned. "It's what I have."

"It's worth trading in. Look, I don't know why you and Susan aren't together, but I do think you've been hasty in deciding you can't work out whatever the problem is. She's worth fighting for." Roxie's brows lowered. "Did you read this morning's 'Dear Bob'?"

He glanced at the newspaper on his nightstand and sighed. "Yes."

"And?"

"Bob is wrong. You can't die from a broken heart."

"She's hurting, Mark."

"So am I, but that doesn't fix things. And she'd hurt even more if I stayed. We both would."

"Know what I think?"

"No, but I'm sure you're going to tell me."

"You're too much alike: that's the real problem." She sighed. "What about the attempts to scare Susan?"

"I asked Nick to keep an eye on her. He promised he would."

"I'm sure he will, but he can't be everywhere. Whoever's trying to frighten her could go too far."

Mark had purposefully not thought about that aspect, though it haunted his nights. "Nick put a watch on Lucy Carpenter and nothing's happened since."

Roxie frowned. "I don't think it was Lucy."

"Why?"

She shrugged. "It just doesn't seem like something a woman might do for vengeance. A woman would plan something more spectacular, something humiliating. Besides, you said yourself that Lucy came looking for Susan right as her boat was sinking. Why would Lucy do that if she knew where Susan was?"

"To make herself look innocent?" At Roxie's annoyed glare, he threw up one hand. "I don't know. If I thought Susan was in any real danger, I'd stay. But she's not." He crossed to the radio and turned it off. "And that's that." He unlocked the door. "I'm going to get some of that apple pie Mother made. You want some?"

Roxie sighed. "You're avoiding the subject."

"As much as I can." He kissed his sister's forehead. "Come on. Last one to the kitchen has to scoop the ice cream."

Susan was so busy getting ready for Thursday's meeting that she barely saw Mark, which good. Just this morning, she'd overheard him talking on the phone to Roxie. Susan wasn't certain, but thought she'd heard him say something about "wanting to leave as early as possible."

Was that it, then? Was he simply going to drive out of her life forever, just like that?

She wondered if he'd even bother to say goodbye. He'd made no attempt to do so as of yet. Feeling lower then she'd ever felt, she made her way to Micki & Maud's a full hour before the meeting time and settled at her favorite seat.

Connie set a pie on the counter and Susan leaned over and sniffed. "Mmmm. Heaven. How *do* you get your pecan pies to smell like that?"

Roxie nudged Susan out of the way. "Forget the smell; I want a taste." Susan had been surprised that Roxie was already at the diner.

She reached out a finger, but Connie swept the pie out of reach and placed it on a pie stand behind the counter. "Nuh uh. This is a birthday pie and it's not for general consumption."

"I bet I know who it's for," Susan said, smiling. "Ethan's birthday's tomorrow."

Connie's face turned a fiery red. "I don't know what you're talking about."

Roxie chuckled. "That's it, deny everything. It makes falling in love so much easier."

Susan nodded wisely. "It's just a short step from denial to stalking. I just read about that on TMZ. Happens all of the time in Hollywood."

"If I were going to stalk someone," Roxie said, "and this is just hypothetical, mind you, it would most definitely be Ethan."

Susan thought Ethan was plenty sexy, but he didn't affect her the way a certain dark-haired, blue-eyed, eyeglass-wearing accountant did. Which was a true tragedy.

"Ethan's a total hottie." Roxie fanned herself with a napkin. "Those eyes!"

"Those arms," Connie enthused. "What does he work out with? Train carriages?"

"Car axles." Susan looked into the pie case. "Are you saving the apple pie for anyone's birthday, or can we have a piece of that?"

Connie pulled out the pie. "Want it à la mode?"

"Yes. Yes. Oh, and yes."

"I'll have the same thing," Roxie added.

They were soon eating their pie. Susan glumly

wished her jeans weren't getting so tight, but since her discussion with Mark—she couldn't bring herself to call it an argument since they'd agreed—she'd been eating nonstop. Pies, cakes, chocolate bars; if it was sweet and rich, she'd been eating it.

The door jingled and Pat came in. She nodded briefly at Susan and Roxie, and found an empty table near the jukebox.

Roxie licked her spoon. "So . . . Mark's packing for Raleigh."

Susan rammed a spoonful of pie into her mouth so she wouldn't have to say anything.

Roxie slid her a sideways glance. "He seems sad."

Unable to swallow the pie, Susan reached for her glass of water and took a small sip.

The door creaked open and old Sheriff Thompson walked in, removed his hat, and took a seat beside Todd Barkins, the president of Glory National Bank.

Roxie reached over the counter and refilled her coffee cup. "It's hard to see him so upset, but he won't even talk about it."

Susan put her glass down. "Roxie?"

Roxie looked at her with a hopeful expression. "Yes?"

"It'll be time for the meeting soon."

Roxie sighed. "You want me to change the subject."

"Desperately."

"Fine. Though you'd feel better if you'd just get it off your chest."

"I doubt it." Susan refilled her own cup. "Do you think all of the folks here are waiting for the meeting?"

"Most of them." Roxie looked around. "There are a *lot* of people here."

Susan eyed the other customers. "I know Pat was invited. She told me this morning."

Roxie nodded to the far table by the window. "Both Pastor Lawrence and Pastor MacMillan were invited, as was Lucy Carpenter."

"Great," Susan muttered.

"I'll protect you. There's more pie in the cabinet and I don't think a little bitty thing like her could withstand a coconut crème between the eyes."

Susan laughed. "I guess not." She turned her stool a bit more. "There's Deloris Fishbine, Mitzi Ketteringer, June Berlitzer, and Doc Wilson."

"He's enjoying being at a table full of women."

"His wife says he's a horrible flirt."

Roxie grinned. "I heard that Robin and the mayor weren't invited, and she's mad about it."

"Looks like she decided to attend anyway."

The door swung open and Robin stepped in, dressed in a too-tight skirt and white knit shirt. The mayor was hard on her heels, smiling vapidly every time she looked his way, which wasn't often. Robin cast a defiant stare around, her gaze locking with that of the new pastor, Scott Lawrence.

To Susan's surprise a flush suffused Robin's face, and she turned away from the empty table near him and led her pathetic boyfriend to a table across the room. That was interesting. Why had Robin reacted to the pastor in such a—

"Here come Nick and Mark." Roxie waved as her fiancé and her brother entered the diner.

Heart aching, Susan turned her attention back to her pie. Tonight was one of the last times they'd see each other . . . It didn't bear thinking about.

"I wonder where Tundy and her gang are?" Nick placed a folder on the counter. "Good evening, Susan. That looks delicious. I might have me a piece—Ethan!" Nick waved Ethan over as the creaky screen door closed behind the biker. "Don't tell me you got invited to this madness, too?"

"Yup." Ethan brushed his long dark hair from his eyes. "Don't know what's going on, but if it has to do with the Murder Mystery Club, you can count me in. That Clara's a character. She pinched me at the Piggly Wiggly last week." His slow, sexy grin made Connie, who was standing as close as she could without being rude, sigh with wonder.

"Clara's a danger to herself and others," Nick said in a severe voice.

Ethan chuckled. "I forget she's your great-aunt."

"I never do," Nick said fervently.

Ethan claimed the stool beside Susan as the door opened again.

This time Tundy came in, pushing Clara in her wheelchair. Clara's cane was neatly stowed across her lap. Rose stomped behind her, scowling as if going to battle. C.J. staggered in after her, carrying a large box.

"The dossiers," Susan murmured.

"Quite a collection," Nick agreed. "And thorough."

"Have you seen them?"

Nick crossed his arms and gave a faint smile. "I spent all afternoon going through each and every one."

Ethan frowned. "They have dossiers on all of us?"

"You wouldn't believe it if we told you," Susan said.

Tundy parked Clara, while C.J. placed the box

on the nearest table. Rose rubbed her hands to-gether as if ready to burst into song.

Susan noted that Clara's hands were even more bejeweled than ever and that Rose's red wig looked recently combed, while C.J. sported a brand-new pair of tennis shoes.

Tundy, resplendent in her pink velour track suit, held up her hands and said in a loud voice, "People, thank you all for coming here tonight. We're very glad to see you—very, *very* glad to see some of you, while the rest—" She suddenly frowned. "Wait a minute. We didn't invite all of you. Some of you will have to leave."

Connie leaned across the counter. "Tundy, I said you could have your meeting here, but I can't close everything down. Some of these people are my paying customers."

Tundy sniffed but, after a brief—and noisy—consultation with her gang, she nodded. "OK. We'll let them stay."

"You'd better," Connie said cheerfully. She turned and tried to catch Ethan's gaze.

"What's this meeting about?" Doc Wilson asked.

"We have an announcement to make." Tundy pulled a crumpled piece of paper from her pocket. She unfolded it, then began to read. " 'We, the Murder Mystery Club, do—' "

"—of the Pine Hills Assisted Living Center," Rose added.

Tundy nodded. " '—do hereby announce that we have done solved a real, bona fide mystery!' "

There was a moment of silence and then Roxie asked, "What mystery?"

"Don't rush us," Tundy said. "You'll find out soon enough." She turned. "C.J., the chart."

The old man smiled gently at everyone.

Tundy cleared her throat. "C.J., the *chart*."

He blinked, his smile fading. "What chart?"

"The one from Rose's room. The one we worked on *all* afternoon."

"I didn't bring it."

"*What?*" Tundy said, her eyes almost bulging.

"I thought we'd finished it."

Clara slapped the arm of her wheelchair. "Damn it, C.J.! We used up all of Miss Moore's pink highlighters on that thing!"

Tundy frowned at C.J., but after shaking her head, she turned back to Rose and Clara. "We'll just have to go on without it." She faced the assembled guests and lifted her hands as if parting the Red Sea. "OK, people, listen up! We've done solved a mystery and we thought we'd go ahead and give you all the down low."

Roxie chuckled. "Tundy, I think you mean the 'lowdown.' "

"Whatever. OK, here's what we know. *Someone* in this town broke into our rooms and tried to steal something. We finally figured out what it was—one of our dossiers."

Ethan straightened and asked loudly, "Tell us about those dossiers?"

Mitzi Ketteringer put down her latte, her expression scandalized. "Dossiers? Like the government does on people?"

"I don't think that's legal," the new pastor said, frowning.

Clara made an impatient noise. "Will you all stop asking so many questions? We can't do our presentation if we're interrupted every two minutes."

Ethan ignored her. "You made dossiers of everyone here in town? *That's* why you were taking pictures of my ass."

Connie whirled to face Clara. "You have pictures of Ethan's ass?"

Ethan turned to look at Connie, whose face flooded bright red. "I-I-I," she stammered, her gaze shooting back to Tundy, "I can't *believe* you'd take pictures of Ethan's ass!"

"Got more than one." Clara patted the box at her feet. "If you want a copy, just say the word."

Connie waited until Ethan was looking another direction before she gave Clara a hearty thumbs-up.

Clara nodded sagely.

"As I was sayin'," Tundy continued, sending Clara a mind-yourself glare, "we put together dossiers on everyone in town—"

"Even me?" Doc Wilson said, looking astounded.

"Yup!"

"I want to see it." He stood.

"Me, too." Deloris Fishbine rose and hurried forward.

Clara hovered over the box, her cane waving in the air like a sword. "Get yourselves back into your chairs! No one's gettin' a peak at these. At least not until we're done with them."

After eyeing Clara's cane, Doc resumed his seat, but Deloris was made of sterner stuff. "I am *not* going to sit down," she announced. "I know my rights! I've been to a confidentiality conference and I know all about privacy and the right to search, and all of it!"

Clara lowered her cane. "Deloris, you've been to one conference in your whole life. That was last year and it was in Raleigh. I know 'cause you told me when you was buying lemonade just a few weeks ago."

"It doesn't matter where or when the conference was. The point is, I went and I want to see what's in my folder. I'm not going to sit down until I do."

"I wish I still had my taser," Clara said wistfully.

"Me, too," Rose agreed.

Tundy sighed. "Deloris, what if we promise to let you see your folder *after* we finish with our investigation?"

"And when will that be?"

"In about ten minutes, if you'll sit your ass down and let us finish our presentation."

After a long moment, Deloris marched back to her seat and plopped into her chair, her color high.

"Now," Tundy said, "back to our presentation. One of the problems with living in Glory is that there's not a lot happening at any given time."

"Amen," Pat muttered.

"Fortunately for all of us concerned—that'd be me, mostly—while we were in the process of making money at the lemonade stand for our new CSI lab and getting all of your fingerprints for our dossiers—"

"*What?*" Deloris gasped.

The new pastor leaned forward, an intense expression on his handsome face. "You got them from the lemonade glasses?"

Ethan's brow lowered. "You did not."

"*Anyway,*" Clara continued, "someone started a campaign to steal our dossiers. They broke into Tundy's room first, and then later into Rose's, though we didn't think they'd taken anything."

"That's what we *thought*," Rose agreed, "until Sheriff Sheppard figured things out."

Tundy didn't look happy that Rose had mentioned that aspect. "Which he *sorta* did, with *our* help. We wanted to capture the thief on our own but—"

"Just get to it!" Clara ordered.

"Yeah!" Rose confirmed.

Tundy nodded. "OK, then. We know who took the file from the dossier box—"

"Which we didn't know was missing until the sheriff thought to go through and see whose file was gone," Clara explained.

Rose nodded. "I thought the thief was after my dentures."

"But apparently this lowdown critter was after something else." Tundy paused dramatically. "The person who stole the file was—"

Pastor MacMillan stood up. "I took the file," he said calmly.

A collective gasp rose across the room.

"You didn't!" Lucy Carpenter breathed.

"Yes, I did. I had to."

Lucy's face was so red it seemed as if she might start smoking at any moment. She stood now, her hands visibly trembling. "No, you *didn't*. I know because *I* took the file."

The pastor scowled. "Lucy, please. Don't say another word."

She reached across the table, took one of his hands and held it tightly. "Please? I need to do this. I have to. It's . . . it's time."

He smiled gently. "Are you sure? You don't have to do this here. We could wait for the next board meeting and—"

"No. It's better if everyone knows. All at once." She was so pale that Susan wondered if the woman might faint.

The preacher patted Lucy's hand and then released it. "OK, then. Remember, Pastor Lawrence and I are right here. We'll back you every step of the way."

"Amen," the younger pastor said softly, smiling encouragement.

Lucy swallowed hard as, clutching her hands

before her, she turned to face the group. "I admit it, then. I-I stole the file."

"We know," Clara said with a satisfied gleam in her eyes. "That's the only one missing."

Susan leaned forward. "But why?"

Tundy shot her an exasperated look. "Because she didn't want no one to have her fingerprints!"

Rose pointed to Lucy. "Admit the rest of it now. You was a criminal before, and you're still one. In fact, you took the missing money from last year's Bake-Off, didn't you?"

Every eye pinned the tiny woman in place.

Lucy straightened her shoulders. "I didn't take the file because of the fingerprints. I took the file because of the receipts you found in my trash can the night you woke up Doc Wilson."

"The receipts?" Clara pondered this a moment. "I don't remember what those were for."

Rose shrugged. "Me, neither. I just stampled 'em in there."

Lucy gave a slightly hysterical laugh. "Lovely."

"What were the receipts for?" Susan asked.

"Gambling. I-I have a problem." Lucy glanced at Pastor MacMillan who smiled calmly. She took a deep breath and continued, "I've always played the slots and such, but last year . . . I don't know what happened, but it got out of control and I-I just lost. And then lost some more and then more. I broke my computer, hoping that would stop me, but then I started going to the library."

Deloris suddenly gasped. "Is *that* what you've been doing in the library every day?"

Lucy nodded miserably.

"But we have locks on those sites and—"

"I know how to get around that." Lucy covered her face for a moment. "I shouldn't have gone, but I just couldn't stop. Before I knew what had happened, I'd lost all of the profit for the year's Bake-Off."

"Thirty thousand dollars," Susan said.

A loud murmur broke out as people reacted.

Lucy nodded, her cheeks bright red against her pale skin. "When I realized what I had done, I told Pastor MacMillan. He was so kind, so nice—" Lucy choked on a sob.

Pastor Lawrence was out of his chair before the sob died. He handed his napkin to Lucy and slipped an arm about her shoulders.

She mopped her eyes and continued, "Pastor MacMillan set up a payment plan so I could fix things."

"And got the board changed out so that no one would know what happened," Mark finished.

Lucy nodded. "I know you are all mad at me, but I didn't mean to do it. It just happened. I'm seeing a counselor now and I'm on medication and—" She gulped. "That doesn't bring it back, though."

A long silence followed.

Doc Wilson rubbed his chin. "Let me see if I've got this straight: you took some money."

Lucy nodded.

"And you've been paying it back ever since?"

"Yes."

"I'd call that a loan, not a theft."

Connie nodded. "Yup, definitely a loan."

To everyone's surprise, Robin Wright spoke up. "So long as you were paying it back, I don't see the issue."

Everyone started nodding.

"Wait a minute!" Rose said loudly. "We got us a criminal. You all can't just uncriminal her like that! It's not Christian!"

The new pastor chuckled dryly. "Actually, it is."

"Damn," Tundy said. "I thought we had us a *real* criminal, and all we got was a gambling grandma."

"Nothing wrong with a little gambling," C.J. said in an unexpectedly clear voice. "Do it myself." At everyone's surprised look, he reddened and added, "Now and then."

"Well," Rose said. "I guess there's only one thing to be done. Nick, arrest Miz Carpenter so we can all go home."

Clara nodded. "There's a *Barnaby Jones* on Nick at Night, and the TiVo isn't working."

Lucy left the shelter of Pastor Lawrence's arm and walked to where Nick stood at the counter. "I'm ready, Sheriff. Take me away."

Nick rubbed his chin. "I can't."

She blinked. "You can't?"

"Nope. No one's reported a crime."

Lucy's eyes were wide.

Pastor MacMillan stood. "That's true! We didn't."

"Wait a minute!" Tundy said. "What about our break-ins? We were invaded, our privacy violated and—"

"Hold it," Nick said. "Tundy, both times you had a break-in, I asked you if you wanted to file a report, and you told me no."

"I didn't have time for no reports then, but you can arrest that thief now."

"Now wait," Clara said. "Miz Tundy, you tol' us you was filing police reports."

"I was goin' to, but those forms are as long as

your arm. I didn't have no time, not with tryin' to get all of those dossiers done, and tendin' to my singin' efforts."

"You and that damn karaoke," Rose said in a disgusted voice. "First, we have to listen to you 'practicing' all day long—"

"Caterwauling is more like it," Clara said.

Rose nodded. "And then we find out you've been derelict in your duties to the club."

Clara shook her head sadly. "Miz Tundy, we are so disappointed in you."

Behind her, C.J. shook his head in the exact same manner.

"That don't matter," Tundy said stoutly. "We've got us a crime, and we have to arrest a criminal or the case isn't closed."

"Bull hockey!" Clara said.

"No kiddin'," Rose agreed.

Tundy frowned at her charges. "What's wrong with you?"

Clara scowled through her thick glasses. "We don't mind being investigators, but I'll be damned if we'll lock up good people. There aren't enough of them out here as it is."

"Yup, and while Lucy may be a snarky bitch," Rose added, "she ain't no criminal."

Nick tucked the folder under his arm. "Tundy, I guess you've been outvoted."

"I guess so," Tundy said sourly.

Nick turned to the pastor. "I'm sorry you didn't come to me and let me know. I could have put your mind at ease."

"We should have," Lucy said, wiping her eyes.

"No kidding," Ethan said, grinning. "If you'd come to me, I probably could have gotten Tundy and her gang to hand over the folder in exchange for some beefcake shots."

Clara turned to Rose. "He could have, you know."

Rose nodded. "I'd have taken that bribe."

"Me, too," Tundy agreed.

"Me three," Connie agreed, blushing when Ethan shot her a surprised look.

Pastor MacMillan wiped his eyes and turned to the new pastor. "These people are why you've got the best job in the world."

Scott chuckled. "I see why you keep saying Glory's a magical place. I am counting on that."

Susan glanced at Mark from under her lashes to see if he'd heard that, but he was frowning at Nick, as if there was something more the sheriff was supposed to have done but hadn't.

Why, even now, with such a wonderful example of the quality of people found in Glory, couldn't he at least *think* about staying here?

Well, *she* wasn't so afflicted. *This* was why she'd never leave Glory. If only he could see that.

"Hold on a moment," Connie said. "Did you guys ever find out who was trying to hurt Susan? Nick?"

Nick crossed his arms. "Actually, I know who it is. I just need a little more evidence."

"Who is it?" Tundy asked eagerly.

"Yeah," Pat said, pulling out her notebook. "Who is this phantom?"

"I'll let you know soon. *Very* soon."

Clara's face fell. "That means you don't know, but don't want to admit it. Don't you worry none, Miz Susan. We'll follow you around until you're killed, so we'll know for sure."

Connie laughed. "Well, that's not effective, but it's certainly a thorough way of catching a criminal." She pulled out a stack of plates. "OK, people, there's a special on pecan pie! Anyone who orders a piece in the next ten minutes gets it, and a coffee, for a mere five-dollar donation to our new Help Lucy Fund!"

Chapter
20

It was a lovely way to end a meeting. Nick slipped an arm around Roxie's shoulder and whispered something into her ear before he turned to Susan. "There's one more thing I need to speak to you about. Would you mind stepping out into the parking lot with me?"

She shrugged. "Sure." She followed Nick outside to his cruiser, where he unlocked the trunk and tossed in the file he'd brought.

"What was in there?" she asked.

He grinned. "My budget report. I didn't want Clara to think she had all of the evidence."

"You handled that really well and I—"

The door opened and Roxie and Mark came out.

Nick lifted his brows. "Hi, you two. Can I help you?"

"Just hanging out in the parking lot," Mark said blandly. "No law against that, is there?"

"No, but I wanted to talk to Susan. Alone."

The door opened again and this time Pat ambled out. She saw the group and stopped, then walked jerkily toward the newspaper building.

Nick watched her. "I also need to talk to Pat." He stepped away from his car and lifted his voice. "*Pat!*"

She froze in place.

"Come here, please! Got a question for you!"

She stiffened, her hands fisted at her sides. Slowly, she turned and walked toward them. She stopped an awkward distance away, an uncertain look on her face. "What?"

"Susan would like to ask you a question." Nick looked at Susan.

Susan grimaced but faced Pat. For a long moment, she just looked at the older woman.

Finally, Nick said softly, "Susan, either you do it, or I will."

Susan rubbed her forehead. "I don't really want—"

"It was me," Pat said.

Everyone looked at her.

Her face was bright pink, her arms crossed tightly over her chest. "I cut the brake lines in Susan's Jeep and drilled a hole in her boat."

Mark gaped. "Why would you try to harm Susan?"

Nick said, "She wanted drama for the paper, didn't you, Pat?"

Her jaw set, she nodded. "I had to do it. We didn't have any good stories and Mark had these charts—"

"Oh, God. *Damn* those charts."

Pat shrugged. "I got to thinking how a spate of seeming murder attempts would get the paper going again." Pat clasped her hands before her and sent Susan a serious look. "I hope you don't mind, but I thought that you, more than anyone else, would understand. This paper is all I have—" Pat's voice broke, and it took her a moment before she could speak again. "I've been working there since I was nineteen, and oh, what an operation it was then. We had two reporters and an editor, and people really *cared*. They'd stop by and invite us to cover their events—not like now, when they want you to come but not ask any questions." Pat sighed. "Things have changed. Somehow we've become—" She looked at Mark. "What was that word you used?"

"Irrelevant."

"Yup. We've become irrelevant, and I just

couldn't let that happen. That paper is necessary to Glory. Without it, no one would ever know what was going on in town, or who won the Baptist Bake-Off, or anything." Pat spread her hands before her. "I couldn't let that happen."

Mark frowned. "But Susan or someone else could have gotten injured."

"I made sure the accidents were things that wouldn't hurt anyone."

Nick sighed. "You'll have to tell that to the judge, Pat."

She paled. "You're going to arrest me?"

"I have to. You understand that, don't you?"

She gave a jerky nod.

"The local prosecutor will have to decide how this goes down. It's possible you might plead to lesser charges; I don't know. It would help if Susan's willing to speak on your behalf."

"I'll do it," Susan said without pause. She locked gazes with Mark.

He read the unspoken question in her eyes and heard himself say, "I'll speak to the prosecutor, too." Regardless of his personal feelings about Pat's actions, he couldn't withstand Susan's pleading gaze.

Nick jerked his head toward his car. "Come on,

Pat. I'll book you and you can post bail and head home. Won't take more than twenty minutes."

She sent Mark a sour look. "I guess this means I'm losing my job."

"I'm afraid so. You crossed some lines, Pat. You're supposed to report the news, not create it."

Nick shut the trunk of his car and carefully handcuffed Pat's hands. "That hurt?"

"No."

"OK, then. Let's take a ride to the station."

They left and Roxie turned to Mark and Susan. "Wow. What a night! I bet you two have a lot to do at the paper."

Mark frowned. "I was going to 1—"

"I'm sure you and Susan can work it out. I think I'll step back inside the diner and get a to-go latte. I just can't get enough of Connie's pie, either." As she spoke, she backed away toward the diner. She waved to Susan and Mark. "See you guys later."

Within moments, Mark and Susan were standing alone in the parking lot. The lone streetlight clicked on, flooding the semidarkness with a golden light as the faint hum of cicadas began to lift from the trees.

Mark glanced around the town square, at the neat rows of petunias that bordered the walk, the arch of tall oaks overhead, the faint outline of the statue of the town founder perched on the square marble base, neat benches surrounding it. "I'm going to miss this town." The realization made his heart ache a little more.

"We'll miss you, too," Susan said softly.

"I have a life in Raleigh." He winced at the almost defiant sound of his own voice.

"I know," she said simply. The streetlight bathed her red hair in a warm glow and highlighted strands of pure gold. "We all have to do what we have to do. It's a cliché, but true."

He rammed his hands into his pockets to keep from reaching out for her once more. He had to stop this craving, this desire. But he couldn't see her without a deep, unfilled ache in the region of his heart. "Susan, I wish . . . I wish things were different. That I didn't have my responsibilities, and that you could leave your dad and—"

"Mark, don't. We are who we are. I . . . I'm a Glory girl." She smiled ruefully. "I used to blame my dad for that fact. I used to be so angry with him for trapping me here." She tilted her head to one side, a peaceful look on her face. "Now I can't imagine living anywhere else. No, I don't *want* to live anywhere else."

"Ever?"

"Ever. This is who I am. It has nothing to do with my dad." She looked around the quiet square, her lips curving gently. "I love this town. I've made it my home. And I need it far more than it needs me. This is where I belong."

Mark nodded and rubbed his chest. For one wild moment, he wondered if he could change, if he could move to Glory and open a branch office. But what if things didn't work out with Susan? There were no guarantees, and he was a man who relied on rock-solid numbers and certainties.

"Susan, whatever happens, I wish you luck. You're . . . you're a hell of an editor."

Something flickered in her eyes. "Thanks. That means a lot." She gave a breathless laugh. "Speaking of which, I'd better head over to the office and get to work. I have a long night ahead of me if I want to rework the front page in time to get it to print. I guess you won't be in again?"

"I still have to empty my desk. I'll do it in the morning."

"I won't be in." She took a swift breath, then stuck out her hand. "Good-bye, Clark. It was great working with you."

He looked at her hand, as elegant and graceful as she was. He reached for it, but the second his skin touched hers, he forgot his decision to make a smooth exit. He grasped her hand, his fingers twined with hers. "Susan, please. We have to find a way to—"

She yanked her hand away, her eyes bright with unshed tears. "Good-bye, Mark. And good luck."

Then she was gone, walking quickly down the sidewalk toward the newspaper building, leaving him alone in the parking lot, cicadas chirping all around.

Chapter
21

"You're an idiot."

Mark put the last folder into the box on his desk.

"A complete and total idiot. An *idiot's* idiot. The idiot of all idiots, and—"

"Roxie, that's enough. I don't want to hear any more."

"Fine, but you know I'm right. That's why it hurts."

He sighed. "You can't stop, can you?"

Roxie leaned forward. "Mark, you're miserable. So is Susan."

"She loves this town."

"And you love numbers. That doesn't mean you two can't find some compromise."

"We're not the compromising sort of people." He handed a box of files to Roxie. "Here. Make yourself useful."

He picked up the final box and looked around

his empty office, his gaze flickering across the aisle to Susan's. It was empty, a mishmash of notes scattered over her desk. "She did a helluva job on this morning's paper."

"It was phenomenal. I think the paper will do well. Susan's going to raise the prices on the ads once circulation increases."

"A few more editions like this morning's, and she'll do it." Mark walked into the hallway, Roxie following.

As he reached the empty reception area, his cell phone rang. He set the box down and pulled his phone from his pocket.

"Mark, it's Doc Wilson. Do you know where Roxie is?"

Something about the brisk way he spoke made Mark stiffen. "Yes, she's right here."

"Thank God. I need to talk to her."

"Is something wrong?"

Doc hesitated briefly. "It's Susan Collins."

The world around Mark settled into a cold haze. From a long distance, he heard his voice, calm and authoritative, ask, "What's happened?"

His soul froze as he waited. *Is she hurt? Was it a car wreck? She fell? Damn it, she has all of those power tools, what if—*

"It's Susan's father. He collapsed this morning."

Relief slammed into Mark, and he found himself sitting in a chair, his knees shaking.

Roxie bent down and looked into his face, her eyes wide with concern.

He shook his head.

Doc continued, "It was a massive stroke. He's alive, but—we just don't know. Susan's here alone, and I thought she should have someone with her."

Mark felt as if every ounce of energy had been sucked from him. *She's okay. She's not hurt or injured or—but that's not true. She loves her dad.* He forced himself to swallow. "Roxie and I will be there right away."

"Good. I'll keep Susan here until then. I don't want her to be alone." Doc cleared his throat, his voice suddenly husky. "She's taking it hard, Mark. Harder than I thought she would."

Mark nodded blindly. Susan always seemed tough as nails, but underneath was the woman who wrestled to maintain the identity of the newspaper she loved, the woman who supported her community and was a good friend to dozens of people around her, the woman who couldn't resist the world's largest puppy, the woman he loved.

He closed his eyes as tears flooded them. *I love her. I've stupidly been fighting it, but I do.*

"Mark? You still there?" Doc's voice was tinged with impatience.

"Of course." Mark stood, galvanized to action. "Rox and I are on the way." He rammed the phone into his pocket.

"Susan?" Roxie's voice cracked.

"No, her father. She's at the hospital and she needs us."

Hold on, Susan. I'm coming.

"Susan?" A Styrofoam cup of coffee was gently placed in her hands.

Susan looked up and blinked, trying to focus. Doc Wilson. Oh, yes. They were in the hospital. Dad had—

Her throat clamped shut, her swollen eyes filled again, and her face crumpled like a wrinkled shirt dropped to the floor. *Like one of Dad's shirts. Oh, God.* "I was doing the laundry."

Doc settled into the chair opposite Susan's. "You were what?"

"I was doing the laundry when Dad—" She closed her eyes, tears dripping down her cheeks. "I heard a thump in the other room and then Krypton began to bark, and I just knew. I don't know how I knew, but I did and—" She held her breath, trying to stop a sob.

Doc took the coffee and replaced it with a handful of tissues. "Don't give up hope. He's fighting. He might make it."

Susan mopped her cheeks. "I left the clothes in the dryer and now they'll be so wrinkled." She gave a watery laugh. "Not that it matters." A sob cut through her words, and just like that, she was crying again, hard. "D-D-Doc, I'm s-s-sorry. I can't s-s-seem to quit."

Doc scooted to the chair beside Susan's and held her hand.

"Please tell me he'll be OK. Just say it. Please—"

Doc patted her hand. "Easy, sweetheart. You're not alone. We all love you, and we're all here for you."

"I know," she said, clasping his hand.

Doc's beeper sounded. He glanced at it and grimaced. "I have to go. Do *not* leave this room, do you hear me? Not by yourself."

"Of course."

The beeper went off again, and he cursed as he strode toward the door. "I'll be back soon."

"OK."

And just like that, she was alone. She was used to spending a lot of time by herself, but this was different. Now she was really alone. It was just her . . . and no one else.

Tears choked her. *Dad, please fight it. Please, please, please.* She placed her elbows on her knees and dropped her head into her hands. *Oh, God, I can't bear this. Please help me carry this. I can't—*

Then she was hauled to her feet, strong hands pulling her against a broad, steady shoulder, muscular arms enfolding her into a wonderfully secure hold. She clung to Mark, her hands fisted in his shirt as she dropped her face against his shoulder and cried.

Mark closed his eyes and pressed his cheek to her head as she sobbed, wet, sloppy sobs like a lost, forlorn child. He rubbed her shoulder and murmured, "It's OK, Susan. I'm right here," over and over. He held her tighter and she burrowed into his arms, leaning against him.

Finally, she was letting him close. And finally, his heart chipped through the doubt that had kept him immobile. *This is the woman I want to spend the rest of my life with. Regardless of the problems that may lie ahead, this is the one I choose to be with, forever.*

It was that easy. That simple. How had he allowed his stupid *thinking* to make it so hard?

Susan finally sagged against him, her knees buckling slightly. Mark swung her into his arms and carried her to the couch, where he cuddled her on his lap and held her, feeling peaceful assurance mixed with deep sadness for her. *She loves her father, as difficult and complicated as the relationship is. Because that's the sort of woman she is.*

He'd been such a fool. He couldn't possibly live without her anymore.

He rubbed her back, his heart aching at the child's wail he heard in her sobs. "Easy, sweetheart," he murmured against her hair. "It'll be OK. I promise. Just hang in there."

He held her close and let her cry. Sometimes that was all a man could do, and he did it with his heart just as full and just as loving as hers. Whatever she needed, he'd provide. He just prayed she'd believe him. Her entire life, people had walked out on her: her mother had left physically and emotionally, and her father had littered her life with broken promises and a lack of care. Then he had demanded the one thing she couldn't give up—the security she'd found in this community—and packed to leave when she refused.

Mark rubbed his cheek against her hair, settling into the couch to engulf her deeper into his embrace. When the time was right, he'd tell her he loved her. For now, he'd just show her.

Chapter
22

Four days later, Susan stood in the kitchen doorway and sighed. Krypton wagged his tail when she looked his way.

She had to smile. "We have to get things ready for Dad, don't we? He'll be back home in a week or two." She dropped to her knees and engulfed the dog in a hug, dropping her face into his soft fur. For a long time they sat there, neither moving, the puppy panting softly. Finally, Susan lifted her face. "You're a good dog, aren't you?"

He wagged his tail and looked eagerly into her eyes.

She chuckled. "I think someone wants a snack." She rose and fetched a treat from the bin by the sink, then Krypton pranced off, his prize held gently in his mouth.

"Hi, Susan!" Roxie's friendly voice filled the house as the front screen door creaked open and slammed closed. Krypton barked loudly. "You home?"

"In here!" Susan called.

"Down, Krypton," Roxie commanded. Footsteps sounded as she crossed through the living room and came into the kitchen, the puppy hard on her heels.

Roxie set several bags on the counter. "I brought you some necessities."

"No food, please. Every Baptist in town has been by already. Just look." Susan opened the fridge door and Roxie gasped.

"Good God, there must be—six, seven, *eight* casseroles in there!"

"And two pots of soup, a pan of lasagna, three salads, and a Boston cream pie."

"Wow. That's a lot of love."

"They're good people. I just don't know how they're not all two hundred pounds overweight."

Roxie closed the refrigerator door and cast a shrewd glance at Susan. "Let me guess—you haven't touched any of this food. Mark said he couldn't get you to eat a thing."

Mark. Until this morning, he'd been with her nonstop since Dad's illness, even sleeping on a recliner in the waiting room at the hospital. She went to sleep knowing he was there, a call away, and when they came home, she awoke every morning to the smell of bacon or pancakes or whatever delicious food he thought might tempt her to eat.

She couldn't imagine what she'd have done without him. She couldn't imagine how she was going to handle it when he left again.

And he would.

He hadn't said anything, but he'd been on the phone more and more lately, discussing work stuff in an urgent, hushed tone. Then, this morning, he'd told her he had to leave but he'd be back.

She didn't expect him to return, despite his words. She felt it in his voice, in his looks . . . the weight of something unspoken.

"I brought Häagen-Dazs." Roxie pulled two pints of ice cream out of the bag, along with dark chocolate sauce, caramel sauce, and a can of whipped cream.

"That can't be good for me."

"Right now, everything is good for you." Roxie's expression softened. "I'm glad your dad is doing better."

"The doctor says it will be awhile, but he's almost out of the woods."

"Sometimes you have to pamper yourself a

little, to ease your way over a rough time. And chocolate sauce is the perfect medicine."

"We'll give it a try."

Roxie caught sight of a huge stack of pizza boxes stacked beside the fridge. "More Baptist generosity?"

"No. Ethan."

Roxie's brows raised as she went to start a pot of coffee. "There must be fifteen boxes here!"

"He comes by three times a day, and every time—" She gestured toward the stack.

"Wow, that man is a gem. Sure wish he'd pay attention to Connie."

"Me, too. They'd be a cute couple, though they are really different." Susan sighed, feeling so bone weary that she thought she could sleep for a week. Yet when she tried to sleep, she jerked awake at every noise, every phone call, her heart pounding.

"So," Roxie said in a casual tone, "have you heard from Mark this afternoon?"

"He called awhile ago."

Roxie sent her a quick glance before turning back to the bowls of ice cream she was preparing. "What did he say?"

"He asked how I was doing about eight times in a row, and then he hung up. It was sort of awkward."

Roxie sighed. "Someone needs to teach that boy some social skills."

"He sounded busy." Susan sank into a chair, her knees as shaky as her emotions. "What's going on at the paper?"

"Ray and I are making it work, though we miss you." Roxie poured them each a cup of coffee, then brought the bowls of ice cream to the table. "It's a lot bigger job than I realized."

"It's fun, though."

"*If* you know what you're doing." Roxie scooped a spoonful of chocolate sauce into her mouth, smiling in bliss. "Hmm. You have to try the chocolate sauce with the ice cream."

"You didn't have any ice cream in your sauce."

"Not this time."

"This time? How much ice cream have you had today?"

"I had a little bowl at home before I came over here, just to make sure it was up to your standards."

"The sacrifices you make for me. I'm astonished."

"Me, too." Roxie grinned.

Susan ate some ice cream, though she couldn't help glancing at her cell phone on the counter.

Mark had seemed so hurried when he'd called. He'd asked how she was, inquiring about

Dad's condition, sympathy in his voice. The last thing she wanted from him was sympathy. She wanted— She covered her eyes. What in the hell *did* she want?

Right now, nothing seemed clear. She raked a hand through her hair and sighed, her heart so heavy it felt as if she'd need a backhoe to haul it back in place. Whatever she wanted where Mark Treymayne was concerned, it was painfully obvious she wasn't going to get it.

Later, as Roxie put the dishes away, Susan wandered into the living room and ran a hand over the worn cushions of her dad's chair. Had she done all she could for him? Should she have demanded that he get help? See a doctor? In the past she'd done just that, but she'd slowly come to the realization that no matter what she said, he'd do what he wanted to do.

You can't help someone who won't help himself, right, Dad? Your favorite saying. Her throat closed and she knuckled her eyes, moving quickly out to the porch, Krypton at her side.

She sank onto the front step and put her arms around the puppy, trying to distract herself by taking in the green lushness of her yard.

A change of scenery was what she needed. She would take a vacation as soon as Dad was back to normal—actually, better than normal. He couldn't drink again; the doctor had been adamant about that.

Her puppy licked her ear and she hugged him tighter. "Krypton, what do you think about going on a fishing trip? We could pack up and go camping on Lake Hope—"

The door swung open and Roxie came out. "There you are! Nick wants me to come home as soon as I can. Something about my mother. God only knows what she's said to him now, because I—"

A red Mustang came down the road. Mark's red Mustang, to be exact.

He came back. Susan's heart fluttered, her stomach tightening. Suddenly, she wasn't only exhausted but slightly ill, her nerves jangling. *Don't get used to this, you idiot. He's just being nice. He'll leave soon.*

"It's about time," Roxie muttered.

"Where are you—"

"Gotta scoot! See you tomorrow. Call me if your plans change."

"Why would my plans change?"

"Life happens, sweetheart." Roxie headed toward her car. "Just call, either way!"

"Yes, but—"

"Bye!" Roxie closed the door and backed out, wiggling her fingers at her brother, who'd parked in front of the house and was now climbing out of his car.

He strode across the lawn, looking calm and collected, his crisp khakis and button-down shirt perfectly pressed. His hair was slightly mussed, as if he'd just run his hand through it, and his eyes were steady through his glasses.

He stopped in front of her, his hands in his pockets, which made his arm muscles bulge. How *did* he do that?

For the life of her, she couldn't think of a darn thing to say. "Hello."

"Hello yourself. I won't ask you how you're holding up, because I asked you already. Probably six or seven times." A deliciously crooked smile crossed his face. "That's enough for one day. Susan, I—" He stopped and rubbed a hand over his face and started again, "Susan, I— Oh, God, I don't know where to start." He gave a rueful laugh.

He's leaving and doesn't know how to say it. She rested her head against Krypton's. "There's really nothing to say."

"Yes, there is. There is a *lot* to say." He put his hands on his hips, unwittingly assuming the

Superman pose—feet planted, hands on his hips, chest thrust out. Lose the glasses and add a cape, and he'd be a dead ringer.

"Susan, we need to talk."

"Mark, you've been very kind to stay with me, but I know it's time for you to return to Raleigh."

She would be fine. Really, she would be. Yet deep inside, a more honest voice cried out, *I want him here. I need him.*

The thought stopped her cold. She didn't *need* anyone. She never had. When something needed to be done, she did it without fuss. She did it because that was her job, her place in life. Dad hadn't been able to provide for her needs—heck, he couldn't even provide for himself. And Mom had left—

A sob began to bubble in her chest. *I am* not *going to cry right now. I refuse to!* Krypton wiggled against her and licked her face, giving her the strength she needed.

She hugged the dog and said softly, "Thank you for all you've done, Mark, but I'd rather you left now."

"No."

She frowned. "I beg your pardon?"

"I can't leave, Susan. Something is holding me in Glory. And I only hope it will hold me forever."

She couldn't swallow, couldn't breathe. "M-Mark?"

Mark stepped forward and lifted Susan into his arms, then sat on the stoop with her snug in his lap. "I'm back, Susan, and I'll never go away again."

"B-but your b-business—"

"I sold it."

She struggled to understand. "*All* of it?"

He nodded. "I sold the whole thing—even the building. As of four P.M. today, I'm officially unemployed."

"But . . . but Roxie said you had a big accounting firm—"

"One of the biggest in Raleigh. I bought it when it was failing and had only eight accountants. Now it has over two hundred, and it just keeps growing. We'll see if John is as good a manager as I was."

"John?"

"John Freeman, my second in command. I sold it to him and a group of investors." He kissed her forehead. "And I made a pretty penny. I may not have a job, but I'm not sure I'll ever need one again."

"Never?"

"Not with twenty million dollars in my pocket."

She choked. "That's so much money!"

"Yup, but I won't get it all in one lump sum. The IRS would eat it all up if I did that."

"Of course," she said faintly, trying to imagine so much money. "If you stacked that in ones—I can't even imagine."

"I took a quarter in cash and a quarter in stocks and bonds, then the rest is coming in a series of payments over a few years. That will give me time to set up new investments to roll those into."

"I thought you *loved* that business."

"I used to, but I lost my taste for it a few months ago." His gaze met hers, and suddenly he didn't seem calm, but barely contained. "I lost my taste for the accounting business—and for Raleigh—when I started working at the newspaper. When I began to know *you*. I was just too stubborn to admit it." He smiled wryly. "I don't accept change well. It's something I'm trying to fix."

Susan swallowed hard. She must look a mess, all swollen eyes and red nose. Damn it, this was no way to have a conversation with a man she . . . she thought a lot about. A *whole* lot.

"So . . . what are you going to do now?"

"That depends on you." He smiled into her eyes. "I hate to tell you this, Collins, but you're stuck. I am one stubborn, tough, crazy-about-you guy, and I'll be damned if I ever leave you again."

She blinked. "Crazy . . . about me?"

"About you. About your delicious laugh. About the way you walk, and how you dress so casually yet look so elegant. About how you fix your own Jeep and can wear a tool belt without even thinking about it. About how you renovated this house, and took care of your father, and fought so hard for the paper, and yet could forgive Pat when she messed up. Susan, I guess I just love you."

Her heart stuttered. "I . . . I . . ."

His arms tightened about her. "I know you've got a lot on your plate. But I couldn't *not* tell you. I know you're worried about your dad right now, but when you're ready to listen to all I have to say, I'll be here."

"Here? In Glory?"

"Here with you. Wherever that is. I sold my business, put my house on the market, closed my bank accounts and moved them here to the Glory National Bank." He grinned. "You should have seen Todd Barkins's face when I handed him a seven-figure check. I don't think they've ever seen that many zeros."

Her heart lifted hopefully. "Mark, why did you do all that?"

"Because I wanted to be ready to do this." He reached into his pocket and pulled out a small velvet box.

Mutely, she watched as he opened the box, a sapphire and platinum ring dazzling her. "One day, when you're ready, I want to be a part of your life. On that day, I'm going to ask you to marry me."

Susan took the box. "It's *beautiful*."

"And colorful and classy and true. Like you."

He kissed her as if he were a drowning man and she was his life rope. He kissed her as if he couldn't bear to stop, as if he loved her dearly, as if he *would* wait for her forever, or longer.

He kissed her as if he loved her as she was, for who she was.

When he pulled back, she tightened her arms about his neck. "Mark, I think you won't have to wait very long. Like, maybe . . . now."

His eyes burned with emotion. "Are you . . . Are you sure?"

"I'm positive. I love you, too."

He laughed with joy as he scooped her up. Krypton gave a bark of approval as Mark whirled her around.

Susan held him tight. She'd found a real Superman. He might not be able to stop a meteor from hitting the Earth, but he knew when she needed a hug. There might be difficult times in the years ahead, but Mark would be there to hold her. A lifetime of happiness with the man she loved and who loved her, too, was better than any fantasy imaginable.

Find out how it all began!
Turn the page for
Roxie Treymayne and Nick Sheppard

in **TALK OF THE TOWN,**

Karen Hawkins's debut contemporary romance.

Available from Pocket Books

On Monday, Roxanne Lynne Treymayne Parker bleached her hair blond, had her navel pierced, and got a tattoo on her right ass cheek. And that was all before noon.

It wasn't every day a woman could celebrate shedding two hundred and fifty pounds of worthless husband. Today was Victory Day, and in honor of the occasion she'd ditched her sober navy blue suit and sensible pumps for a pair of dangerous, four-inch do-me heels, black miniskirt, and low-cut top.

She straightened her shoulders before she marched up the courthouse stairs. For once, prim and proper Roxanne Lynne Treymayne Parker wasn't going to stand meekly aside and let life hand her leftovers. This time, she was going to take life by the throat and choke its scrawny ass until it cooked her a four-course meal.

She grabbed the heavy glass door and heaved it open, stepping into the courthouse foyer. She was immediately rewarded when the security guard's eyes widened appreciatively.

She flicked him a smile as she whisked through the metal detector, collected her purse, and headed for the elevator. She'd been sensible her whole life, and look what it had gotten her—a cheating husband, a boatload of pain, and the loss of her sense of femininity. With one bold, selfish move, Brian had snatched it all away while she'd been busy being a "good wife."

To hell with being good. She'd tried it and had gotten nothing in return, so now she was going to be bad. No, bad wasn't enough. She was going to pass bad and jump right into *wild*. Even better, she was going to do it in a court of law.

The elevator opened and she strutted into the final hearing to end her marriage. Head high, she hid a satisfied smile when her lawyer gasped at the sight of her. Her whole body tingled with bitter happiness when Brian and his lawyer stopped talking in midsentence to stare at her and her *incredibly* naughty Dolce & Gabbana heels. She took her seat, adjusted her short skirt to an even more scandalous level, and then winked at the judge.

Judge Kempt, who looked to be all of a hundred years old, turned a pleased pink and within twenty minutes had granted her the lion's share of her requests, leering at her greedily while ignoring Brian's lawyer's endless objections.

For Roxie—once Glory High School's most popular Homecoming Queen, the first Glory resident to be voted Raleigh's Debutante of the Year, and current Chair of the Raleigh Lakes Country Club Women's Organization—it was further proof that good girls finished last, while bad girls got whatever their little hearts desired.

As they all waited for the final signatures to be added to the piles of paper that represented the rubble of her marriage, Roxie crossed her legs to make sure Brian saw exactly how short her skirt was, how great her do-me pumps made her calves look, and how her scanty stretch shirt lifted just a bit to reveal her new navel ring.

Maybe she should have gotten her tongue pierced, too. It would have been priceless to stick it out at Brian and see his reaction. But she'd been afraid a tongue-piercing might have made her lisp, which wouldn't have fit with her "badass" image at all.

She sent Brian a glance from under her lashes. He sat rigidly, his manicured hands gripped together in his lap, looking so startled that one good puff of air might topple him over—Armani suit, Prada shoes, Rolex watch, and all.

Good. It was about time someone other than her got shocked by life.

After the last signature had been added to the towering pile of papers, Roxie's lawyer took her arm and practically waltzed her out to the hallway.

There, she turned down a not-very-subtle pass from the heavily cologned man, then clicketyclicked down the hall on her to-die-for heels to the waiting elevator.

She drove straight home, an odd whirling noise in her ears. *I've won*, she told herself. *Soon I'll feel it, and things will be better.*

She parked her car, went inside, closed and locked the door, stopped in her huge, Italian marble kitchen to collect every bag of chips in the cupboards, then climbed the grand stairway to her bedroom. Once there, she stripped off her new, uncomfortable clothes, kicked off her tippy shoes, and yanked on her favorite jersey sleep shirt. Then she unplugged the phone from the wall, fell into bed, and piled the bags of chips around her in a protective wall. She ripped one open and ate a handful, savoring their salty comfort.

Somehow she didn't *feel* like a winner. During the last few weeks, as this day had approached, she'd thought the moment of release would lighten her painful sense of failure. She'd thought that when she won the huge settlement, she'd be vindicated and would no longer feel so . . . empty.

Instead, sitting in her bed in the middle of her huge, silent house, all she felt was lonely.

A tear landed on her wrist. It was followed by another, and then another. Suddenly the enormity of the last few months hit her, and she pushed away the chips, curled onto her side, and sobbed into her pillows, weeks of anguish pouring out.

Finally, her face salty with tears and chips, she fell into a deep, dreamless sleep. She slept for the rest of the day and the entire night. She might have slept for most of the next day, but at ten in the morning she was awakened by the insistent doorbell.

She slowly opened her eyes, aware that something was wrong . . . oh, yes. The divorce. Her heart sank again, but she refused to cry anymore. She scrubbed her face with the edge of the sheet. The doorbell rang again and her heart leapt with hope. Perhaps one of her neighbors had come to check on her? But no, that would never happen. She might have "won" the divorce and gotten a very generous settlement, but that meant nothing to the inner sanctum of Raleigh society. To the socially elite that made up her snooty neighborhood, Brian was a man with a future, while she was nothing more than an "ex."

Damn it, she had a degree in political science and could have gone to law school herself if she'd wanted; she'd had good grades. But that would take years—and in the interim, she was positioned for a painfully slow social exorcism. Besides, after three months of emotional upheaval, she didn't have the energy to start again. Right now, she barely had the energy to eat chips. Thank God the bags were easy to open.

The doorbell rang again, even longer this time.

Roxie pulled the blankets over her head. *I don't need them anyway. I have friends like . . . like . . . !* She bit her lip. The closest thing she had to a friend was her housekeeper, Tundy. Roxie had been too busy being Brian's chief cheerleader to find any real friends.

She swallowed the lump in her throat. "Screw the lot of them!" she told the ceiling defiantly. "Tundy's always been better company than the Raleigh Wives, anyway." Thank God for Tundy. The housekeeper was always cheerful, always ready to help, and—right or wrong—always willing to give her honest opinion. Tundy's frankness was a trusty compass while navigating the unpredictable ocean of guile and Southern politeness that made up the Raleigh Wives.

Brian had snickered when Roxie had named the aimless, avaricious women who populated their exclusive subdivision "the Raleigh Wives." From the tops of their salon-colored hair to the tips of their perfect nails, the Raleigh Wives were worse than Stepford Wives: they were Stepford Wannabes. At first Roxie had avoided them, until Brian had pointed out that it was her duty to help his budding legal career by accumulating "useful friends." Pasting a smile on her face, Roxie had submerged yet another part of her pride and made an entire subdivision-worth of false friends. Mother would have loved every minute of it; they were her sort of people.

But Roxie knew what a vicious gaggle of griping, sniping geese the Raleigh Wives could be. After Brian's defection, far from rallying around her, they had collectively ignored her, all the while continuing to invite Brian to their houses, where, she was sure, they'd cooed over him and offered their "support." She shouldn't have been surprised; they went with the money, and despite the generous settlement, in the long run that would mean Brian.

The doorbell annoyingly rang again. "Go away!" Roxie snuggled deeper into the womb she'd treated with 600-thread-count sheets, an embroidered silk comforter, and her wall of chips.

But the doorbell didn't stop. It got more insistent, then *more* insistent. Roxie glared at the ceiling. Didn't anyone respect anyone's privacy anymore? Didn't people know she had A Situation on her hands that required complete and total despair?

If she left the house from the terrace door, she could drive into town and buy a gun. It was only a fifteen-minute drive. Then she could put a final end to the annoyance.

There was a long silence, then she heard the click of a key in the lock and then her brother's voice, calling from the foyer, "Roxie, I saw your car in the drive! Are you here?"

Damn it, Mark must have heard about the divorce. She hadn't told anyone—not Mark and certainly not Mother. Mark might get angry at Brian, but Mother would have a cow. Treymaynes did not get divorced. Why, when Arlene left Mark, Mother had almost disowned him, saying that if he didn't find Arlene and patch things up, the family name would be "smirched." Though, if anyone had besmirched the family name it was Arlene, who'd ridden off into the sunset with a rodeo rider.

"Roxie?" Mark's voice was on the stairway now.

She struggled to sit up and yelled, "I'm up here. What do you want?"

She should have left straight for Paris yesterday and had a passionate rendezvous with a mysterious Frenchman in a dark café. Or perhaps found a bedroom-eyed Italian to sip wine with in a trattoria in Florence.

Mark appeared in her bedroom doorway, his clothes rumpled, his hair mussed, his tie askew.

He opened his mouth to speak, but his gaze locked onto her hair. He just stood there, mouth ajar.

She frowned. "What?"

He rubbed a hand over his eyes. "You're *blonde*."

"Did you come to compliment my new 'do, or did you want something?" She dug through the bags of chips, opened a fresh one, and munched a handful. "I suppose you've heard about what's happened?"

He ripped his gaze from her hair with obvious difficulty, coming further into the room, looking relieved. "You already know? That's good."

"Of course I know. How could I not?"

"I don't know. I've been trying to call you since I found out, but no one answered." He frowned. "You seem very calm."

"I am. I'm glad it's over."

He paled. "*Over?* Mother didn't—"

"Please don't bring Mother into this! It was hard enough going through a divorce without knowing how Mother was going to take it and—"

"Divorce?" Mark gaped at her. "But . . . why? You and Brian were the perfect couple!"

"Someone forgot to tell Brian." Roxie forced

the words from her stiff lips. "He fell in love with someone else."

Mark winced and suddenly looked exhausted. "Jeez, Roxie. I don't know what to say. I'm so sorry."

"That's OK." Though nothing was OK anymore. She rubbed her forehead with a weary hand. *I should miss Brian, but I don't.* She frowned. *Is that normal? Maybe I don't miss him because I was already sad and lonely when I lived with him. Now I feel angry and betrayed, but that beats sad and lonely by a huge, scary margin.* She cleared her throat. "Since you didn't know about the divorce, why did you come?"

Mark rubbed his eyes. "Oh, God. You don't need to hear this, but—Roxie, it's Mother."

Time shuddered to a halt. Roxie clutched her bag of chips like a shield. "What happened?"

"She had a heart attack, but Doc Wilson says she'll be fine."

Roxie breathed a relieved sigh. "Thank God!"

"No kidding. It happened yesterday."

"Why didn't someone call me?"

"I tried! Your phone just rang and rang."

She looked at the cord, where it hung over a chair in the corner of the room. "Oh, yeah. I never thought something might happen."

"None of us did. Doc said it was a very mild attack, but you know how Mother is." Mark sent her a grim look. "Rox, we have to go home to Glory and get her back on track."

Roxie looked down. This certainly put a crimp in her budding plans to be bad, but that was what she got for hesitating. She shoved the chip bags aside and climbed from her bed. "It'll just take me a few minutes to pack."

Mark smiled tiredly. "I don't know how we're going to do this. Mother'll want someone with her night and day, and—" He blinked. "Hey, do you think you could talk Tundy into helping us? She's got more sand than any woman I know."

Roxie paused with one hand on the closet door. "That just might work. Tundy'd do anything if you paid her enough, and she knows Mother from the times she came to visit."

Mark fished his cell phone out of his pocket. "I'll give her a call. What's her number?"

Roxie let Mark make the call. Tundy was a sucker for a smooth man, and when Mark was on his game, no one was better.

Roxie threw clothes into a suitcase; sensible, sober clothes for "With Mother" and fun, playful clothes that showcased the new Roxie for times "Away From Mother."

Frowning, she looked with distaste at a high-necked yellow dress suitable for an episode of *Father Knows Best*. She set her jaw, then pulled out every last sober and sensible thing she'd packed, leaving nothing but her flirty new clothes. Then, chin high, she zipped up her suitcase. Like it or not, Mother was just going to have to adjust.

It was time someone other than Roxanne Treymayne compromised on life.

Sheriff Nick Sheppard knew the little town of Glory better than any human should. He knew every car and pickup, every house and shed, and every last tree for a ten-mile radius. He could recite names, relationships, and even the birth dates for most of the citizens. He should have been able to—he'd been born and raised in Glory and, except for a twelve-year move to Atlanta, he'd never lived anywhere else.

Glory, North Carolina, was the exact opposite of his experience in Atlanta. Here, being sheriff was a personal sort of job. Just this morning, he'd had to *personally* unwedge the head of Mrs. Clinton's fat pug from between the spindles of her front porch railing, then he'd *personally* investigated a report of a stolen lawn mower over on 5th and Elm, which had turned up in a neighbor's garage, having been borrowed but forgotten. After that he'd very *personally* answered yet another emergency call from Deloris Fishbine, the city librarian, about a supposed noise she'd heard in her attic late last night.

That was the third call she'd made this week, and he'd already half-decided that the old woman had a thing for men in uniform when he'd caught her at the bottom of her attic ladder, shining a flashlight up at his ass. It didn't get much more personal than that.

The distant sound of a car approaching fast made Nick lift his radar gun and look down the road.

A red-hot '68 Mustang roared into view. Oh, yeah. That was a good one. He clicked the trigger and was rewarded with a rising squeal. Twelve miles over the limit.

He reached into his squad car and flipped on the lights, then waved the car over. The Mustang's rear lights flashed on and the car whipped to the side of the road, spraying gravel. Nick caught a glimpse of the driver, a hot blonde wearing huge hater-blocker sunglasses that would look less out of place in L.A.

Well! That was a sight he hadn't seen in his two-year tenure as town sheriff. And a good thing, too. If he knew anything, it was that women could be trouble, especially hot blondes who thumbed their perfect noses at the law. He'd seen the damage a woman could do if a man got too mixed up and lost his objectivity. He'd sworn to never succumb to such dangerous temptation.

He approached the car, noted the Raleigh plates, and counted at least two other occupants besides the driver. To keep his hands free, he tucked his ticket book into his back pocket and walked to the open window. The driver was turned away from him as she dug through her wallet, obviously looking for a license. His gaze dropped to the space between the woman and the door, instinctively looking for a weapon—old training from when he'd worked somewhere far busier and far more violent.

As he expected, he didn't find anything of interest. Well, that wasn't entirely true. That long expanse of smooth, tanned thigh and, at the curve of her hip, the hint of a tattoo peeking from the edge of her white shorts were very interesting.

His gaze lingered appreciatively.

Whoever she was, she definitely wouldn't fit in with the grayhairs and shiny domes who sat around Micki & Maud's Diner, complaining about the weather.

Nick bent down to the open window. "Ma'am, I'm going to need to see your driver's license and registra—"

The woman looked up and flipped her sunglasses to the top of her head. In one blinding moment, Nick forgot everything he was going to say. Sitting before him was the reason he'd left the idyllic little town of Glory in the first place— Roxie Treymayne. "You changed your hair color!"

It was a stupid thing to say and her reaction was immediate.

Hot color flooded her cheeks, but her chin immediately notched up a level as if ready for a fight. "You think?" she asked in a cool, faintly sarcastic way he immediately recognized.

Nick flicked a glance at the creamy blond hair lifting up into a ponytail, hair that had once been such a deep brown that it had bordered on black. He might not know that new hair, but he did know those wide, pale blue eyes, thick black lashes, and pouty, kissable mouth, just as he knew that too-stubborn chin. At one time, he'd showered them all with kisses. "Roxie Treymayne."

"Nick Sheppard." Her gaze flicked over him before she met his gaze, humor lurking in her expression. "A cop. I never saw that coming."

"Yeah, well, neither did I. Though my mother's

glad I'm in charge of the jail rather than residing in it." Though he tried not to, his gaze drifted, noting the low-cut halter top and . . . the twinkle of a navel ring above the waistband of her short shorts.

Once a too-good-for-anyone brunette ice queen, Roxie Treymayne had returned to town as a hot, sexy blonde. A hot, tattooed, navel-pierced blonde, at that.

Hot damn.

Nick's mind reeled. Growing up, he'd watched little Roxie Treymayne prance about Glory, so pure and perfect that it had almost hurt to see her. He'd watched her grow from a leggy sprite wearing a Peter Pan collar to a supremely confident homecoming queen with a large blue satin bow on her shoulder. Just breathing, Roxie had kept every male for miles around panting. Except him.

He hadn't panted. He'd dreamed, desired, longed for . . . and had had the good sense to make a run for it before he'd made even more of a fool of himself.

Now, he met her icy blue gaze and realized just how much things had changed. At one time, she'd been the town's hottest and most unavailable virgin, while he'd been Senior Most Likely to Be in Jail During the Reunion. Now he was a by-the-book cop, while she, by all appearances, had returned a sultry scofflaw, the exact sort of woman he avoided like the plague.

"Well, Officer?" Roxie's voice traced across his skin like warm fingers. "Am I getting a ticket?"

Nick shoved away his far-too-strong reactions and pulled his ticket book from his back pocket. "You were going twelve miles over the posted speed."

A snicker from the other side of the car made Nick look across Roxie. In the passenger seat sat a rotund, squat woman dressed in a pink velour sweat suit that clashed with her short, curly red hair. She gripped an oversize bag of barbecue pork rinds in one hand, her fingers orange from the rind dust. She pulled her heart-shaped neon-pink glasses to the end of her freckled nose, and flashed an orange-tinted smile. "Well, hello there, Officer."

Nick blinked. Had she just winked at him?

He grinned and tipped his hat, then glanced in the backseat and saw a familiar man with tousled dark hair and blue eyes; who was hiding a smile.

"Mark!" Nick exclaimed.

Mark grinned. "Nick! I haven't seen you since . . . I don't know when."

"Your wedding."

A shadow crossed Mark's face.

Oh. So it was like that, was it? "What are you doing back in tow—oh, right." Everyone knew Mrs. Treymayne had taken ill, and he should have realized what that would mean. "Sorry about your mother."

"Me, too." Mark glanced at Nick's uniform. "I thought you were in Atlanta."

Roxie glanced his way, but Nick kept his attention on Mark. "I came back here a couple of years ago."

"Not paying enough?"

"Not enough peace."

A question flickered through Mark's eyes, but all he said was, "I suppose that's as good a reason as any."

Nick thought so, too. He was glad Mark didn't ask any more questions; he wasn't ready to talk about Atlanta. That was a time best forgotten, just like he should forget Roxanne Treymayne. Only . . . it wasn't Treymayne now, but Parker.

Which was a good thing. He wanted to stay in Glory and make a life here. He didn't want any trouble, and the new Roxie Treymayne looked like trouble with a capital T. But at least she was someone else's Trouble.

Nick opened the ticket book. "I'm afraid I'm going to have to issue you a warning."

"Roxie, how fast were you going?" Mark asked.

"Oh, she was flyin'," the redhead in the front seat said. "Just flyin'! I warned her, too, but she wouldn't have none of it. No, sir, she told me she knew the speed limit and—"

"Thanks, Tundy," Roxie said through clenched teeth.

Nick raised his brows. "Tundy?"

Roxie showed him her teeth in a saccharine-sweet smile. "Nick, this is Tundy Spillers. Tundy, this is Nick Sheppard. He used to be one of Mark's friends back in high school."

He'd been Roxie's "friend," too, if four weeks of mindless, all-absorbing passion warranted the term. But Roxie hadn't been willing to publicly claim him as such, of course.

To his surprise, the old hurt returned and, jaw tight, he touched the brim of his hat. "Nice to meet you, Miss Tundy."

The redhead grinned. "Nice to meet you, too. I'm Miz Parker's maid."

Nick sent a quick glance at Roxie. Who in the hell would come to Glory with a maid?

"Tundy's come to take care of Mother," Roxie said impatiently, her blue gaze pinning him in place, as if she'd been able to read his thoughts. "She has a lot of experience tending older folks."

Tundy leaned forward to tell Nick in a confidential voice, "I make corn bread and soup beans, and they like that. Keeps 'em regular and—"

"Tundy," Roxie interrupted, "Nick's not here to hear about your recipe for staying regular."

"No," Tundy said, crunching on another pork rind. "He's here 'cause you were drivin' like a bat outta hell."

Roxie sent an accusing look at Nick. "Someone changed the speed limit."

"The city council did it last month because we've been getting a lot of vacation traffic whizzing through here on weekends. I've been giving out warnings ever since."

"Lovely. Just give me that warning and we'll be on our way. We've things to do." With that, Roxie settled her hater-blocker glasses back onto the bridge of her patrician nose and effectively relegated him to the level of security guard at Costco.

Nick took his time finding his pen. "I'll be glad to give you the warning, Mrs. Parker."

"I prefer Treymayne," she said tersely.

Nick lifted his brows, but before he could speak, Mark sighed. "Rox, just pay attention to the signs next time, will you?"

Tundy snorted. "I tried to tell her, but you know how stubborn she can be. How completely pigheaded and—"

"Thank you, Tundy," Roxie said abruptly before saying to Nick in a voice most people reserved for repelling telemarketers, "Can you hurry, please? Mother's expecting us."

Heaven forbid anyone keep Lilah Treymayne waiting. If there was one thing Nick disliked about Glory, it was the fact that Roxie's mother, the widow of and mother to the sole descendents of the town's founding father, General LeeRoy Treymayne, thought she owned the whole place. And Lilah wasn't shy about invoking the spirit of her long-dead husband whenever she felt she wasn't being treated with enough deference.

Nick refused to treat Lilah Treymayne any differently than he did anyone else, which was one of the many reasons she couldn't stand him. "I'll need your license and registration, and then you can be on your way."

Nick filled out the warning while he tried not to stare at Roxie's smooth, tanned thighs and remember the time when he'd kissed his way up them to— He blinked at the ticket and scowled. He'd written his name in the date slot, and he'd be damned if he'd let her see it. He flipped the page over and started a new one, hoping she didn't notice. It took all of his concentration, but he filled it out correctly. "Here you are."

She reached for it and their fingers met. For a long moment, they stared at each other, their fingers clenched over the same paper. Nick's heart gave an odd gallop, and then, with a wince, as if she'd burnt her fingers, Roxie snatched the paper from his hand, almost tearing it in two.

Nick stepped away from the car. "Watch the signs from now on," he said in a voice that matched hers for terseness.

She threw the car into gear.

"See you around, Nick!" Mark called as Roxie hit the gas and wheeled onto the road.

"Bye, Officer!" Tundy yelled out the window, waving a pudgy, orange-fingered hand.

Nick watched the Mustang until it disappeared and the gravel dust settled into a low haze.

"I'll be damned," he said aloud. Glory was definitely less predictable than it had been a few minutes ago—and all because of a hot blonde in a red Mustang.

Nick jabbed his pen back into his pocket and turned toward the squad car. If Roxie Treymayne had returned to town as she'd left it, innocent and pristine as the rising sun, he might be worried.

Fortunately for him, she'd come as the one thing he was now immune to—a woman in trouble. He didn't know what kind of trouble, but he recognized the signs, every tempting, tattooed one.

He tossed the ticket book onto the car seat, lifted his hat, and raked a hand through his hair, realizing his shoulders were as tense as if he'd been facing an armed murderer. "Hot damn," he told the warm breeze that ruffled the trees overhead.

Once again, Roxie Treymayne was off limits. Only this time, it was for an entirely different, and far more interesting, reason.